To S.T.

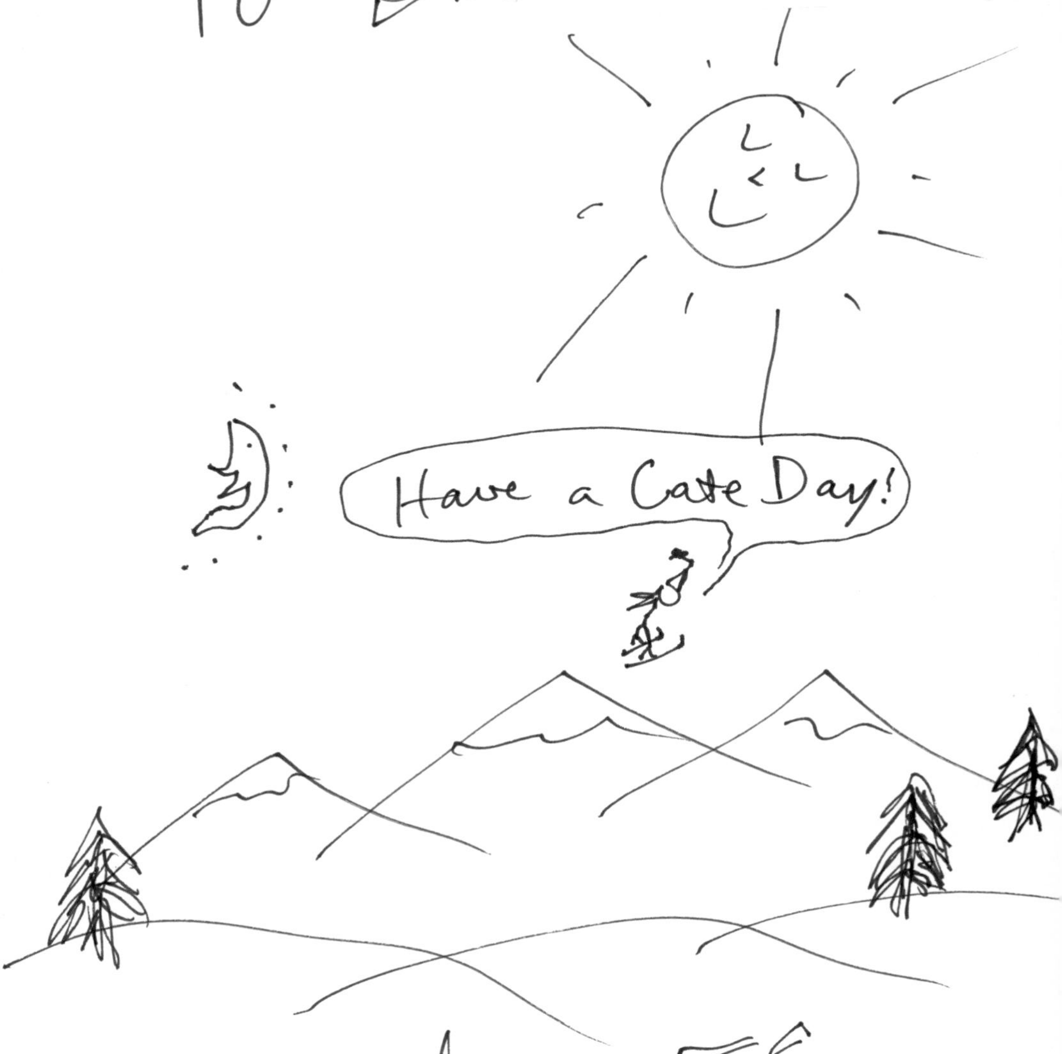

Sincerely, M.T.S.

Matthew Thomas Stember

Sally Stember

CATE

DARRINGER

Stember, Sally
Cate Darringer / by Sally Stember

ISBN-13:978-1540562999

BISAC: Young Adult Fiction / Action & Adventure / General
A plucky, young girl growing up in Indian Territory (modern day Oklahoma, c. 1892) Cate hungers to see the world. When a botanist comes to the ranch to take her brother James with him to Nigeria to search for a cure for cancer, she determined to convince the botanist she is the better candidate. In a case of mistaken identity, her father's testimony has condemned a mentally challenged man to the noose. Cate must uncover the facts to save her innocent friend. In the interim, she has a marriage to arrange, pheasants to raise, villains to hogtied, a horse to break, a skunk to apologize for, pigs to tie-dye, and Jimmy Davenport to lick some sense into. Is it any wonder some of her plans go awry?

This is the first in a series of "Cate Darringer" books. 288 pages, illustrated.

Published by Sun Bear Theaters. Printed in the United States of America.

Author's Prayer
Please forgive my typos as you would have others forgive yours.

Cover Photo: Shannon Stember, photographer. Julia Pitts as Cate.
Interior Art work: LuAnn M. Conant.

Table of Contents

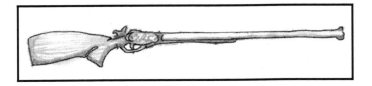

Thanks!

I thank my Mother for all things, but particularly for telling such exciting, adventurous tales of her childhood home. She may not have gotten the children she deserved, but she loves the children she got, and that is the more important truth.

I thank my sister Janet. She has always had more good ideas than anyone else I know. She is, in no small way, the inspiration behind Cate.

I thank the Multnomah County Hillsdale Branch Librarians. They are the best.

I thank the PDX Playwrights without whose critique and encouragement I would never have pursued authorship.

I do not have enough years left in me to thank all the people I should. It would be a fair assumption that if we have met, you taught me something, whether I made good of it or not, and your name should rest here.

Foreword

A few years ago, a lifelong friend asked if I would like to perform in a radio play written by his wife, Sally, for The Fertile Ground Festival that winter. He approached me because of my background as a professional actor. I was excited about doing my friend a favor, and after seeing the script I was enthused to be involved with the project.

Sally had written a radio play that featured a young girl named Cate Darringer, who had her own way of looking at things. Rehearsals went off without a hitch and when the big day came the live performance was fantastic! An amazing cast, complete with foley artist and an African drummer, brought Cate's story to life. Our audience response was in sync with every line. We actually had to pause several times to let the response settle down. I am proud to have been a part of that performance. Me thinks the favor was for thine own self.

Sally has that gift of taking the written word and placing them in such a fashion that the reader shifts from reading the scene to seeing the scene. People talk about "page turners" not knowing what it is that makes us want to move to the next page, to the next chapter. We can not explain it, yet we know it when we have it in our hands, in our hearts and in our minds.

I know you'll enjoy her storytelling as much as I do.

~ Brendan Quinlan ~ a.k.a. Ian Darringer & Sheriff Dole

CATE

DARRINGER

Chapter One: The Wait

The native grass had grown tall enough to hide a man on horseback. If Cate were to climb down to a lower branch, the bottoms of her feet could brush the tops of their maturing blooms. As it were, she preferred the view from the higher roosts on the living side of the Lightning Tree.

The tree was ancient and split between Life and Death. The old were forever cautioning the young to stay out of its gnarled limbs lest God be tempted to strike it again. Cate was never quite sure whom the caution was meant to protect: her, or the tree? Not that it mattered. If lightning had not stopped the tree from growing, then Cate saw no reason why it should stop her from climbing. That such behavior gave her mother palpitations was hardly her fault.

The warm late afternoon was drenched in eerie silence: no mockingbirds sang, no hummingbirds darted restlessly, even the ever-hungry crow had vanished from his perch. There was a sense of foreboding in the calm before the storm. Cate had been born during a tornado. Such a child can never truly fear the wind. The rest of the world, however, held its breath, desperate to go unnoticed by the approaching fury.

Cate peered through the thick leaves. The sun was hot and the air breathless. Through the heat haze, she imagined the world before her was Africa and she was a cheetah watching proudly over her savanna.

She pulled a hoof pick from the pocket of the hand-me-down pants she wore and used it to clean under her fingernails. The Warden, Cate's secret name for her mother, had emphasized on more than one occasion the important role clean fingernails played in making good impressions. Cate was desperate to impress the man she waited for, although why a botanist on his way to Africa would care about dirt under fingernails was beyond her. Surely, he would not expect his assistant to have clean fingernails all the time? When she was finished, she pocketed the hoof pick and gazed out across the expanse. There was no sign of him.

She pried a few leaves from a nearby branch. Weaving the stems together to make a fan, she thought of Cleopatra. The Egyptian queen never had to lift a finger to fan herself; she had slaves for that. Cate had not been a born a slave (a fact her mother blatantly ignored), but she had strong opinions on the matter nonetheless.

Slavery had torn the South apart when her parents were children, and the land and its people had yet to truly heal. That Indian Territory did not belong to either side, had not kept it safe from the horrors. The bloodshed, suspicion, fear and hatred had sent ripples of pain across the land like an earthquake that could not be contained by lines drawn on a map. The scars it had left behind were invisible but pronounced.

To Cate's way of thinking, the new laws had not gone far enough. They had not kept mothers from telling daughters how to behave. That this provision was absent from all government constitutions was proof: governments were shams.

At last her keen ears caught the sound of the slow, heavy steps of a tired man plodding along the dirt wagon road. Cate swelled with satisfaction. How ashamed her family would feel for doubting her, and for making their guest walk in from the crossroads. They easily could have hitched the buckboard and gone to fetch him.

Plod. Plod. Plod.

Cate was curious. For all the talk regarding his arrival, there had been none on the topic of his physical appearance. Would he be as tall as the Watusi? Or as short as a Pygmy? Would his eyes glow in the dark like a cheetah's? Or would his neck be stretched out as long as a giraffe's with layers of metal rings around it? Would he have a stick through his nose? Or maybe a scar running down his face from a lion's claw?

Cate climbed higher still for a better look, way up into the top of the Lightning Tree where only the reckless dared go. She parted the leafy coverage to peer out. She caught only a glimpse of a man's dark, wide brim hat through gaps in the tall grass. His head bobbed up and down with each laborious step. Maybe he had been injured. That would explain why he was so slow. Cate considered climbing down and rushing to meet him, but she stopped herself. Eagerness could be off-putting. It was better to be coy.

Cate shimmied back down to her favorite perch to wait. Her thoughts raced towards all the wonderful adventures she would have in Africa once he was convinced to take her with him. Cate was so lost in her daydream that she was startled when the man flung his travel bags on the ground beneath her bough and collapsed in a heap beside them. His weathered, dusty hat hid his face. His hands were brown, but that was hardly an indicator of what the rest of him would be. The Southern sun browned the hands of many a laborer much darker than the rest of the body.

After a bit, he pulled a flask from one of his travel bags and took a swig. Cate knew it was water. Her father would not have spoken so highly of a man who imbibed spirits.

She wondered if his face would be covered with tattoos that told the story of his many travels. Or better yet, smothered with ornate welts depicting his status as an explorer. She had met many Negroes who told such tales of their ancestors. She itched to go to their native lands and see the many faces there. She waited, but he just sat like a tired old lump, breathing and sighing.

Cate had brought a few nuts along to eat. She pulled some from her pocket and tossed one on the brim of his hat. He flinched, but that was all. She tossed another one with the same result. She tossed a third.

The man reached over and picked up one of the nuts. Cate held her breath. She suddenly remembered she was sitting in an oak tree and the nuts she tossed were pecans! The man studied the nut a moment, then looked up. He looked straight at Cate but gave no sign of seeing her. Perhaps it was because the glasses he wore needed cleaning, but then again, perhaps not. People seldom see the things they are looking for let alone the ones they are not. Either way, he had not seen her and Cate felt safe watching him.

He was as ordinary as any of her father's friends and he was old; at least as old as her father. How could there have been so much talk over someone so uneventful? It was common for the Gossip Brigade to make a to-do out of the ordinary, but her father? He was not one to embroider the truth and yet this man looked no more worldly wise than a farm hand.

He was white. There was nothing particularly wrong with being white; she was white herself, at least the parts hidden from the sun were. It was just that this man could easily pass as a clerk in the telegraph office whereas, she expected an African explorer to be exotic and bold!

He tsked. Cate's heart raced. She had heard of an African tribe that spoke in clicks and gulps. Was he speaking to her in an unknown language? She was about to ask him what he had said when he muttered something about "miserable squirrels."

He gave a sigh, and then ate the pecan! He turned his head to look around. After a moment, he pulled out a pocket watch from his shirt pocket.

Cate wondered why anyone would bother with a timepiece? Cate could tell the time from the position of the sun and the stars and from what flowers were blooming and which birds were singing. She mused, wouldn't it be fortuitous if something were to happen to his watch? Say a horse stepped on it or a pig ate it? Then she could amaze him with her natural timekeeping skills. Without a timepiece to argue the point, he would have to accept her word.

Cate thought a bit, then realized it would do no good to wish misfortune on a timepiece. She would surely be blamed for its demise, even if she were clear on the other side of the ranch when it happened.

The man stood up and gathered his bags. With a deep sigh, he continued his journey down the rutted wagon road. Cate waited for the man to be out of sight. When he was a safe distance ahead, she slithered down the tree's well-worn trunk and followed in pursuit.

Chapter Two: The Meeting

It was an easy matter for Cate's young legs to catch up with the tired old man, but she hung back and kept a respectful distance. She wanted to get a better measure of this man. She found his laborious struggle amusing and she mimicked him. Her bare feet matched his clumsy gait and her shoulders the roll of his as he struggled with the weight of his load. She mimed his every movement for several minutes before tiring of the game. She silently moved in closer until she was just behind him. Her Southern twang broke the silence, "You'll need to take bigger steps."

"Oh!" he cried, dropping his bags.

She had not meant to startle him. She wondered if he was always this jumpy. He turned slowly and faced her. Cate wondered if his cheeks were red from the heat or from embarrassment.

He studied the waif before him. Her voice pegged her as a young girl, yet she had the hair and the clothes of a wild boy. Her bare feet were camouflaged with earth, and the rest of her was as brown as a berry from the Southern sun. Shoulders squared back, head held high, she had all the confidence of a man. Her face carried a soft, earnest expression.

He considered her a moment. She looks harmless enough, he thought, but so does an asp. Looking around for a logical place, he finally asked, "Wherever did you come from?"

"Teota," she said surprised, as if the entire world knew she had given the Lightning Tree a grownup name; it was after all a grown up tree. Seeing his blank face she added, "That scarred Lightning Tree back yonder. The one you drank your water under."

He shivered. "Gracious, you've been following me that far? You're like a svelte lioness stalking a lumbering wildebeest." His heart raced at the thought of being prey.

"Cheetah," she corrected politely, "I'm a cheetah, not a lioness." She hoped he would be impressed with her knowledge of African wildlife.

He pulled a handkerchief from his pocket. He pushed his hat back to mop his brow. Cate could see he had a thick head of hair belying his aged face. Except for his glasses, he looked disappointingly ordinary to her. He, on the other hand, thought she was far from ordinary. She was eyeing him like a predator deciding which part to devour first. A shiver ran down his spine.

"Ah, yes," he stammered, "either way, I'd have been shred to pieces to feed your hungry cubs."

Cate considered his remark. She shrugged, "No, not a scrawny thing like you, not enough meat for my cubs. I'd kill you just for sport and leave you for the hyenas."

"Hardly a comforting thought," he shuttered. He had seen hyenas feasting and it was not how he would leave this world if given a choice. He took a long look at the massive tree in the distance that dwarfed even the tall grass. He narrowed his eyes as he looked at her and then asked, "I don't suppose you noticed any extremely large squirrels in that tree, did you?"

"Oh yes," she said earnestly, "they grow monstrously large in the territory. They grow so big, they aren't even afraid of a cheetah. A feisty one was throwing nuts. It's why I had to leave my perch. Cheetahs don't like to be pelted with nuts."

He looked at her innocent face and had he been less irritable from disappointment, he might have been inclined to believe her. He studied her then said, "If you're a cheetah, prove it."

"Prove it?" asked Cate. She thought a moment and then snarled. "Ggggrooowwwl!"

"No! No!" he pleaded, shrinking back as if he was afraid she might pounce. "Run! Run like the wind! Prove you are the fastest animal alive!"

Cate's young legs lite down the rutted dirt road. The man hardly had time to blink before she disappeared out of sight. He was momentarily glad and congratulatory on how cleverly he gotten rid of her. Now he could wallow in his world of self-pity without distraction. Then a horrible truth dawned on him. He well could be lost. The girl, or cheetah, or whatever creature she may have been playing, probably could tell him where he was. He quickened his pace in hopes of catching up.

Suddenly, she did it again. She came out of nowhere to startle him anew. She brushed passed him, knocking a bag out of one hand and causing him to drop the other. She ran up the dirt road, stopped and turned. He stood stock still, astonished. How had she gotten behind him without his knowing?

"I've just circled the globe. Is that fast enough?" she asked.

"The globe?" he mused. "Yes, that would be an amazing feat. You put the cheetah to shame."

"Lots of animals are faster than cheetahs," she said nonchalantly, raising her face to look up at him. His wire-rimmed glasses did give him the appearance of worldliness, she thought.

"Oh? Such as?" he asked. He wondered if new discoveries had been made in the Territories during his absence.

She shrugged, "I've been a cheetah dozens of times and my horse Kiwi can outrun me any day of the week."

His spirits lifted at the mention of a horse. He peered around. "You have a horse?" he asked hopefully. He craned his neck in all directions hoping to catch a glimpse of it hiding in the tall grass.

"Of course. The fastest horse in all the land!" boasted Cate. She could tell by his enthusiasm that she had sown the seeds of intrigue well and piqued his curiosity.

"May I be so bold as to inquire where she may be?" he asked politely.

"At home, resting." It pained her to confess this. Cate did not want the man to think Kiwi a lame horse; she expected Kiwi to be part of the deal of her going to Africa. "Nebraska Jo said I'd wear her legs to nubbins if I didn't let her rest now and again." Durn that Nebraska Jo.

The man was crestfallen. "And today, of all days, is the day she needed to rest?" he observed sadly.

"Had to be today," she affirmed with a solemn air. "Nebraska Jo got out the growth stick and proved to me she's getting shorter." One could feel the concern she held for her horse.

"I see. Well, we can't have Kiwi's legs being worn to nubbins," he sighed, a little deflated. He felt as though the closer he came to his destination, the further away it became, eluding him like a mirage in the Ténéré desert. He felt near to weeping.

Then the cheetah girl smiled at him. It was the sort of smile one would gladly travel a thousand miles just to see. In his case, he had traveled even farther. He smiled back. "Earlier you said I'd need to take bigger steps. Just where is it you think I'm off to?" he asked.

The question surprised her. The answer was obvious – unless he was not the botanist she was waiting for. She looked again at his dusty bags and his weathered face. She could not be wrong. She would never live it down if she was. "The Darringer's ranch," she explained, adding, "It's the only place out this way."

"Ah, yes," he said, relieved. "That would make you Ian's lovely daughter Cate."

"It would, and you are 'Dr. Livingstone, I presume.' " Cate spoke quite grandly, as if she were quoting a line from a play.

He marveled at her. How quickly she moves from cheetah to reporter, as fluid as water, he thought. He had a soft spot in his heart for actresses, having given his heart to one many years before. He was flattered by her remark and sighed. "Ah, alas, no, though undoubtedly, I feel that I am as lost as he."

He tucked his handkerchief into his pocket. Finally removing his hat, he spoke theatrically, "Allow me to introduce myself. I am Ralph Mahoney, daring explorer and humble botanist at your service." He made an elaborate bow, for he had a flare for the dramatic as well.

Her smile broadened. Her family would be dining on crow tonight! Cate fluttered her leaf fan in front of her face, hoping he would notice how clean her nails were. Speaking with all the grace and dignity of nobility, she curtsied and replied, "Charmed, I'm quite sure, Sir Ralph."

With delight he responded, "I as well, for the Queen herself hath never met a more delightful noblewoman." Even barefoot in hand-me-down boy's clothes, the little ambassador before him held herself with the poise of a Southern lady.

He stooped to pick up his bags, but she quickly took one. He thought to object, but she lifted it with such ease he gladly allowed her to carry it. She is like an ant, he thought, able to carry objects many times her size. He smiled. Picking up the other bag, he offered Cate his arm, "Shall we?"

"We shall," replied Cate, delicately placing her hand on top of his forearm. She hoped again he would notice her clean fingernails, but he said nothing. She had noticed his were well cared for and wondered if his mother checked them every night before bed.

She gazed up at the clouds as they commenced to stroll down the narrow dirt road. The sky had grown a field of cotton and some invisible hand was gathering it all up into a bale. The eerie calm would be ending soon. They would have to get a move on.

Sir Ralph was as oblivious to the approaching weather as he was of Cate's clean fingernails. He was just glad to know he was close to his destination. Nothing else mattered. It had been ages since he had escorted anyone as lovely as Cate. It had been donkey years since he had done anything as giddy as role play. He was home, back in the land of his childhood. He could be forgiven for a moment of play. His spirit felt refreshed, the length of the road no longer mattered.

"I am pleased to tell you," Cate confided, "I have followed your exploits with great interest and I am quite prepared to assist you in your further adventures. When do we leave for Nigeria?"

For a moment the question sounded like a playful one and he almost gave it a playful response. However, he had long ago learned women have a habit of holding men to their words, no matter under what circumstances they might have been uttered. He considered the question, "I'm afraid..."

"Oh, you mustn't ever be afraid," Cate chided. "It's a

complete waste of energy, unless it's done for fun. Do you enjoy being afraid, Sir Ralph?"

"No, quite the opposite," he sighed, "I meant only it injures me to disappoint you, for I am forced to tell you, I come not for you, milady, but for thy brother, Sir James."

"Oh, you don't want James," she blurted. "He's something of a coward." She had not meant to be so blunt, but some things cannot be candy-coated.

"Oh?" The idea caught Sir Ralph off guard. "Then my sources have been unreliable. On what do you base this harsh assessment?"

In a conspiring tone that would have put the best of the Gossip Brigade to shame, Cate loudly whispered, "He's been in love with Ida Sue Williams since the first day he laid eyes on her and hasn't the guts to tell her."

Sir Ralph could tell from the look on Cate's face that she considered this to be an unspeakable act of cowardice, akin to deserting one's post in the field of battle. The world holds cowards in low regard, but in the war-ravaged South, they were beyond contempt. "Well," Sir Ralph sighed thoughtfully, "One mustn't be too hard on a young man on the matter of love, for a woman's beauty has weakened the will of many a Hercules."

"Speak thou from experience?" Cate asked, raising an accusing eyebrow.

"Sadly, yes," he ceded. He would rather be chased by a thousand hyenas than a single woman in love. It was a fact he was sore to admit, but he had been warned Cate could charm a turtle from its shell and thought it best to surrender early in the skirmish. Perhaps such an admission would soften her view of James.

"This lady, was she fair?" Cate asked, although she knew the answer. Lost ladyloves are always so.

"Like a summer day," he sighed. "Never have I found fairer, though I have searched the world over." He noticed the sun on Cate's chestnut hair and the spark in her dark eyes, and thought how soon it would be she would have knights on white steeds jousting for her hand.

"What became of her?" Cate asked. "Did she find another? Or did she spend her days a spinster, pining away for the love you denied her?" Her tone was part melodrama and part accusation.

"I'm afraid," he began slowly, reaching up to loosen his collar.

"You mustn't be afraid. We've already discussed that," she asserted.

"Alas, it is an accurate term, for I have been a coward." In truth, he was a coward still. He would run from this conversation and Cate's inquisition in a heartbeat if he had the legs of a younger man. He wished wishing could make him brave, then he would gather up all the wildflowers along the road and travel back in time to lay them at his true love's feet. If only he had a second chance.

On the one hand, Cate had long found cowards deplorable; but on the other hand...a coward would need a brave person like Cate to look after him. She waited for him to say more, but it seemed that he had lost the wool of his thread so she prompted him. "You were saying?" she asked.

"Yes," he continued, "I was divulging my weakness." He spoke theatrically, with his hands as well as with his tone, to make light of his shame and pain. "There is no scenario that would suit both my ego and my desire for her happiness, so I have chosen to comfort myself with ignorance. I have no knowledge of her now, only memories of then."

Despite the discomfort in his face she pressed on, "Is that what you'd want for James? Only memories?" she asked.

"It is not for me to say," he shrugged. A cowardly response, albeit, a true one.

"Because," she continued, "now Ida Sue is seeing George McGillicutty and more's the pity, I say."

"Ah, well," he hesitated, "perhaps it's for the best James has no one to pine for him. No broken heart left behind."

"No reason to leave her behind," Cate started, but then stopped, because she was far more interested in her own cause than Ida Sue's.

"Of course there is," remarked Sir Ralph, surprised he would have to explain, "Africa is no place for a woman."

Cate stopped in her tracks and looked at him curiously. "Do you mean to tell me the women of Africa have all packed up and left and the only people there are men?"

The concept startled him. "No, no, there are plenty of women, as well as children. I mean only, it's a dangerous place crawling with disease," he said gravely.

"Diseases like tuberculosis, smallpox and cancer?" Cate pressed. "Mother says cancer is the worst disease in the world. Aunt Muriel died of it last May, you know."

"Yes, I was sorry to hear that. We used to play down by the creek, your Aunt Muriel and I," he reminisced.

"Creek?" asked Cate.

"I meant crick," he corrected.

"Then you ought to have said," declared Cate.

"Yes, you are right. I ought to have," agreed the African explorer. He wondered how much of his childhood language had he lost while on his travels? How many memories with them? He cast his eyes across the fields and wondered if he had walked right past the crick without even knowing. Cate cleared her throat and he looked back at her. He could almost see a bit of Muriel in Cate's face, and the thought brought back memories of a simpler time.

"I'm sure your aunt is, in part, why James is so eager to join me in my search for the cure." The botanist hoped his reasoning would appease her queries.

"She was every bit my aunt, too," Cate protested, "Makes no sense to take James and not me."

He saw a hardness in her expression that reminded him why he had remained a bachelor. Why were women, even small ones, so difficult to reason with? "But Africa is full of dangerous predators that would gobble up a girl your size in one bite!" he blustered.

"Hmm," huffed Cate. "Any animal large enough to eat me in one bite could eat you in two. If that were the case, it stands to reason they would have already eaten everyone in Africa to sate their enormous appetites. Then, once the food was all gone, they'd have died off from starvation. You exaggerate," she stated firmly.

"Perhaps a bit," he conceded, "but African animals are vicious nonetheless."

"Worse than pumas, wolves, and bears?" she queried.

Cate put down the bag and released his arm to animate her story as she enacted both prey and predator. She stalked down the road, claws at the ready. "A puma was stalking Papa in the woods last week and just as it leapt for his throat, BAM! Right between the eyes! I want to make a necklace of the claws, but Papa says it wouldn't be ladylike. But if I were in Africa, no one would think twice of it, would they?"

"True," admitted Ralph. Then he thoughtfully added, "Which is precisely why you shouldn't go! Some of the African tribes can be quiet savage."

"Like the Shawnee, Apache and Comanche?" she asked. She wanted to add "and the Blue Coats, the Grey Coats, and the Settlers," for she knew they were just as bad, but she had no desire to appear disloyal. Loyalty was a survival skill in these parts.

He considered her remark. "Yes, Africa must seem like a walk in the park to a child raised in Indian Territory."

"Oh, I hope not!" blurted Cate. She picked up the bag and offered her arm to him. He took it and they recommenced their stroll. "Parks are the contrived, pitiful attempts of men to control nature, which is idiotic at best, and the worse of it is, they're boring!"

Spoken just like her father, thought Ralph.

Cate went on with her pronouncement. "I think the Bible is amiss that it didn't list boring as a deadly sin."

"Ah! But it does! Sloth!" He beamed, pleased the conversation had veered off at last. He felt much more at ease discussing the Bible than he did discussing romance, or having to explain to a headstrong female, whatever her size, why he couldn't be taking her to Africa with him.

She looked at him curiously, "Laziness is not the same as

boring." She leaned in and spoke enthusiastically, "Did you know sloths have moss growing in their fur? If animals can be part plant, then surely," she theorized, "there are plants that are part animal."

"Gracious, and what would be the good of that?" he asked. He considered plants dangerous enough without giving them animal parts. What an active imagination, he thought.

"I've heard tales," she confided, "of man-eating plants that swallow Hottentots whole!"

This story obviously delighted her. Still, he could not resist. "Just a moment ago, you said an animal of that size couldn't exist, and now you claim a plant can, but wouldn't it also suffer the same fate of mass annihilation?" he mused.

"A plant has a much slower digestive system," she declared with offhand authority. "It would be a good decade eating the first Hottentot, by which time they'd have more than replenished themselves. Since no one would suspect a plant for being the cause of disappearing tribesmen, it would never occur to anyone to hunt them, would it? They would simply continue to flourish. I'm eager to be the first to find proof! What sort of ship shall we be sailing on?"

Ah, back to the ship, are we? he thought. How so like a woman to find a way to circle back to a topic, like a buzzard circling over the dying. He thought a moment, then beamed a smile as he spread his hands to welcome her grandly to her invisible ship, saying, "Oh, that I could build you a ship out of clouds and sail with you across the skies!"

She looked again at the clouds which were beginning to darken and wondered what sort of ride they would make, but before she could ask, he added somberly, "I'm sorry, Cate, but it is James who will be accompanying me. You, my dear child, will be headed for school soon, I imagine."

"School!" she huffed. "I'd hardly call that imaginative. All you learn in school are facts, figures, and dates of deeds of old dead men. Hardly anything useful."

"Really?!" pondered the botanist. Ralph was amused that he had found a way to needle her at last. "I would think you could make use of any fact tossed your way."

"Such as?" she asked. Her tone carried a hint of dare to it.

He thought a moment, desperate to recall what he had learned when he was her age. "Well," he stalled. "If I were to say, ' A pint's a pound the world around,' then you would say?"

"That your world doesn't include Slider Johnson's still," quipped Cate. "Papa says it only takes half a pint of his Red Mash to leave one's head pounding for days."

"A fact best learned second hand," Ralph grimaced. He had been young once. And foolish. Some of his exploits were best forgotten. Looking into the direction of the late afternoon sun, he quickly changed the subject, "If I were to say, 'East is east and west is west and never the twain shall meet,' you would say?"

"That Kipling never stood on the shores of Cape Reinga where the Pacific Ocean crashes headlong into the Tasmanian Sea with a force that is both felt and seen for miles." Cate whipped her arms in a crashing motion for effect.

"How is it you know such a thing?" he marveled.

"I read, Sir Ralph," she boasted.

"Ah," he smiled and pointed out, "one of those useless skills you learned in that useless school of yours."

"School wasn't built 'til last spring. Papa taught me at home," Cate exclaimed proudly. Her father was a better teacher than the school marm she had now. He never called her 'impertinent' or 'sassy', or whipped her for speaking her mind, and he didn't expect her to sit still and be quiet all the time.

Ralph sighed. He imagined Cate kept the school marm quite busy. "Nonetheless, my point is made. No fact is too rigid, no truth too stern, you cannot bend it as easily as a willow sapling in spring. See those clouds?" He pointed skyward.

Of course she had, but Cate merely asked, "What about them?"

"If I were to tell you those are cumulus clouds, what would you say to that?" posed Ralph.

"What I said earlier, 'You'll need to take bigger steps.'"

"Oh? Why is that?" wondered the African explorer.

"Because in these parts, when cumulus clouds accumulate, it's sure to mean thunder and lightning. So unless you want to get drenched, I suggest you keep up with me!"

With that pronouncement, Cate sprang down the road like a springbok and was out of sight in an instant, leaving a startled botanist behind to wonder if he had just imagined her.

Chapter Three: Not a Word

Cate no more slammed the door of her home behind her when the first peel of thunder rumbled across the sky. She placed Ralph's case against the grandfather clock in the parlor. He should have kept up, she thought. She turned and nearly collided into her mother in the hallway.

Ann's ivory snow hair was pulled back severely into plaits as neat as a pin. She could not abide a hair out of place, while her daughter's hair went to great lengths to do just the opposite. Cate once asked her mother why she bothered to have hair when all she ever did with it was bind it out of the way. Cate never found out, but she did learn not to ask that again.

Her mother wore her usual sleeved apron and her usual look of displeasure. Ann stood stock still for a moment, eyeing her obstinate daughter. If her eyes had been knives, the family would have been attending a funeral.

"Your hands need washing and the table needs setting," seethed The Warden.

"But," Cate started.

Her mother drew herself up and bristled. Cate always marveled at how such a small woman could make herself appear ginormous. The Warden was in full form.

Cate cast her eyes to the floor as she hurried past her mother and into the kitchen where she was surely meant to be.

The Warden followed close behind, rushing to the cast iron wood stove and the milk gravy cooking on the back burner. She beat the gravy with the whisk so hard it was a wonder any stayed in the pan. Cate's mother began yammering on about how she had enough to do without Cate running off, forgetting her chores.

Cate had not forgotten them, she had just chosen not to do them. Lord, that woman can prattle, thought Cate as she scrubbed her hands clean in the wash basin. Why she bothered to clean her nails when clearly no one noticed was beyond her. She shook her hands dry and walked to the cupboard.

Her mother was so busy listing all the ways Cate had wronged her that she failed to notice Cate had gotten out the best plates, five sets in all: one for her, one for James, one for Mother, one for Papa, and one for Ralph.

Cate had dropped the "Sir." Less knowing folks may have wagged their tongues over their botanist house guest *before* his arrival, but he obviously was unworthy of the title if he could not see straight-off that he should be taking her instead of James.

Despite her mother's diatribe, which was preferable to her silence, Cate refused to believe it was her fault her mother was worked to the bone. Her mother was never satisfied with the work accomplished. Cate was sure it was her mother's mission in life to be worked to death. If her mother didn't like being bone-thin then she should eat more and work less.

Thunder vibrated the window panes and lightning lit up the room brighter than day. The rain came down like a waterfall. If there had been the slightest hint of a funnel, they would have run for the storm cellar. This storm brought more rain than wind and no alarm was warranted. At least, not yet.

When the meal was on the table and the evening lanterns lit, Cate walked out to the covered porch and clanged the iron triangle in the pattern of the dinner call. She wondered why it was so important to have the food on the table before calling the men when the fact was they seldom came when called.

There was just no training a man the way you could an animal. An animal would come running for grub, but nine times out of ten a man would think of one more thing to do before heading in. Cate was kept busy washing the cooking pans while waiting for the men to come in.

Sure enough, it was a full quarter of an hour before her brother James hung his coat on the porch to dry and came inside. His thick, dark hair hung close to his blue eyes. James favored his father in many ways, both in manners and in looks, although he had yet to grow as tall.

Cate secretly hoped he never would. She already envied him everything else. Him shooting up like a bean sprout would not help her feelings towards him any. He was old enough to travel. He was old enough to marry. Not that she wanted to marry, she just wanted to be "old enough" to live her life.

James took one look at Cate and grinned. "Well if it isn't the wayward girl coming home, *alone*," he smirked. He reached out and mussed her hair.

"I wouldn't," Cate started.

"Hush!" thundered her mother. "Not a word from you, not one word."

Cate buttoned her lip. Wait, she thought. Just you all wait.

A few minutes later, her father, Ian, finally hung his coat out on the porch and walked in the door. He walked over to the wash basin, washed his hands, then rolled his sleeves down and buttoned the cuffs.

Her mother marched Cate into the dining room to stand and wait by the table. James came in and patiently stood opposite Cate. The extra plate for Ralph was next to James. Ann stood at the end of the table closest to the kitchen.

Ian acknowledged the family with a nod and took a seat.

Like MacGregor, where Ian Darringer sat was the head of the table. While his size intimidated most people, it was his confidence that held their attention. Once he was seated, the rest of the family took their places.

"Good," nodded Ian, acknowledging his daughter. "I would have hated to go looking for a lost girl in this weather."

Cate sat quietly. Ian looked from Cate to his wife. He wished he could ignore their petty feuds, but he knew better. Cate had a lesson that needed learning. Lots of folks would get out the stick to discipline a willful child, but that was not Ann's way. Being told to be quiet made a person want to talk all the more. Ian sometimes wondered if a good whipping would be less painful than the intolerable silence that filled the room. Certainly, it would be over quicker. He could see the agony on his daughter's face.

He loved his daughter's independent ways, boasted of them in fact, but it wouldn't hurt her none to tell folk where she was going. It did not matter that Cate could take care of herself, better than most adults. It was that Ann would worry herself sick. A few summers back, Cate had disappeared for a fortnight. Cate had been swept away with a wild notion to go to "Peru." She traveled as far as Gup's Bend and decided to camp in the abandoned mine shaft. Who knows how long she would have stayed if Stumpy had not found her and tricked her into coming home. In the two weeks she was gone, Ann's hair had turned from a vibrant chestnut to a soft ivory. Cate needed to learn not to worry people like that.

When she disappeared after the noon meal, he had tried to tell Ann not to worry. If Cate had gone far, she would have taken Kiwi with her. That only worried Ann all the more. In her mind, if Kiwi had been left behind, the only explanation was that Cate had been abducted. Now, there his women sat, nearly vibrating from the strain of holding in all them womanly emotions.

Well, best get at it, he thought. Ian clasped his hands together and bowed his head.

The family followed his lead. Eyes squeezed shut and head

bowed, Cate listened to her father speak the familiar prayer. Cate loved his voice, and she was sure God loved it too. If ever there was a voice that could reach God's ears, this would be the one. It was both calming and authoritative. Even Cate seldom questioned him, although that had all changed since the murder trial. His testimony not only condemned Stumpy Gilbert, it had invited doubt to eat away her faith in him like termites in pine.

Once grace was finished, Ian, Ann and James began passing the food around and loading up their plates. Cate continued to sit quietly. "Mother," Ian hinted to Ann, "I believe a seam is about to split. You might want to see to that."

"And there's a list of things you might want to see to, too, starting with that daughter of yours," snipped Ann.

Ian raised an eyebrow. Questioning his authority in private was one thing, but he did not take well to it in front of the children. Husband and wife locked eyes in a silent, heated power struggle.

Cate would have joined in, but she could not decide which parent to stare down. She remained quiet, waiting for the outcome.

Finally, with eyes still firmly on her husband, Ann spoke, "Alright Cate, what is it you want to say?"

"Nothing," shrugged Cate, "Just wondering why nobody has asked why I set an extra plate."

It had been a coon's age since Cate had set an extra plate or two for her menagerie of imaginary friends. Nonetheless, without missing a beat, James remarked, "It's Tuesday, so it can only be for the ever charming and delightful Mrs. Needleheimer." He turned and addressed the extra plate, "We're extremely pleased to have you back, Mrs. Needleheimer, you've been away far too long."

Cate let out a gasp of exasperation. "For the tenth time, it's Wednesday, not Tuesday, and the plate is for Ralph."

"Who?" puzzled her mother. She could not recall having an imaginary Ralph for dinner before.

"Ralph Mahoney," answered Cate, as if it should have been obvious, which it should have been. He was due today, after all.

Then, because they continued to look puzzled, she explained further. "The botanist coming to take James on a safari with him. Though I don't know why he'd pick him over me, when clearly he doesn't even know what day of the week it is." Cate folded her arms across her chest and glared at her brother with a raised accusatory eyebrow.

Ian thought they had discussed the matter enough for one day at breakfast. He began replaying the week. "Sunday we went to church. Monday we dug post holes, then yesterday…"

"Was Tuesday," Cate glowered.

Ian sat with a puzzled look on his face. "James, was it Monday we dug those post holes, or did we do that after church on Sunday?"

James was serving himself some more skillet potatoes. He paused with the spoon in mid-air while thinking. He was tired and hungry. He wished his sister would learn to leave things be at meal time because a man has got to eat. He was wondering what he could say to get her to drop the subject and let him finish his meal in peace.

"Oh for pity's sake," grumbled Cate. She jumped up and headed to the parlor.

"Cate," snapped her mother sharply, "Cate, you haven't permission to leave the table. Ian, you tell her to come back here!"

Ian did not have the chance to say spit. In a flash Cate was back with Ralph's travel case. She plopped it down heavily on the empty seat.

Cate flopped down into her chair and spoke as much to herself as to the rest of the table, "I told him to take bigger steps. It ain't my fault he couldn't keep up."

Surprise spread across the faces of her family. They all stared at the bag none of them had ever seen before. In unison, everyone but Cate dropped their forks and bolted from the table.

"Catherine Mariah Darringer, why didn't you say something?" fumed her mother. Ann rushed to get her coat.

"You said 'Not a word, not one word,'" Cate called after her.

The Warden turned and stomped back. "You pick the strangest times to be obedient," she snarled.

"Ann!" barked Ian, "That's enough. You can take it up with her when we get back. James, go get Kiwi and hitch her to the buckboard."

"No!" protested Cate, "You can't take Kiwi, she needs her rest!"

"She's been resting all day," Ian thundered. He had been swallowing too much backtalk from Cate and he had just about reached his limit.

James knew when Pa gave an order, it was carried out. He was out the door in a flash, leaving Cate to call after him.

"James! No, don't do it!" she protested. With the door slamming between them, she took it up with her Pa again. "Nebraska Jo said we'll wear her legs to nubbins if she doesn't get to rest!"

"If that happens between now and the time we get back, I'll buy her some new legs," promised Ian, hotly.

"Cate!" snapped her mother. The Warden grabbed Cate by the shoulders and pointed her towards the kitchen door. "Get in that kitchen and boil some water and warm up a blanket for our guest."

"But…" A crestfallen Cate tried to stand her ground. When that failed, she stormed into the kitchen on her own accord.

Not one of them cared that she had been right all along. As the rest of the family scrambled to get lanterns and hitch Kiwi to the buckboard, Cate slumped into the kitchen to heat up a large kettle of water for Ralph's feet. She placed an iron on the wood stove to heat up so she could warm a blanket like she had been told. Not a soul could hear her mutter beneath her breath. "I tried to tell them earlier it was Wednesday. It is not my fault they all are just a pack of stubborn mules who cannot listen."

Cate spilled some of the kettle water as she lifted it to the stove. She grumbled profusely. Keep that up and she would need to go out to the well for more.

"It don't seem right to be in trouble for being obedient," she fumed to herself. "Why even bother to do what you're told when half the time you're in as much trouble for obeying as you are when you don't listen at all."

She used a heavy towel to grab the iron handle of the wood stove door and slung it open. She angrily stoked the fire inside with more kindling and logs. "At least when you don't listen, you get to do things your way before you're in trouble," she muttered. "I didn't save up Kiwi's legs all day long just so y'all could hitch her up for a nighttime gallivant you wouldn't even let me go on."

She laid a towel on the kitchen table to protect it from the hot iron she would use when she ironed the blanket. "Even if you could buy a horse new legs, which I am fairly sure you can't, they wouldn't be as good as the ones she has now."

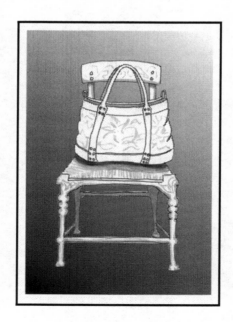

Chapter Four: Carrots for Kiwi

Despite her reputation as being "slower than molasses on a cold winter morning," Cate managed to finish her chores before the rescue party returned. This left her plenty of time to continue her sulk. When the heroes finally appeared, Cate listened skeptically to their explanations.

Mr. Mahoney claimed he had heard the dinner bell clanging in the distance and tried to take a short cut through the pasture. The darkened sky and the heavy rain had rendered his glasses useless and shortly after leaving the road he became turned around. Cate questioned the validity of a man turning north when the dinner bell was clearly west, the direction he was already headed. Although, by her way of thinking, if that were true, it was just more proof that he needed her in Africa. He needed someone with good tracking sense.

When the brave trio failed to find him by the time they reached the Lightning Tree, they doubled back and worked their way slowly over the road. Ian jumped out and looked for foot prints with his lantern. James stood on top of the driver's seat with another lantern, calling Mr. Mahoney's name, while Ann drove. They moved at a snail's pace. Finally, Ian saw what looked like a path cutting through the pasture grass and he signaled the family to wait. Ian followed the trail of trodden grass 'til he found his childhood friend. Ralph was lost, confused, drenched and grateful for having been found. Ian had looked at his friend and quipped, "Dr. Livingstone, I presume."

The whole family reveled in his wittiness. Cate glowered.

Ralph Mahoney's reception may have been delayed, the food may have been held over, but it was Ann's cooking, and so it was nutritious to the soul as well as the flesh. The blanket was warm, new burn hole notwithstanding, and he was glad to be soaking his feet in a pail of warm Epsom salt water. With good humor, he accepted each heartfelt apology for the confusion.

While Ralph basked in a halo of family friendship, Cate suffered a different fate. The Warden's eyes were throwing daggers at her while Cate continued to stew.

The four of them discussed Ralph's visit, the point of which was to get reacquainted with James. James was a babe in arms when Ralph had left for his first journey. While that had been a long time ago, he knew both Ian and Ann well. As far as he was concerned, being their son was recommendation enough.

Why this attitude failed to apply to their daughter was beyond mystifying to Cate, as was his belief that she would require a chaperone. Cate needed no chaperoning to live her life in Indian Territory. She certainly would not need a chaperone in Africa, either.

The men sat next to the fire, trying to outboast each other. Cate found Ralph's stories as dull as the history books in her new school. Any fool could see that he needed her to come along with him to make Africa the adventure of a lifetime!

The discussion turned to politics. Cate had little patience for politics. Everybody west of the Atlantic knew President Harrison was a spendthrift. Heck, even a botanist lost in a wheat field knew that. As far as his opponent was concerned, Cate believed anyone named Grover Cleveland ought to be out planting trees, not stumping his opinions all over states and territories. Besides, he all ready had his chance. And a whole town shared his name. What did he want? A whole state?

To Cate, politics was nothing more than one fool trying to out-dumb the next fool. It made little difference to Cate which fool was in office. She lived in a territory, not a state. She failed to understand why she should care about the policies of a foreign nation, which was what the United States of America was in her mind: a foreign nation. A hostile foreign nation at that, imposing its will on 'Territories' it did not rightfully own, but wanted to boss around.

Any country that did not allow women the right to vote was just plain barbaric. When she growed up, she would build her own government, one where all people have the right to vote, including children, even those who cannot spell and had a "propensity" for adding punctuation for decoration!

The more she listened, the more she wanted to veer the conversation in the right direction. Cate was about to open her mouth when The Warden relegated her to the kitchen. "Slavery was abolished," Cate muttered sourly.

"Yes it was," agreed Ann, "in the United States of America. But as you are so fond of pointing out, you live in a Territory. And in this Territory, in this house, you will do as you are told."

Cate slunk into the kitchen. She reluctantly concluded it was best to be out of sight before The Warden could think up more chores. For awhile, Cate played at being a galley slave in a ship on a tempest sea, but then she heard Kiwi out in the barn.

Seeing that The Warden was extremely busy with the extremely uneventful house guest, Cate reckoned her absence would go unnoticed. She grabbed a lantern and quietly slipped out of the house and headed to the stables. The light from the lantern drew attention from the other horses. They knew which horse Cate was looking for, but still, it never hurt to ask.

Cate grabbed a bunch of carrots kept in a bin by the door and quietly walked to the first stall. Lep, a pig-eyed, blotted excuse for a horse, snorted at her. He was always stabled closest to the door. Cate suspected he was afraid of the dark because he would not go any further into the stable without having a fit. He was hardly her favorite, but Cate liked to stay on the good side of an ornery horse. She held out a carrot for him and he grabbed it in his usual rough manner. He eyed her with disgust. One of these days, thought Cate, I'm gonna teach that horse some manners.

She worked her way down the stalls, handing out carrots as she went. Each horse snuffed a greeting and took the carrot as the casual gesture of good will that it was. Finally, she came to her heart's true love.

There she was, the most beautiful Marsh Tacky ever to walk God's green earth. In the dim light from the lantern, she looked pure black, but Cate knew when the sun shone on it, the fiery color of her coat would shine through. Her father described Kiwi's coat as "liver chestnut" and her mane simply as "orange," but Cate didn't much care for that description. It lacked poetry. She had spent many hours trying to think of a better way of expressing the passion Kiwi's coat evoked, but time and time again, words failed her. Cate knew only that Kiwi was the most beautiful of all horses, and she was hers.

James had done a good job of rubbing Kiwi down and putting a blanket on her. As envious as she was of James at times, Cate did appreciate the good things he did.

Kiwi shook her beautiful mane and bobbed her head in greeting. She nuzzled Cate. Fact was, Cate meant as much to Kiwi as Kiwi did to Cate, and they hadn't seen much of each other that day. Cate brushed her hand against Kiwi's neck. She felt warmed and reassured. She gave Kiwi her carrot. It disappeared quickly. The other horses may have only received one carrot, but Kiwi knew she deserved two. She nuzzled Cate and Cate obliged. Cate put her ear against Kiwi's chest and listened to her breathe. It was like listening to her own heartbeat.

ʊ

The next morning was bright and beautiful, as if the storm from the previous evening had never existed. While in future tellings it would always be known as the storm Ralph arrived in, or sometimes as "The Mahoney Storm," it didn't hold a candle to the storm Cate had been born in. Cate's storm had carted away the small house where her family lived. While Cate had been born in the root cellar, her early life was spent living in the barn and she was to be forever attracted to the smell of hay. The new house was slightly more than a frame when the rest of the family gratefully moved in. Cate, however, would return to the barn time and time again.

At first, Ian would carry his sleeping daughter from the barn to the house. He would patiently carry her up the flight of stairs to her room and tuck her into her proper bed. He would lovingly wish her sweet dreams.

Even a small child can become heavy. After awhile the thought of carrying in a child who considered being carried in ill-treatment, appealed to him less and less. When she began sneaking back down in the middle of the night, he quit fetching her altogether. Once she had a horse of her own, it was a small move from barn to stable. Getting Cate to sleep in the 'people stable', as Cate called it, was a tiresome battle that Ann rarely won.

Despite her mother's insistence that Cate sleep in her room while they had company in the house, and despite Cate's good intentions of doing so, Cate had fallen asleep in the stable with Kiwi.

Cate lay in Kiwi's warmth, dreaming of Africa. Kiwi sputtered mildly. She nuzzled Cate half awake. A morning bird cooed, and Cate became alarmed. Her mother would be none too pleased that she had slept in the stable, while a guest stayed in the house.

Cate peered out of the stable in the pre-dawn light. From across the yard, she could see a lamp being lit in her parents' room. Cate quickly scurried out of the stable, made a mad dash across the yard, and took a flying leap onto the magnolia vine that wound its way up to her room. She climbed as nimbly as a spider on web, straight to her bedroom window on the second floor of the house. Holding onto the pinky-thin vines with one hand, she pushed back some of the vines to search for the secret stick that keep her window open.

"Stuffin' on it," muttered Cate. The stick was gone. Somebody had locked her window.

Chapter Five: A Boubou

Cate stood up and pressed herself tight against the magnolia vines. She scooted along the narrow ledge, holding on tight. A cat would envy both her sense of balance and her endless supply of lives. Cate tapped lightly on her brother's window. "Psst!" She whispered.

James was already dressed and about to leave the room when the tap caught his attention. He turned and looked back at the window. His sister's silhouette against the early shades of dawn reminded him of shadow puppets.

Why she couldn't just use a door like everyone else, he would never know. It weren't like nobody knew what she was up to. He walked over and pulled the window up to let his sister crawl through. He watched as she used her hands to 'walk' her way across the floor, until her legs cleared the window ledge. When they flopped on the floor, she stood up and smiled at him.

He smiled back. For all her peculiarities, James was going to miss his Little Peanut, but he was not about to let on.

A light breeze came through the window and James was blessed with a good whiff of his sister. He waved his hands around and scrunched up his face. "Pee-ew-whee! Cate, your horse smells better than you do," he teased. He did his best to hide a smile.

"Of course she does," quipped Cate. "There ain't a horse alive than doesn't smell better than a human."

She pulled her clothes up close to her nose and sniffed. Her face screwed up. She grabbed another section and sniffed again. After the third whiff, she had to concede that with company in the house, she had better wash up.

She walked over to the wash basin on the stand by her brother's bed and splashed her face with water. "Got a clean pair of hand-me-downs?" she asked him.

"None I'd lend a girl that smells like a horse. You could use some soap," he stated matter-of-factly. He held a bar of soap out for her to take.

Cate eyed the soap in her brother's hand like it was diseased. "I used soap Sunday," she retorted.

"And you'll use soap today if you don't want to have breakfast with the chickens," he teased. They both knew such elegant dining would suit her just fine. "For Ma's sake," he prodded.

She frowned and reluctantly took it from him, grumbling to herself. Cate found soap repugnant for many reasons. One of them was that soap fouled the water, necessitating more frequent changes. Who had to lug all that water up all those stairs? The person with the young legs, that's who. Did anyone care if her young legs were worn to nubbins? No. Did The Warden, who insisted upon living in a two storied high-rise, have a room on the second floor? No.

James watched in amusement as his sister talked to herself. Her facial muscles had a habit of twitching even when she was silent, and her hands fluttered around like butterflies trying to dance out the words she was keeping to herself. All that extra hand-waving was slowing down the washing and causing a fair amount of splashing. He quickly removed two hand towels from his top drawer, one to clean up the spilled water and one to give to Cate.

"Ma's going to expect me to look nice," explained Cate. She started to dry her face off with her shirt, but James quickly handed her the hand cloth.

"So wear a dress," he answered, a little pleased to see her in a quandary. "Your chifforobe is busting full with them."

"Yeah, from when I was five. You know Ma stopped sewing for me," Cate snapped.

"That's because you kept getting tar and pitch and manure all over them," he teased.

"Not my fault she can't sew a dress that's practical. Always making more work for herself sewing up bunches of sissy frills and dandy buttons every which way," she muttered.

Ann had been certain Cate would quickly grow tired of

wearing her brother's old hand-me-downs and would come begging, grateful for even the most sissy of frills in no time at all. She underestimated Cate's lack of fashion sense. Mother and daughter were locked in a stalemate.

"Come on, James, you've got to have something that's clean," Cate pleaded.

James smiled. He knew she knew he would soften. He walked over to his dresser and opened a drawer. He took out a shirt and handed it to her, wondering how many of his friends had sisters who borrowed their clothes?

"Much obliged," Cate squealed. She clutched the clean shirt in her hands and ran for the door. She took a quick peek down the hall. The Warden was down in the kitchen by the sounds of it. Her young legs carried her quickly to her room.

James snickered as he descended the stairs to light the morning fire. He had a feeling his sister was going to be in trouble before she even had a chance to say "Good morning." He was just adding the kindling to the fireplace when Cate came flying down the banister. James often wondered how fast she would go if someone were to oil it with pig's fat. With enough grease, an open door and a little tail wind, it was completely possible that she would sail out the door, up and over the stable and land in the horse trough on the far side of the barn. leastways, that was the general consensus.

Ann rounded the corner and saw her daughter standing in the doorway of the parlor. For the shortest of moments, Ann mistook the shirt for a dress. "Catherine Mariah," she fumed, when she realized what her daughter was wearing, "Whatever are you doing in that?"

The reproach startled Cate. She had thought she had done a good job of making herself presentable. She looked the shirt over to be sure. "It's clean," Cate responded, puzzled by her mother's clear disapproval.

The day had hardly begun and already Ann was exhausted by her daughter's inability to understand even the most basic of social dignities. Ann's voice quavered with exhaustion from trying to remain calm, "You're not coming down in an old night shirt, clean, or otherwise. Now get backup to your room and get dressed properly."

Cate slunk backup the stairs and stomped into her room. Her mother wanted her in a dress. Fine. She would wear a dress. None of the dresses she owned fit proper. The best she could do was to wear one that opened in the front over another one that opened in the back to hide the fact she couldn't fasten either one of them. She had to snip a few threads to loosen the seams so her arms could move. It seemed a little disrespectful to Cate to mistreat garments this way but her mother wanted her in a dress, what else could she be expected to do?

When Ann saw Cate come into the dining room, she didn't know whether to laugh or cry. How could someone be so good at being so bad at following directions? Why was Cate not in the dress she had borrowed from Juliette Davenport for the occasion?

"What?" Cate asked in response to her mother's expression.

Ann was struggling for words when Mr. Mahoney entered the room in full African regalia.

Ann's face lost all its color.

Cate's eyes popped and it was all she could do to suppress a belly laugh. A full grown man in a dress?

"I hope you don't mind," Mr. Mahoney said, smiling broadly to Ann, "but my other clothes need washing, and I find this to be quite comfortable for casual occasions."

"Not at all, Ralph," croaked Ann. Her face hid her true feelings on the subject. "You make yourself right at home." She smiled a terse smile.

It isn't bad enough I have a daughter that wears pants, thought Ann. I have to have a male house guest running around in a dress, too? She was struggling to think what she must have done to deserve this when Cate interrupted her thoughts.

"If I wore a bed sheet to the breakfast table you'd tan my hide!" Cate protested. How could her mother be so unfair?

"Cate!" snapped her mother. "If you feel uncomfortable with the company at this table, perhaps you'd prefer to have breakfast with the chickens."

"No, no," Mr. Mahoney intervened, "No need to be so hasty. I'm sure she's more concerned over the mystery of my rights to do as I please, while she must listen to her elders."

Yes, that was precisely her point, and for a moment, Cate smiled. Adults rarely took her side.

Then he had to go on. "It is rather simple, Cate. It is the way of the world that children must abide by the rules of adults, no matter how it displeases them. It is as true here as it is in Africa." His eyes twinkled as he smiled.

Cate seethed. She was NOT a child!

Ralph made himself at home in what he obviously considered "his" chair at the table. Cate couldn't believe his rudeness! He had not waited for her father to sit first; he had not even waited for Ian to come into the room. Cate waited for her mother to set him straight, but Ann said nothing. This lack of admonishment left Cate dumbfounded.

Ralph reached across the table and grabbed a biscuit from the basket that was on the table. He then proceeded to scoot the jam bowl closer to his plate. He spoke while slathering his biscuit with jam, "This 'bed sheet' as you call it, is a boubou. It is one of many traditional clothes in Africa."

Cate had to suppress another laugh. "I think it's quite lovely," Cate declared enthusiastically. Seeing that her mother was in a position of forced politeness, she dared, "I can't wait to wear one."

"You'll do no such thing," snapped Ann. "No daughter of mine will be wearing a bed sheet for a dress."

"Why not?" asked Cate, surprised at her mother's tone. "You make your dresses from flour sacks."

The remark cut Ann deeply. What fabric she used was no one's business but her own. How could Cate embarrass her like that and in front of company?

"If I find one of my good sheets cut up for your play clothes…" fumed Ann. She had more to say, but being a Christian woman, thought it best to cut her words short.

James smirked. The family hadn't even sat down for breakfast and Cate was in a heap of trouble.

"Now, now, Ann," Ian interceded as he walked into the room. He put his strong arms around his petite wife. "It's a little harsh to take her to task for something she hasn't done. I'm sure she has no intention of doing such a thing."

Cate had every intention of doing such a thing; she just had to figure out whose bed sheet she could cut up. If she could get James to marry Ida Sue, that would kill two birds with one stone. James would stay in Indian Territory, leaving Ralph no choice but to take her to Africa instead. Once James married Ida Sue, she wouldn't need her old bed sheet, so Cate could have it. That settled, Cate just had one question. "Ralph, I mean, Mr. Mahoney, how do the Nigerians dye the cloth with so much color?"

Ralph poised his lips to answer, saw Ann's face and then tactfully said, "I'm sorry, but you really are asking the wrong person. My interest in plants is medicinal, not textile." He was surprised to see his answer seemed to please Cate considerably. Anyone who actually knew Cate at all would have realized that he had just given her a challenge. By her way of thinking, all she had to do was find the right plants to use as dyes and she would win his heart and thus her cause and find her way on a ship headed for the Dark Continent!

Ian raised an eyebrow when he noticed Ralph had started breakfast without him. Meals starting without him was something that had not happened since his wedding day.

Cate waited for her father to say or do something, but he only smiled. He spoke heartedly, "I hope you made enough biscuits, Ann. I have a feeling we're going to need them!"

"There's plenty of biscuits," said Ann, "But we might run low on jam."

"Can't have that," stated Ian. He sat down at the head of the table. He took hold of the napkin and spread it on his lap. Cate was about to sit down, too, but then her father spoke up. "Cate, why don't you run down to the cellar and get more jam before we say Grace." He posed it like a request but Cate knew it was an order.

"But I'm wearing a dress!" Cate protested. "I might get

dirty."

Ian looked over the calico concoction covering his daughter. She was getting into a habit of defying him at every turn. He was not going to have it, dress or no dress. He turned to Ralph. "Do women in Africa wear dresses?" he asked.

"Oh, my yes they do," gushed Ralph. He obviously found them well attired.

"And do they work while wearing these dresses?" asked Ian.

"Definitely," agreed Mr. Mahoney.

He had made his point. Cate took off like a race horse to go fetch more jam.

Cate's mother would never go down into the cellar – not to store things, not to retrieve them, not even to clean up the dust. She always claimed that Cate's legs were younger than hers and better suited for the stairs, but Cate never bought that. She figured her mother just hated spiders. That woman was always getting out the broom and batting down spiders from the corners and ceilings of every room of the house. She would carry a broom with her to go out to the barn in case a spider spun a web in the way of her path overnight.

Cate on the other hand, loved spiders. The cellar was absolutely crawling with them this time of year. Cate wondered who her mother would get to do her leg work once she was in Africa and James was married off to Ida Sue.

Cate knew the cellar blindfolded. In a flap of a blue jay's wings she brought back two jars: one of peach and one of apple butter. She reckoned Ralph to be an apple butter man, although what she based that on she couldn't say. As for the peach, that was her favorite. She figured with company around, she would get away with bringing up the last jar.

After breakfast, Cate wandered out to the fence Nebraska Jo was mending and asked him if he knew what plants made good dye. He was one of her favorite ranch hands and for the most part, if Nebraska Jo didn't know a thing, it weren't worth knowing. He was also three quarters Creek Indian. By Cate's reckoning that meant he was three quarters more likely to know plants. If he did, he was mute on the topic.

By Nebraska Jo's reckoning, if Cate was asking him questions she should have been asking her mother, then it was because she did not want her mother to know. He knew all too well where that would lead. He was smart enough to know when it was wise to be ignorant.

Cate persevered. Over the next several days she picked all manners of plants and then laid them out to dry.

Chapter Six: Tomato Plum Grannies

Mr. Mahoney enjoyed the soft life he had at the Darringer Ranch. Cate noticed he found sidling up to the table easy enough. Yet when it came time to push himself away, his strength failed him as surely as Samson's did when Delilah cut his hair. Ralph claimed food could be scarce in Africa and it was best to stock up when one could. Cate reckoned he was working on eating a decade's worth.

Ralph further made a habit of stretching out on the front porch swing to "digest." One morning after a particularly satisfying meal, he was "digesting" when a large polecat came strolling into the front yard. Mr. Mahoney was a little nervous to see the odiferous two-toned vermin headed his way, but Cate reassured him.

"That's just Stinky Pot," she shrugged. "He used to belong to Mick Turner. I've sort of adopted him. leastways, he shows up here once in awhile looking for food. He used to be thin too," she remarked pointedly, looking at Ralph's growing paunch.

Ralph remained uneasy as Cate stepped into the house to get food. Stinky Pot wobbled straight up to him, effectively pinning him into the swing. Stinky Pot sniffed Ralph inquisitively, his

40

musky aroma wafting up into Ralph's nostrils. The musky
aroma was faint, but offensive.

Mr. Mahoney had once searched for a corpse lily along the
Kaduna river. The smell the tribesmen had described turned out
to be a baby bush elephant that had drowned. The creature was
bloated and foul, such that even the predators had left it alone.
While a horrendous stench, as long as one was upwind, the
smell was tolerable. Ralph put his finger in his mouth to wet it.
He held up his finger, but there was no discernible wind, so no
upwind to escape to.

"Cate," Ralph whispered. "Come quickly!" He was afraid
shouting might startle the animal.

The door opened and Cate came out with pralines. The door
slammed with a bang and Ralph jumped. Stinky Pot lost interest
in the man and wobbled towards Cate. She knelt down and held
the pralines out. Stinky Pot came up closer and sniffed at the
sweetened nuts, then quickly snatched a nut with his teeth and
began gnawing on it.

Cate stroked his coarse fur and wondered if it would be
possible to get a brush through it. Her mother was always
yammering on that Cate's hair needed braiding. Maybe braiding
Stinky Pot's fur would sate this odd desire. She wondered what
the skunk would look like with his white fur braided into
elegant cornrows down his spine.

"He's really tame," said Cate. "I've taught him how to do
tricks even."

"Hmm," squeaked a nervous Mr. Mahoney, "Could you
teach him the trick of disappearance?"

"Not much of a trick," shrugged Cate, "seeing how he does
that on his own once he's been fed."

Cate sat up and walked on her knees a few steps back,
holding a praline in front of her. "Come on, Stinky Pot," she
coaxed, "show Ralph, that is, Mr. Mahoney, how you can stand
on your hands. Come on Stinky, you can do it."

Stinky Pot hesitated. He sniffed the air, then wobbled
directly to Cate for more pralines. "No," said Cate. She held out
the pralines close enough for the polecat to smell them, yet out

of reach of his greedy mouth. Stinky Pot came closer. "On your hands," she said, pushing him back.

"Cate," whispered Mr. Mahoney, "I would advise against agitating him." He considered being on the south side of a north-facing skunk a precarious position.

"He's not agitated," said Cate, "He's just stubborn." She was far more interested in getting Stinky Pot to perform than she was with Mr. Mahoney's comfort. She failed to notice his nervousness.

"Really, Cate," said Mr. Mahoney, half pleading, half warning, "I think it best if you leave him alone."

"I do leave him alone," insisted Cate, "He's the one who came to see me. Come on Stinky, up on your hands." She showed him the pralines again, keeping them out of his reach. She had gone to a great deal of trouble to teach him this trick and she was determined he would do it now.

Mr. Mahoney sat wondering if he were still spry enough to leap over the railing and get out of harm's way. Stinky Pot reluctantly stood on his front paws and walked over to Cate. Cate smiled and gave him his reward. Ralph was actually slightly impressed.

Four days later, Stinky Pot showed up looking for food and Cate was no where to be seen. Mr. Mahoney attempted to be friendly, but as he had no pralines to offer, he ended up sprayed.

The smell reached the kitchen surprisingly fast. Ann was peeling potatoes at the time and she nearly doubled over from the stench. She had told Cate a hundred times not to feed that skunk! The Warden bolted out of the kitchen bound and determined to hang that pelt on her barn wall by the afternoon. She opened the porch door and nearly ran into Ralph. He was horrified, drenched and gasping for breath.

"Oh, dear Lord!" cried Ann. She wanted to reach out and give him support but the smell kept her back.

Ann ran to the side of the porch to escape the odor and take in a quick gasp of clean air before it was polluted.

"CATE!" roared The Warden, in a voice that traveled far and wide. Ralph winced and covered his ears for protection.

42

Ann apologized and was immediately sorry for the words as she drew in a new breath of skunk. Walking around him, she sidestepped to the other side of the porch and shouted again, "CATE!"

Cate grumbled at the tone of her mother's voice. The Warden had no right to be angry. Cate was where she was meant to be, doing what she was meant to be doing, which was behind the house taking down the laundry. There is no satisfying that woman, thought Cate. Cate picked up the laundry basket and walked to the front yard with it, where she was met by her mother's flashing, angry eyes.

"Cate," Ann said tersely, trying to keep what little temper she had left, "go pick a bucket of tomatoes, and be quick about it!"

Cate was in the process of forming the words "What for?" when the smell drifted her way and she knew what for without asking. Stuffings on it! thought Cate. Some folks get all the luck. She had been handling Stinky Pot for who knows how long and he had never once sprayed her. Why do all the best things happen to other people? At this rate, she was never going to have any good stories to tell her grandchildren.

"NOW!" bellowed The Warden.

"I'm going, I'm going," lamented Cate. She carried the laundry in, then searched to find a basket for the tomatoes.

Ralph was beside himself. The world could avoid him, but everywhere he went, he took the smell with him. There was simply no escape from it. He was drowning in odor. His skin crawled, trying to flee his bones to seek safer quarters. His worries took a macabre twist as he feared what the smell might do to his gray cells should it travel through his blood system to reach his brain!

"Do you mind terribly if I use your bath for awhile?" he politely asked Ann, edging towards the door, hoping to be let into the house.

"I do mind," admitted Ann with pangs of guilt. She rushed to the porch door and barred his way. She could see his face twisted with suffering. She knew that turning him out was an un-Christian thing to do, but hot places would freeze before she would allow that smell to wander into her house. "I'm afraid you'll have to bathe in the horse trough."

"Oh, I see," he said meekly. "Might I at least be given a towel and perhaps a dressing gown?"

"Yes, yes, of course," said Ann, and she sincerely meant it at the time she said it. "I'll get right on that. You go ahead and head for the trough."

He stood on the porch, flummoxed. He had hoped she would get him the towel first. She smiled weakly and remained fixed at her post. He returned the weak smile. He nodded and walked towards the barn. She waited for him to be out of sight before chancing to go inside the house.

Ralph had actually bathed in worse conditions in Nigeria, but that didn't make this bath any less humiliating. He stumbled out to the trough behind the barn. He looked into the water. Clean enough for horses to drink, no doubt, but gracious, what sort of bugs were those swimming about? Water skippers? Tadpoles? His stomach turned. He searched the barn for buckets and took them to the well. He had filled the last bucket when Cate came into the yard with the tomatoes.

"Cate," implored Ralph, "kindly carry those buckets up to the house. I shall need a second bath after I'm done with this one."

"Two baths in one day?" Cate had never heard of such a thing. "You'll have to skip your Sunday bathing at that rate." As soon as she said it, she thought, hmm, if taking two baths in one day meant skipping the Sunday bathing she was all for it.

Sunday bathing always came with smelly soap, which all too often had been made by her. The more folks bathed with soap, the more soap she had to make. She would have been perfectly happy if soap bathing was restricted to an annual event. Now, how lovely would that be? She wondered if she could get Stinky Pot to spray her on command.

Cate said nothing, but the smile spreading across her face wounded Ralph. She doesn't seem to be taking my plight seriously, he thought. It would have saddened him had he known just how true that statement was. He took the basket of tomatoes from her, then stood and watched her.

Cate grabbed the buckets by the handles and carried the well water to the bath inside the house. He watched until the porch door slammed behind her, and then he took the tomatoes to the trough behind the barn.

The Warden barked out orders as soon as she laid eyes on Cate. "Take this out to Mr. Mahoney."

Please, thought Cate. I have to say please, why don't you?

The Warden handed her a towel Cate was sure her mother had been saving for when the sows had piglets. Cate raised her eyebrows but said nothing. "And when you're done filling the bath I want you to go pick as many of the ripe Plum Grannies you can find and bring them in."

"Yes, ma'am," nodded Cate. What Plum Grannies lacked in flavor they more than made up for with their powerfully pleasant fragrance. Cate disappeared with the towel. She returned shortly, carrying more buckets. With a smile on her face, Cate reminded her mother, "Ralph, that is, Mr. Mahoney, would like a dressing gown. He says he'd prefer not to bathe in his altogethers."

Ann was horrified he had said that to her daughter, but it was her own fault for forgetting to send a dressing gown out with the towel. She hurried to her room while Cate took the buckets of water to the bath.

Ann opened the lower drawer of her dresser and put her hand on her old dressing gown, the one she wore when she was with child. She pulled it out and looked at it. She thought of all the times it kept the chill off of her as she dressed beneath its billowy form. It had seen better days. It was threadbare now and nearly transparent. If it had been anything else, she would have shredded it and used it for rags long ago. She imagined what it would look like once it was covered with tomato juice. It would be ruined. She would have to throw it away and she could not risk that.

Ann knew what every woman in the world knew: The surest way to become with child was to get rid of your last remaining maternity clothes. Ian liked to poke fun at superstition, but Ann had seen the supernatural up close in all its unholy glory. She was a little more prone to believing in old wives' tales.

Ann stood by the dresser lost in thought for too long. Suddenly Cate asked, "What's that?" Ann was startled to see her daughter standing at the doorway, still holding the full water buckets.

"Never you mind," she snapped, "just an old rag not worth wasting a breath on." Ann hurriedly stuck the dressing gown back into the bottom drawer and shoved it closed. "Don't stand there gaping," barked The Warden, "Get those buckets to the bath and be sure not to spill any water on the floor."

Cate huffed and shrugged, "Alright, alright!"

As Cate continued to the bath, Ann hurried to James' room, where Mr. Mahoney was staying. She found his boubou and gave that to Cate to give to Mr. Mahoney. "This will have to do," sighed Ann.

Mr. Mahoney was rather horrified when Cate showed up with his boubou and repeated, "This will have to do." He thanked her nonetheless and advised her to go play down by the crick.

Cate smiled and stood anchored before him, deaf to his words and clueless to her improprieties. He was about to reiterate the "suggestion" with a little more vigor when Ann's voice could be heard calling from the porch, "Cate!" Cate's smile disappeared and with it, Cate.

Mr. Mahoney looked at his Nigerian shirt, the one Cate had recently called a "bed sheet." It was all laid out so nicely on a fresh bale of Timothy hay. The tomato juice would ruin his lovely boubou. The colors would never be the same. It had been such a good, useful boubou. As much as he dreaded being in his altogether out in front of all the world, he dreaded spoiling his boubou more.

He had no choice but to strip down to his essentials behind the barn. He looked down into the trough water and shuddered. He rummaged through his pockets for his pocket knife and laid it on the bale as he disrobed. Once he was one with nature and his clothes folded and out of the way, he opened the knife and began to cut open the tomatoes and squish them against his body. They were warm, and sticky, and watery and mushy and pulpy all at the same time.

Behind the barn was a meadow divided into two paddocks. One contained Cate's horse because Cate was convinced Kiwi needed her rest. The other contained a blotted lummox of a horse Ralph believed was called "Lep," although he was not one hundred percent sure. Horses were not his specialty.

It was Ralph's understanding that Lep had been left behind because he was a difficult horse that resisted training. Ralph looked over at the horses. Both were on the far side of the pastures, minding their own business, which was just as he preferred it to be.

The thought had no more leapt from his mind when Kiwi turned, and seeing him, meander towards the barn. She stopped at the split rail fence and stared at him. She had never seen a man without his clothes before. Hmmph, she sputtered, no wonder people wear clothes.

Red-faced, Ralph turned his back to her and continued rubbing tomato mash over every inch. After a moment, he heard more sputtering. He turned to see that Lep had joined the unintentional peep show.

"Shoo! The both of you," cried Mr. Mahoney. Neither horse made a move to leave. While Kiwi seemed to have a bemused look on her face, Lep looked bored and unimpressed.

"I may be lacking by stallion standards," declared Mr. Mahoney, "but I can assure you, by the standards of my species, I am a most satisfactory specimen!"

Lep sputtered and swung his head back and forth. Kiwi nickered. Ralph was sure she was laughing at him. He turned his back on them once again and continued his bath. He washed his hair and face and even his wire-rimmed glasses with squished tomatoes.

He patted the surface of the trough water to cause the water bugs to dive down deep so he could fill his buckets with confidence. He poured the water over his head and body to wash the tomato off. He was thorough. When he was done, he dried off with the towel.

The horses were still gaping at him. Kiwi looked anxious to tell every horse in the territory about what she had seen. Lep took quite a different view and yawned his disapproval. Mr. Mahoney yearned to say something witty and sharp to Lep, but what does one say to humiliate a horse? He thought it best to hurry and get the whole ordeal over with quickly. He patted himself again with the towel to be sure he was as dry as he could get. Then he slipped on the boubou. The colorful "bed sheet" fluttered wildly as he strode across the yard and towards the house for a proper bath.

Ralph was horrified to find Ann guarding the door to the house. She actually sniffed him before allowing him inside. They were childhood friends for goodness sake! That should have warranted a little consideration. Luckily, he passed the test the first time around. Had he failed, he was sure she would have sent him straight back behind the barn with more tomatoes.

He walked inside with as much dignity as he could muster and strode straight to the bath. The tub was made of metal and it had hinged doors that acted as a lid to keep the heat in. Cate had made no effort to heat the water, and it was on the cold side. Nonetheless, Ralph closed the lid in an effort to obtain a bit of modesty. He had hardly closed the lid when a crow flew up to the window and landed on the windowsill. Its black eyes focused on the bather.

"Caw! Caw! Caw!" cried the raucous bird.

"Shoo! Go away!" Ralph ordered.

The cawing and the shooing brought unwanted help.

The door burst open! Ralph gasped! Ann filled the doorway with her sense of indignation. Around her skinny throat was a Plum Granny suspended in a small crocheted bag hanging on a ribbon. He shuddered. In his travels, Ralph had met people who wore garlic around their necks to ward off evil spirits. He felt slightly wounded that Ann had a similar reaction to him, particularly since he had already bathed once.

"Cate!" thundered Ann.

Footsteps pounded down the hall. Mr. Mahoney sunk deeper into the cold water, his nose just above the water line. Cate appeared at the door. She, too, was wearing a Plum Granny about her neck.

"What?" she asked fearfully.

Her mother pointed to the window. "Your crow!" she stated firmly.

"What about her?" asked Cate.

"Remove her," ordered The Warden.

"Oh," said Cate.

Neither females acknowledged Mr. Mahoney's presence in the bath. He could have been on the moon as far as either of them were concerned, and indeed, he wished he were.

Cate walked right past Ralph and straight to the open window. "Come on, Maggie," coaxed Cate. "Come with me and I'll get you some cracked corn."

Maggie jumped onto Cate's outstretched hand and Cate turned and carried her out of the bathroom as if it were an ordinary occurrence, which it was.

Mr. Mahoney may have gone unnoticed by Cate, but

Maggie found him fascinating. The crow eyed him hungrily as she was carried past.

Cate walked out of the bathroom and started down the hall.

"Contrary to all your hopes and dreams," bellowed The Warden, "you were not born in a barn."

Cate rolled her eyes to the heavens. She stomped back, grabbed the bathroom door handle roughly, then silently closed the door. Ralph could hear Ann's chastising mantra through the door as she followed her daughter down the hall.

Ralph wondered if he should dare to get out of the water and lock the door. Then he remembered that there was no lock on the door. Cate had once locked herself in the bathing room and her parents had ruined the lock getting her out. Ian had installed the window after that as a secondary escape route. Mr. Mahoney waited, listening carefully for the next intrusion.

When he was finally convinced there would be none, he relaxed. He leaned back against the tub and sighed. He glanced up. In the corner of the ceiling sat a spider. No doubt a friend of Cate's, he thought.

"I suppose you're waiting for her to bring you some flies?" he rhetorically asked the spider. He slunk further down into the cold water and pouted for a moment. Eventually, he decided that even if the spider told all the other spiders she knew that she had seen him naked in a bath, it still would never make the front page of the *New York World*.

He was reaching for the soap when the door burst open, again. It was Cate. She was carrying an empty Mason jar and a piece of paper. Without a by-your-leave, she nimbly climbed up and stood on the metal lid of the bath as if it were a platform. She reached up and brushed the spider into the Mason jar. She climbed down and was halfway out when The Warden appeared at the door with a cloth-covered broom in her hands. Cate looked at The Warden's broom. The Warden looked at Cate's Mason jar.

"I'm going to feed it to Maggie," lied Cate. She was hoping to sneak the spider down into the cellar.

The Warden said nothing, but her eyes scrutinized their prey as Cate brushed passed quickly and escaped out into the hall.

Ann stood at the door for a moment searching the ceiling in case Cate had missed something. Deciding she could leave spiders for another time, she turned to catch up with Cate.

Mr. Mahoney was unsure which was more offensive: the intrusion? Or the fact that he seemed to be invisible? He decided to get his bath over with as quickly and efficiently as possible. He meticulously trimmed and cleaned under each nail, and he thoroughly scrubbed behind his ears. He used a nit comb to be sure he removed every last tomato seed out of his hair. He had no desire to be like Cate's sloth and grow plants from unkempt crevices.

The thought of washing Ralph's afflicted clothes turned Ann's stomach. She gave Cate the duty of taking them to the burn pile. Mr. Mahoney's childhood friend was to regret this decision as the odor mingled with the smoke and clung to every branch and twig in the surrounding area. The smell lingered like an unwanted guest.

As Mr. Mahoney was in the habit of traveling light. The burning of his clothes meant that he had to borrow suitable attire from James until he could get to town and purchase his own. Naturally, Cate would be paying for them, which also meant she had to do extra work to earn the money. This greatly annoyed Cate because as far as she was concerned she was not the one who had sprayed him.

Chapter Seven: Chasing A Pig-eyed Horse

After "The Stinky Incident," as it came to be known, Cate had to work harder and harder to prove what a great, self-sufficient, independent, indispensable apprentice she would make.

Ralph was sitting on the porch swing, snacking on a bowl of sweetened nuts. His nose was in a book. Cate sat beside him with a rope in her hands, demonstrating one knot after another.

"This here is a bowline." Cate gave an elaborate explanation as to when and how one would use such a knot, but Ralph had stopped listening a dozen knots ago. He was not a sailor, he had no interest in fishing, nor had he any plans to become a cowpuncher and rope cattle.

Cate untied the bowline. She needed a more impressive knot. She thought a moment. She made a series of loops, then more loops around those, and still a few more, then pulled and dressed it up neat.

"And this one is called a monkey's fist," she continued. He looked over casually.

"Hmmph," he snorted. He scrutinized the knob at the end of the rope she held. It looked like some form of a Celtic knot made into a ball. "It doesn't resemble any monkey I've ever met. What's it for?"

"For adding weight." replied Cate. "If you need to toss a rope up into a tree to climb it, you add this to the end. This a way, when you toss it up and over a branch, it'll come back down."

He considered the knot and its application a moment. It could be useful, he supposed. "Who taught you that?" he asked.

Cate shrank. "James."

"Hmmm," replied a pleased botanist.

Cate pondered. There had to be a knot she knew that James did not. Maybe she could make one up. She untied the monkey's fist.

"A knot in a rope is all well and good," said the botanist, "but a hot iron can be the difference between life and death. A hot iron kills all sorts of bugs that might otherwise thrive in one's clothing. Pity you can neither iron, nor cook."

That really fried Cate's grits. "James can't cook. And he can't iron," she protested.

Ralph merely smiled. "James did not abandon me in a thunderstorm."

Ooooh! Why won't anyone see it was not my fault! Cate fumed silently. She played with the rope, trying to come up with a new knot, one nobody had ever tied before.

Suddenly, a lost little dogie wandered into the front yard. Cate stood up and walked slowly down the steps with the rope in her hand. Ralph was expecting to see her rope and tie the stray calf in record time, but instead, she just stood still.

"Hey, little fella, whatcha doing here?" she asked softly.

Ralph watched as Cate untied the knot currently on the rope and retied it into a lasso as she inched towards the calf. The calf watched her, but made no move to run away. Everything was going well, until Lep appeared and snorted. The calf turned, took half a look at the pig-eyed horse and bolted away in fright. Lep snorted. Then he chased after the frightened dogie like a fox after a rabbit.

"Who let out that pig of a mule?" thundered Cate.

The calf could be heard bellowing on the far side of the house. Things were being knocked over and hooves were thundering. Cate put her fingers to her teeth and whistled long and loud. Out in the pasture, Kiwi's ears pricked. The Marsh Tacky turned, ran towards the fence and took a running leap over it.

The terrified dogie bolted around the corner of the house. Lep was almost on top of the little fella, and would have had him for sure if the calf had not suddenly stopped and kicked its hind legs up into Lep's face. Lep reared up in a fury. The calf bucked a few times, then turned around and stampeded back the way it came. Lep twisted and snorted and went after it.

Kiwi rounded the corner of the barn and headed to Cate in a broken trot. She leapt onto Kiwi's back in one swift movement. She rode Kiwi in small circles in the front yard. Together they listened and waited.

Ann came out to the porch with a broom in her hand. She stopped and surveyed the scene. The frightened calf came screaming around the corner of the yard with the pig-eyed horse in hot pursuit. Timing was critical. Cate twirled her lasso and together, she and Kiwi took off after the wayward horse. Cate wasted no time in lassoing Lep. That was the easy part. Lep continued to race around the outside of the house after the calf. Kiwi and Cate followed in pursuit.

Lep never much cared for Cate, nor for her silly mare.

Kiwi would just as soon lead Lep off to the tanners, if truth be told. She sputtered insults at him. Boot leather. Cat food. Toad breath. You son of a shoeless mare. This only enraged him all the more. He raced faster. No uppity girl and her uppity horse was going to get the best of him!

Ann rang the triangle in the "Get Here Quick" pattern. The horses had gotten ahead of the calf by the time they came around to the front of the house again. Cate was standing in a crouch on Kiwi's back. Cate leapt from Kiwi and landed on Lep, startling him. He reared up and tried to dislodge the unwanted creature from his back. Cate held on.

Pappy Michaels came running into the yard. Pappy was old and grizzled, but very spry. He was often left behind to work near the house and tend to Ann's needs because of his ability to respond quickly. Cate tossed the ranch hand her rope while her other hand clutched Lep's mane.

Lep reared and tried to paw at Pappy with his hooves. Pappy stayed well clear of him and held on to the rope. Nebraska Jo came running up and Ann tossed him another one of the ropes Cate had left on the porch. He quickly tied a lasso and started twirling. Cate could see from his eyes who his target was.

"Don't you dare lasso me!" she fumed. "I'll get off this horse when I'm good and ready."

"I wasn't going to lasso you," Nebraska lied. "But you'll pretty foolish riding that bronco all the way to the Malcolm's shop."

"He ain't going to the tanner," swore Cate.

Lep continued to paw the air.

"You know he'd make a better jacket than a horse," yelled Neb.

"He ain't a jacket yet," snapped Cate. Her fingers were buried so deep into the horse's mane that she could not have jumped off if she tried.

The calf was still running around the house and it nearly knocked Nebraska over in its panic. Lep attempted to give chase. Pappy hung on tight, but was having a time of it. He was glad his gloves kept the rope from burning through his hands. Nebraska dropped his rope, and grabbed a hold of the rope Pappy was holding. Nebraska braced himself, with the rope going behind his back for added staying power. Lep continued to fight against the restraint. Ann came down the stairs with the broom and started poking Lep with it. That only made Lep all the more angry.

"Ann, you're not helping," called Nebraska Jo. Ann stopped poking and ran to the gun shed.

"Come on," cried Pappy Michaels, "let's get him tied to the iron post."

The men worked their way towards the iron post, which held a pulley system for loading hay into the loft. Pappy tied the rope to the iron post, then tried to calm Lep down with soft words. Nebraska ran back and picked up the second rope. He lassoed it around Lep's neck, then tied it to a hitching post nearby. The horse was now tethered by ropes in opposite directions and his movement was restricted.

Ann came running up with a rifle. Oh, dear Lord, thought Nebraska. The Creek Indian was familiar with Ann's aim, or lack of it.

"Cate, get off that horse!" Ann shouted.

"No," cried Cate. She had not an ounce of affection for Lep, but he was not who she was mad it. "Ain't his fault no one's taught him any manners."

The inability to teach a hard-headed creature manners was a tender issue to Ann and she took the accusation as a direct insult. She raised the rifle up to her shoulders. "I said, get off that horse!"

Nebraska ran over to Cate. "Come on Cate, be reasonable," he pleaded, trying to coax her off the still snorting horse.

"I ain't the one being unreasonable," she retorted.

Pappy walked cautiously over to Ann. "Now, Ann," he said soothingly, "everybody knows Lep is just a dumb horse that ain't worth the skin that's on him. Killing is too good for him. Just put that rifle down and I promise, me and Neb will teach him a thing or two." He put his hand gently over the barrel of the rifle and Ann lowered it.

"See that you do," sniffed Ann. "And get a cow poke on that calf. I don't want to see it in my yard again."

"Yes'm." Pappy nodded in agreement. It never paid to disagree with The Boss's Rib, especially when she held a rifle. He felt his heart pounding inside his chest.

Ann reluctantly handed Pappy the rifle. He took it and whispered a quiet prayer of thanks. Ann squared back her shoulders, held her head high and stomped back to the gun shed.

She picked up her broom, then stormed into the house.

Pappy opened up the rifle. Empty. All the same, somebody needed to tell the Boss he needs to take away his Rib's key to the gun shed. Unfortunately, not a hand on the whole ranch wanted to bell that particular cat. Pappy closed up the rifle and shouted at Cate, "Next time, you do as your mother tells you. Durn near gave me a heart attack."

This started a rousing exchange of allegations that impugned the character of all involved. It was good they were all thick-skinned or some hard feelings might have formed. Finally, everyone agreed that the future was more important than the past and that the men would train the horse, and more importantly, the men would mind their own business when it came to Cate and her mother.

That settled, Cate slide off Lep. The ornery horse was left between the two tethers to cool off on his own, while Nebraska set to work mending the gap in Lep's side of the pasture fence. Cate soothed and calmed the little dogie, who had pretty much run himself out. When it was roped and ready, Pappy led the calf back to where it belonged and Cate took Kiwi back to her side of the pasture.

Watching the events made Ralph glad he had chosen botany as his field of study. He was grateful his guest status had yet to wane and he was not expected to aid in such arduous activities. Mr. Mahoney could not imagine anything more disastrous to his studies than a female assistant who was dogged by adventure like spring following winter.

An hour later, Ralph sat on the porch swing with a plate of biscuits and jam slowly disappearing beside him. His wire-rimmed glasses were perched on his nose, which was stuck in yet another book. The corner of his eyes caught a glimpse of Cate as she came around the outside corner of the house with a water bucket in her hands. Seeing him lazing about, she put the bucket on her head and paraded back and forth with her arms out. He gave no indication that he had the slightest clue she existed.

Cate put the bucket down and suddenly flipped onto her hands and walked on them in front of the porch, up the front steps and to the door. The screen door was loose and she easily opened it with her feet. The front door was a bit trickier but she managed to wrap her toes around the knob and turn it. Ralph's nose stayed firmly entrenched in his book. As she scuttled through the door he absently called to her, "Cate, you forgot your bucket."

She stomped back out on her hands, across the porch and down the steps.

"I'm sorry, Cate," he said, hiding a smile, "I can think of no situation where I would need a young lady to behave like a polecat." It was an unkind barb but he was still nursing his tomato bath humiliation.

"Did you know," asked Cate, completely undaunted, with one foot high in the air while the other tried to wrap toes around the water bucket handle, "that the natives wear masks on the back of their heads to confuse the lions?"

He looked over his glasses at her. Did he know? He was the one who had told her!

"Imagine how confused a lion would be to see a head where the knees should be," she continued.

"Even confused lions manage to eat," he answered, putting his nose back in his book.

Cate sprung off her hands and righted herself. Walking over to the porch, she peered between the railings to look at him.

"What if a tribal chief refused to allow you to enter his territory unless you were able to answer an ancient riddle that had perplexed his family for generations and the answer was to walk on your hands?"

"Ah! But a tribal chief would be shamed if you solved a riddle generations of his family could not. Far better to act ignorant." He winked mischievously at her. "A trait you seem incapable of, might I add."

What nonsense.

The Warden appeared at the door. "Cate, stop dawdling and bring in that bucket," she snapped. "Honestly, if all Mr. Mahoney needed was a layabout, he certainly wouldn't need to have come this far to find one."

Cate stalked back to the bucket, picked it up, carried it up the steps and into the house, fuming every step of the way.

Chapter Eight: Guilty, but Not as Charged

That afternoon, Cate slipped into her brother's room and took paper and pencil from his desk. She dug a little deeper and found his old homework.

Earlier in the year, Cate had spent countless, beautiful, sunshiny hours indoors copying James' "perfect" handwriting because the new school teacher, Miss Barris, considered Cate's writing "chicken scratchings." All those torturous hours she could have spent doing just about anything else would finally serve a purpose. Certainly, if it was permissible to copy James' handwriting to please her teacher, it would be an acceptable thing to do to please herself. Copying his writing now was almost second nature, almost.

Cate still preferred to place the original against the window to trace it with the light shining through. She also preferred to find the whole word if she could, rather than construct it letter by letter. It looked prettier that way and was less likely to have spelling errors. Prefect James, Cate thought, always doing everything right.

Cate had tried to tell Miss Barris "Tis a poor man who knows only one way to spell a word." Benjamin Franklin had said that. Miss Barris countered, "Well then, I shall only be able to accept one way of spelling until the town doubles my pay." Thankfully, Cate knew James' work well and could find most of the words she was looking for quickly.

Cate had a habit of sticking her tongue out when she concentrated. It was unladylike and she had endured a good deal of teasing for it, but it seemed to her the only logical place for her tongue when her "thinking brain" was engaged. She was definitely thinking now. Occasionally she would repeat the word as she wrote it, "mead-ows... da-an-ce..."

Cate smiled as she finished the poem. She was one step closer to Nigeria. Her plan was simple. She would hide the love

poem in James' library book. Then she would ask Ralph to
return the book to the town library. Mrs. Whipple was a
thorough librarian, who inspected every book upon its return.
While inspecting the book, she would find the paper, and hand it
back to Ralph to return to James. Ralph, being a scientist, would
naturally be curious. He would read the poem and instantly
understand that James was madly in love with Ida Sue and it
would be a sin against love itself to cause them to part. Since
Ida Sue would never dream of leaving Henryetta, James would
be forced to stay put. With James out of the way, Cate would be
the obvious choice to become his assistant.

Cate tucked the paper discretely into James' library book
and quickly shoved the old homework papers back where they
belonged. She closed James' bedroom door slowly and quietly
behind her. She slid down the banister and was about to escape
to the great outdoors when The Warden's hands caught her
square on her shoulders and spun her around.

"Just what have you been up to?" The Warden asked sternly.

"Nothing," lied Cate with the most innocent face she could
muster. She slowly hid her hands behind her back.

"Show me your hands," demanded The Warden.

Cate was wishing now she had washed them in the basin.

"Show me," repeated The Warden.

Cate lifted up her hands. They were covered in pencil lead.
She could not help it. She had no idea how other people kept
their hands clean while writing. It wasn't her fault pencil lead
was so messy.

"You've been making posters again," accused Ann in a hurt
tone.

"I haven't!" Cate protested.

"Don't you lie to me young lady," snapped Ann. Her face
was hard and stern. Her white hair against the dark wall gave
her the appearance of an apparition.

"But I haven't!" repeated Cate. She was the picture of pure
innocence. A picture her mother had seen far too often to trust.

"We'll just see about that," said Ann suspiciously. She spun
Cate around to face the stairs. "Your room. Now!"

Cate gave a sigh of exasperation and stormed up the stairs with Ann in close pursuit. The two of them burst into Cate's room. Cate opened her desk drawer and snatched up her latest bit of art and handed it to her mother.

Ann looked at it with surprised interest. "What is it?" asked Ann. She turned the paper in different directions in case she had the orientation wrong.

"It's a flower," explained Cate, a little miffed.

"I see, yes, of course," said her mother.

Cate could see the lie on her mother's face. It was a lie that hurt more than the truth. Cate had meant to give it to her mother, but seeing how she didn't seem to care for it, Cate added, "It's for Mrs. Whipple." Cate took the paper back from her mother. "It isn't done yet."

"No, no, of course not," said Ann. As odd as the drawing was, she was a little hurt that it was for Nell and not her. She didn't like to sound childish and so she said nothing.

"Well?" asked Cate.

Ann felt both shame and relief. Shame for doubting her daughter, and relief she had been wrong. The flurry of posters Cate had been putting all over town had caused the family a great deal of embarrassment. Ann felt she was one straw away from a broken back.

Chin up, Ann cleared her throat. Crow was a hard meal to swallow, but a Darringer admits when she is wrong. "I'm sorry I assumed the worst. It is a nice drawing. I'm sure Mrs. Whipple will enjoy it once it is finished."

"Thank you," said Cate. She placed the drawing back into the drawer and closed it. She was hurt her mother did not like her drawing but she was not about to let on.

"Can I go now?" she asked.

"Cate," snapped The Warden.

"*May* I go now?" Cate rephrased.

"Yes, of course," sighed her mother.

Cate slowly walked towards the door. Her mother made no move to leave. Cate felt uncomfortable with the way her mother was looking around the cluttered room.

To Ann, the disarrayed mess looked more like a rat's den than a bedroom for a young lady. Ann wished she could seal it off and forget it existed. The chifforobe stood tall against the wall but the path to it was far from clear.

"Cate, where's the dress I borrowed from Mrs. Davenport? I should be returning it if you aren't going to wear it," Ann reminded her.

Cate gulped. She had put the dress on the burn pile with Mr. Mahoney's clothes, but now was not the time to confess.

"It's around here somewhere," lied Cate.

"Where?" asked Ann.

Cate shrugged.

Ann shook her head slowly. "I don't know why you wouldn't wear it. It was plain enough, not an inch of frill on it."

Cate looked at the sadness weighting on her mother's face and felt a pang of guilt. "You can't expect me to wear something that Jimmy Davenport touched," declared Cate.

"You know durn well Jimmy Davenport doesn't go around wearing his sister's dresses," said Ann sourly.

"No, but he's got an evil mind all the same. He could have rubbed the insides with itching powder. Itching powder can drive a person insane. I heard on good authority that's why he's the way he is, 'cause someone switched out the talc powder for itching powder and his Mama sprinkled too much on his diapers when he was a baby."

"Would this good authority happen to be Opal Tamsen?" asked Ann. Her eyes were full of suspicion.

"That don't mean it isn't so," defended Cate.

Ann sighed. "Itching powder notwithstanding, I need to return it to Mrs. Davenport."

"I know. It'll turn up. I'm sure," Cate lied.

The Warden's eyes turned dark as they narrowed in on their victim. "I am sure as well. You are not to leave this room until it does."

"Yes, Ma'am," nodded Cate.

The Warden strode out the door and down the hall. Cate envisioned dying of old age, alone and forgotten in her cell.

Chapter Nine: The Set-up

The next morning, Mr. Mahoney was sitting at the breakfast table listening to James and Ian recount one of Cate's many antics. Cate entered carrying a library book. Ian stopped in mid-sentence to look at her.

"Speak of the devil," smiled James.

"Why?" asked Cate, "Is he going to Africa, too?"

The three men chuckled. "I would say he's already well entrenched there," observed Mr. Mahoney.

Cate laid her book by her plate. Her mother promptly reminded her it did not belong on the table and so she had to place it on the hutch. Cate waited through grace and half of breakfast before bringing attention back to it.

"Ralph," Cate began, then, seeing her mother, corrected herself. "I mean Mr. Mahoney, since you said last night that you'd be going to town today I was wondering if you'd be so good as to return my library book for me."

"Cate," her mother injected, "Mr. Mahoney has more important things to do today than run your errands." Ann didn't much care for how easily Cate could manipulate others.

"No, no, I'd be delighted!" insisted Mr. Mahoney. "Cate has been days telling me all about it and I've worked up quite an appetite to go explore the library and..."

"You mean Mrs. Whipple?" Cate interrupted. "You know, she really isn't a missus. We just call her that because it would be rude to call someone her age 'Miss.'"

"Cate!" cried her mother.

"Not," continued Cate, "that she's all that old, mind you, I reckon she still has more than a few good years in her."

"Cate!" warned Ann.

"And judging by her collar, she's right handy with an iron," Cate barreled on.

"Catherine Mariah Darringer, that is enough," thundered

The Warden. Cate paused. They stared at one another briefly. Then Ann turned and spoke to Mr. Mahoney. "I apologize for Cate. I haven't a clue how we got on to the topic of Mrs. Whipple."

"You should listen more carefully, Mother," Cate chided, "Mr. Mahoney was saying he had quite an appetite to explore the librarian, so naturally..."

"He said no such thing," claimed her mother.

"He did. I'm sure of it," retorted Cate.

"And I'm just as sure he didn't," Ann insisted. "I'm quite sure he has absolutely no interest whatsoever in 'exploring' Mrs. Whipple or... or... or..."

"Why not?" asked Cate. "She's quite pretty for a woman her age and the only reason she didn't win last year's baking contest was because you did and..."

At this point, a stunned and red-cheeked Mr. Mahoney interceded. "Actually, what I was saying, prior to this interruption, was I'd like to explore the library AND catch up on my reading. One doesn't see much of the printed page in Africa and 'Man cannot live on bread alone.' I would be happy to return Cate's book for her."

"Cate," said her mother smugly, with her chin tilted slightly up, "what do you have to say to Mr. Mahoney?"

"Much obliged, Mr. Mahoney, I'm most appreciative," Cate said. She beamed her sweetest smile.

"And?" prompted her mother in a terse tone.

"And James has a book to go back as well," said Cate.

"Cate!" snapped her mother.

"Well, you have, haven't you, James?" asked Cate, as innocent as a lamb.

"Yes," sighed James.

"Well, then," said Mr. Mahoney, "I'd be delighted to return the both of them."

"Much obliged," said James, reaching for more skillet potatoes. "I'll get it to you right after breakfast." He had mixed feelings. On the one hand, he was glad to no longer be the focus of the conversation. On the other, returning a book was often his only chance to visit a certain young lady without having to endure too much town gossip.

"Cate," snarled The Warden. She expected better manners from her daughter.

"I'm sorry you have no interest in exploring Mrs. Whipple," Cate said sweetly and quickly, in the hopes her mother wasn't truly listening.

The Warden bristled.

"Mother," Ian interjected calmly, "I believe we have a young lady who's interested in stirring things up."

Cate paled.

"Why, yes," said Ann pointedly, "I do believe we do."

"But I made soap less than a month ago!" protested Cate, "We can't be in need of it."

"I'm sure we'll find someone in town who'd appreciate it," answered her father. "The money you make selling it can go towards paying for Mr. Mahoney's new wardrobe."

Cate slumped in her chair. She loathed making soap. As far as she was concerned it ran a close second behind picking cotton. No amount of money could compensate for the hours lost in its labor. Cate opened her mouth to protest, but then reconsidered. James' book would be going back to the library. It would be just a matter of days that she would be going to Africa.

Completely out of the blue, James turned to Mr. Mahoney and inquired, "I don't suppose you'd have time to drop something off at the Furrs Mining office would you? Seeing how you're going to town, anyway."

Cate gasped! He knew!

James enjoyed the horror on his sister's face. Of course he knew. He was the one in charge of burning the burn pile, wasn't he? She had ruined his chance to go see Ida Sue. Seemed only fair to make her squirm a little.

"Of course!" agreed Mr. Mahoney. "I shall be delighted."

"Oh, no," blustered Ann, red-faced. "I'm sure what James is referring to is a dress I borrowed from Mrs. Davenport. She's the secretary for the mining office," explained Ann.

The Warden's eyes darted over to Cate and she shrank into her chair. That Ian had given Cate amnesty and permission to leave her room did not mean Ann was going to let *her* daughter off the hook. The Warden smiled wickedly. "I prefer to take it back to her house personally, sometime when Cate can go along with me."

Cate's smile quivered. She was a dead girl walking.

Chapter Ten: The Face on the Poster

Frank Merrill leaned against the outside wall of the Okmulgee branch of the National Bank. He was a dark man: dark hair, dark eyes, dark beard, dark heart. He had left the territory some months back in a state of drunken fear. Folks had a tendency to jump to conclusions when a person dies from a bullet wound. He had no desire to have that particularly accusatory finger pointed his way.

A recent "misunderstanding" at the card table filled him with a sudden impulse to continue his migratory manners. He could have headed almost anywhere, but curiosity brought him back to the territory. Rumor had it another man was getting ready to hang for the death of Mick Turner and Frank wanted to get a look at him.

Frank was surprised anyone cared enough about Mick to go to the trouble. He was certain that the rumored hanging spoke more to the dark nature of the human soul than it did to anyone's sense of justice.

In truth, he could save this man. He knew Mick's death had been an accident. As Frank was a wanted man himself, he doubted his word would count for much. Coming forward might only give the town a different neck to stretch. Frank had no desire to have that accusatory finger pointed his way.

Frank reached into the pockets of his gray coat and felt the small, smooth river rocks. Rolling them around in his hands was both soothing and mind clearing. With the life he led, clearing the mind was a great deal easier than clearing the soul.

He liked the coat. It fit well. He liked the way the wool scratched his skin even through his shirt. Even worn as it was, the coat kept off the chill of the morning dew. Best of all, it enabled him to blend in. Who would take notice of a Southern man in a gray coat? The only thing to distinguish him from all the others was the top button made of elk antler. It had been poorly sewn on, and was barely hanging on by a thread when he found the coat in the bushes.

The minute he had laid eyes on it, Frank had hurriedly removed his own coat, the one stained with Mick Turner's blood, and had swapped it for the one sitting atop the scrub. He pulled off the elk button and nearly tossed it away. Then he stopped. This new coat was his saving grace. Sewing the button back on was the least he could do for it. He pocketed the button to sew it on later. He did a good job of it, too. That button would would outlast the coat.

Frank was contemplating his next move when he noticed an old cowpuncher coming out of the print shop. The grizzled old goat was carrying a roll of posters. Posters typically meant bad news either to someone Frank knew or to Frank himself. Frank backed into the alley to watch from the shadows.

Not that Frank would have cared one way or the other, but the cowpuncher was actually Pappy Michaels, a part-time hand on the Darringer ranch. Pappy's trip served two purposes. He was picking up supplies unavailable in Henryetta, and he was picking up Cate's posters. He had taken one to the printer on the sly during his last trip to Okmulgee, and had ordered up a number of copies. Pappy was sympathetic to the cause. It was unthinkable to him that such a kind-hearted soul like Stumpy could murder so much as a fly. While Pappy considered Mick to be lower than a fly, he was still pretty sure Stumpy would have done his tormentor no harm.

Now that the posters were ready, Pappy was in a quandary over what to do with them. Pappy preferred Ian stayed ignorant of the hand he played in the widespread distribution of posters. Ian was his Boss, and a powerful and well-respected man. While Pappy was not afraid of him, he did not relish going against him, either.

Pappy spied a young boy walking down the street and decided to approach him with a job offer.

From the shadows, Frank watched the old man work out a deal with the young boy. The old cowpuncher gave the boy some money, the posters, a bag of one penny nails and then a small hammer from his back pocket. The boy was instructed to post the posters in prominent areas of the town. He could keep the hammer as part of his payment. The old man watched the boy post the first one on the outside wall of the grocery store. He seemed pleased enough with the work. He thanked the boy and went on his way.

Once both the boy and the cowpuncher were out of sight, Frank came out of the shadows and walked down the street to have a better view of the poster. Well, I'll be, he thought. Isn't that a fine kettle of fish. He was looking at the smiling face of Stumpy Gilbert, but he might as well have been looking at himself if he had been clean-shaven.

Large letters shouted out, "FREE STUMPY GILBERT!" Below that was the contact information of Stumpy's court appointed attorney and a request to petition Judge Isaac Parker over in Fort Smith for his release.

Frank snorted. He knew Stumpy. He had met him more than a few times at Mick's. He was a simpleton. No matter what torment Mick dreamed up for him, he was always in good humor. Mick had often speculated that if they were to shave their beards, they might pass as brothers. Mick would rest easy in his grave to know he had been right.

Seems a shame to hang a man before his prime, thought Frank, especially one as useful as Stumpy. He pulled the poster from the wall and rolled it up so he could take it with him and study it more closely in private. He knew of an abandoned mine shaft near the river bend folks named after Stumpy's dog. Gump? Sump? Dump? He could not recall the name exactly, something stupid. Seemed like a good place to hide a man for awhile while another man robs a few banks. He wondered how many banks he could rob before the reward was "Dead or Alive." The town was planning on killing Stumpy anyway; Frank saw no harm in profiting from their likeness first.

Frank wandered the streets a bit until he came across a dubious tavern. If he was going to bust Stumpy out of jail, he would need a few accomplices, a couple of men no one would miss once they had served his purpose. He walked into the tavern and knew right away that he had come to the right place.

Chapter Eleven: A Narrow Escape

The time had come for Mr. Mahoney to visit his patrons in Oklahoma City. Dreary dinner parties with inquisitive financiers scrutinizing every cent were not at the top of his list of relaxing activities, but on the grand scale of things, a small price to pay for his research. He packed a small bag and borrowed Shadow, Ann's horse.

Shadow was a Morgan with a grullo coat, the color folks often referred to as blue. When she was a filly, Shadow would follow Ann around like Ann was her mother. They were as devoted to each other as Kiwi and Cate. Shadow was familiar with the surrounding areas. Should Ralph get turned around, he need only give her her head and Shadow would find her own way home.

The ride to town was uneventful and much quicker than his walk in from the crossing had been a fortnight prior. It was early and the town was still asleep. Ralph dismounted and tied Shadow by the water trough. He grabbed the books out of the saddle bag and began to stroll down along the store front.

Ralph marveled at how the settlement had blossomed into a town. When he was a child, it was little more than a few crossroads with a massive oak tree known as the Meeting Tree. "I'll see you at the Meeting Tree," was as fancy as folk got with their social engagements back then. Now, modern civilization was reaching its long arm far out west. There were stores with windows and even the side roads had wooden sidewalks! He looked up and down to see how many stores he could identify. There was a post office with a telegraph office inside! There was a tanner's and a smith's! And of course, Opal's Boutique and Curiosity Shoppe. Ann had alluded to the shop owner's penchant for gossip. He believed Ann's intent was to encourage avoidance. He, however, had a curious nature and he planned pay Opal a visit later.

He noted the sheriff's office and cringed. Even law-abiders preferred to avoid such places. There were stables and an office for the Furrs Mining company, and best of all, a grocer! With a liquor store on the side. He shivered at the thought of Slider Johnson's Red Mash.

Mr. Mahoney pressed his nose to the window and wondered when the general store would open. Cate had raved about the penny candy, and his mouth was watering for some. The sign in the window read "Closed." He saw no one around, so he thought he would walk around a little and come back later. Mr. Mahoney had planned to spend a few hours at the library prior to heading out.

With two books in his arms, a stone's throw from the library, he heard singing. He froze. Only two people could be expected to know that tune. He knew it, having composed it himself. That left only one person who could be the source of the melody. He ducked behind a cigar store Indian and peered slowly in the direction of the sound.

There she was, walking towards the library, singing absent-minded, blissfully unaware anyone was around. Her hair was the color of clover honey. It was swept up into a soft bun and atop it was a small hat with a feather plume. Even out here, far from East Coast influence, she maintained a sense of fashion. He was too far away to actually smell her perfume, but that did not matter. The scent was indelibly imprinted in his memory. He nearly swooned to recall it. Ralph felt now as he had so many years ago. He yearned to speak to her, but his feet had grown roots.

Ralph was sure the pounding of his heart could be heard from miles away. Please do not look this way, he begged quietly. What would she think of a grown man hiding behind a statue? He felt foolish, and yet, unable to move. She fished out a set of keys from her purse, unlocked the library door, and went in.

The terrified paramour let out a deep breath. Ralph was still dazed when he became slightly aware of a young man standing just behind him, asking him something. "Pardon?" asked Mr. Mahoney absently. His eyes still lingered on the door she had walked through and he had yet to focus on the young man.

"Are you alright?" repeated the young man.

"Yes, yes, of course, why wouldn't I be?" snapped Mr. Mahoney. He grabbed his handkerchief and mopped his brow. He was silently congratulating himself on his narrow escape. One of the books slipped from his grip and thunked onto the sidewalk.

"You should be careful with library books," explained the young man. He bent over and picked it up. "They'll charge you for the damage. A penny a page and a nickel for the cover." The young man handed the book to Mr. Mahoney. Mr. Mahoney looked at the book as if it were a savage hyena ready to bite off his arm. He made no attempt to take it from the young man, who had such a kind, helpful look about him. An idea popped into Mr. Mahoney's head.

"How would you like to earn a quarter?" he asked.

"A quarter?!" asked the young man. "Well, gosh, who wouldn't? What did you have in mind?"

Mr. Mahoney reached into his pocket and fished out a

quarter. Pressing it and the second book into the young man's hands, he asked, "Could you take these books back to the library?"

"That's it?" asked the young man. "But that's easier done than said. The library is just right there."

"It's closed," blurted Mr. Mahoney. "I haven't the time to wait."

"Closed?" asked the young man, "That's odd. You can set your clock on Mrs. Whipple. I'm sure she'll be here soon."

"I'm in a bit of a hurry. I'd really appreciate it," said Mr. Mahoney, beating a hasty retreat. He tipped his hat and hurried down the street. He was wishing now that he had taken Cate's horse, Kiwi, rather than old reliable Shadow. While Cate tended to stretch the limits of truth to its outer edge, she was accurate about one thing: the speed of her horse.

Chapter Twelve: Winter Coats & Cast Iron Skillets

The young man stood by the wooden Indian a moment pondering his good fortune. This was the easiest quarter he had ever earned. He carried the books across the street and waited for Mrs. Whipple to come by. When she failed to appear right away, he walked back and forth for something to do.

After a few minutes, he spotted Donna Tucker sashaying her way towards him. He hurriedly combed his hair with his fingers, then he opened a book to appear as if he was reading.

Donna strained to hold back a smile to see him preen. She walked straight up to him. "Hi, George," she beamed, "Whatcha doing?"

"Oh! Hi, Donna," croaked George. He stood staring at her as she swayed back in forth in her summer dress. She got prettier by the minute, but he lacked the courage to say-so. A mass of soft curls the color of sunshine framed her heart shaped face. Her ruby lips parted into a wide smile.

"George, I asked you what you were doing," she said. She loved how easy it was to make him nervous.

"Oh, um… I'm just waiting for the library to open. I've got a few books to return," he answered. She had a nosegay pinned to her dress and its scent wafted up to him. She smelled heavenly.

"Oh? Well, that's really sweet, George, but don't you have to actually go inside to return them?" she mused.

"Oh, sure, Donna, it's just Mrs. Whipple hasn't opened it up yet," he answered. Gosh, the sun was so pretty on her hair.

With her skirt bouncing with each step, Donna turned and walked up to the door, opened it, and peered in.

"Hello, Mrs. Whipple," she called.

"Hello, Donna," replied Mrs. Whipple. Donna shut the door and sashayed back to George.

"Mrs. Whipple is already inside, George." She smiled again

and George thought for a moment he would melt into the sidewalk.

"Thank you, Donna, I guess I should be getting these inside." Instead of moving, he stayed frozen to the spot, gazing at her. "Donna?" he asked nervously.

"Yes, George?" she said, pressing up close to him to watch him sweat.

"Donna, I was wondering," he hesitated. It would be so easy to reach down and kiss her, but what would she think if he did?

"Yes, George?" she cooed with honey dripping in her tone.

"I... I... I was wondering if you'd ask James Darringer to the dance," he stammered.

She stepped back, a little affronted. She knew he could be slow on the draw but this was a little much, even for him. The softness of her voice took on a hard edge that surprised, and even panicked George. "Why, George, you know it wouldn't be proper for a girl to ask a boy to a dance."

George's eyes widened and his jaw dropped as he struggled with an explanation, "I... I... I know that Donna. It's just, I'm... I'm taking Ida Sue, and well," he gulped, "It's just... it's just. I'd really like for you to be there and since no one has asked you..."

"What do you mean, 'Since no one has asked me'?" exclaimed Donna. Her temper flared and her voice climbed an octave. "George McGillicutty, I'll have you know, I've had several inquiries."

"Yes, Donna," said George. George felt like the time when he was five years old and stepped on a rattlesnake and got bit. He had been wearing boots at the time and so he was more surprised than injured. He was wearing boots now, too, but he doubted they would be of much help. Donna was prettier than any snake he had ever seen, but somehow, he was pretty sure, she was a lot more dangerous.

"I can go to any dance I please with any man I choose," she continued. Her face was flushed and her eyes had narrowed.

"Yes, Donna." George gulped, taking a small step back.

"Why, any man would jump at the chance to escort me," she fumed, taking a bigger step forward.

"Yes, Donna." repeated George. He took another step back.

"Even a thick-skulled ape could understand why it would be an honor," she snapped, taking a step forward.

"Well, sure, Donna, everybody kn... kn... knows, you've got the prettiest ha... ha... handwriting in all the t... t... territories," George stammered, taking another step back.

"Handwriting!" shrieked Donna. Dear Lord, she thought. Just how many cobwebs are in that handsome head of his? "George, men don't take women to dances because they have pretty handwriting."

"No?" pleaded George. He could clear an entire hay field and stay dry and yet Donna that could break a sweat out of him with just a smile. He could feel the moisture on his back.

"No," said Donna in a definite tone. She crossed her arms and stepped back to look at him. Her eyes took him in and her anger melted. George was not the brightest penny in her bank, but he was handsome. And strong. And loyal. And easy to manipulate. All good traits in her book. "No, George," she cooed, uncrossing her arms and getting closer to him again. "Don't you think there's something else a man might notice about me?"

There was her perfume again, wafting up to his nostrils. Her heart face, her beautiful lips, so close to him. A girl can't expect a man to be able to think when she's standing so close to him, can she?

"George," repeated Donna softly, "I asked you, don't you think there's something else a man might notice about me?"

His mind scrambled to work. "Well, your mother says you can darn a sock right nice," he offered.

"Sock darning?" shrieked Donna. Lord give me strength, she thought. She moved in even closer. "Honestly, George, isn't there something about the way I look you think a man might take note of?" she pressed.

"Well, sure Donna," he expounded, "You got straight legs, a good set of teeth and..."

"Straight legs and good teeth!" she protested, her temper returning. "George, you don't pick out a girl the way you would a horse."

"But you asked me about the way you looked," he explained. He could see a storm brewing on her face and he hurried to backpedal, "And... no... no... now Donna, I ain't saying you look like a horse. It's just... if you were a horse, you'd fetch a mighty fine price." He gulped.

"George McGillicutty, has anyone ever told you you're a lot smarter when you don't open that mouth of yours?" she fumed, narrowing her eyes.

"Well... I..." he uttered, backing up just a little more.

"I think you ought to try for an 'A plus' right about now," she said, her finger drilling a hole in his chest. "How would you like it if girls went around talking about boys like we were shopping for a winter coat or a new cast iron skillet?" she snapped.

But you do, thought George, only he must have actually said it, because she a shocked look spread across her face and she squealed, "We most certainly do not!"

"Well, sure you do, Donna," said George. "A gal wants a fella who'll keep her warm and well fed, doesn't she?"

"Oh, it's well fed am I?" snapped Donna, her hands on her shapely hips.

"No! No, I meant, a g... g... good wool coat would look good on you," he stammered.

"What about a nice summer dress," asked Donna in a haughty tone. She held her skirt slightly out as she twirled around in it. "Would that look good on me, too?"

George failed to understand how anyone as beautiful as Donna would need to be told how beautiful she was. Surely, she would notice it herself when she looked in the mirror, wouldn't she? "Donna," George swooned, "you could be wearing a sack of beans and still be the prettiest girl I've ever seen."

She sighed. He really was a hopeless case. "I'll keep that in mind in case pintos and limas ever come into fashion." She peered down at the books in his hands and asked, "So, what books are those?"

"Oh, um," George fumbled with the books, "This one is 'The Adventures of Tom Sawyer,' and this one is 'The Sonnets of William Shakespeare.'"

"You're reading sonnets and the best you can come up with is to compare me to a horse, a thick wool coat and a bag of beans? Did you even read that book?" she scoffed.

"Well, no," he admitted slowly.

"Why am I not surprised?" she sighed.

"But, they aren't my books," he explained. "You see, I was over there this morning when a man..."

"What man?" snapped Donna.

"I don't know, a stranger," shrugged George

"Uh-huh, go on," said Donna, eyeing him with suspicion.

He felt her eyes dissecting him. "Well, this stranger gave me a quarter to return these books for him," he said.

She sighed. "You expect me to believe that a total stranger

walked up to you and gave you a whole quarter to deliver two thin books to a library not twenty feet away?"

"Yes," he said hesitantly. It sounded foolish to hear her say it, like he was telling tall tales, which he wasn't.

"Show me the quarter," she demanded skeptically. Honestly, did he think she was thick?

George fished the quarter out of his pocket to show her, "Here it is, Donna, see?"

"Hmm, so it is," she said, a little surprised. She plucked the quarter out of his palm. Taking the books from him, she cooed, "Thank you, George, I could use a quarter."

George stood mute as he watched her waltz towards the library. Donna glanced back as she opened the door. She smiled like the cat that ate the bird then vanished inside.

George headed down the road thinking, money and women sure do have a way of disappearing.

Chapter Thirteen: Full Steam Ahead

Donna walked straight to the librarian desk where Mrs. Whipple sat writing. Town librarian was really only a part time position so Mrs. Whipple often took in other work to do at the library. She was writing a letter on behalf of the town council and going ever so slow. Donna knew Mrs. Whipple knew she was waiting for her, and was testing her patience and politeness.

Libraries were for librarians, as far as Donna was concerned. She only brought in the books to tease George. Now that she was standing by the desk alone, she felt foolish. Donna sighed loudly, hoping Mrs. Whipple would hurry up.

Mrs. Whipple put the pen down slowly and closed up the ink bottle at a deliberate pace. She liked Donna just fine, but she saw no reason to hurry on her account. Finally, she looked up. Donna was a beautiful young woman. Seeing her often reminded Mrs. Whipple that she had been a beautiful young woman once, too. She looked at Donna's soft blonde curls and wondered, would Donna end up as she had? A dry old spinster in a dusty old library?

When Cate had given bestow the moniker "Mrs." upon her, the town librarian had done little to correct the error. She saw no point in falsely advertising herself as "available" when her heart was given to a man long ago and far away.

Mrs. Whipple found it difficult to imagine Donna carrying a torch for any man, nor could she see her ever giving up the notion that a better one was just around the corner. Donna would thrive on the attention that comes from being single and desirable. Yes, she just might end up a spinster, whether or not she became a librarian.

"Yes, Donna?" Mrs. Whipple said politely.

"I'm just returning a few books," Donna explained, handing the books over.

More likely just waiting for George to follow you in like a

pup on a lead, thought Mrs. Whipple. She did not recall Donna checking any books out recently, but took them nonetheless. She did her best to hide her surprise at the titles. Sonnets, she could understand, but Tom Sawyer? Well, it was not for her to judge.

Donna looked around the library. Nothing of real importance is in here, thought Donna. Men wrote all the books and when was the last time a man wrote a book on how to apply makeup properly, or how to design clothes that flattered the figure? Men had no real understanding. Take George, thought Donna, just now comparing me to a horse.

"What's the matter, Donna?" asked Mrs. Whipple noting Donna's expression.

"Oh, nothing, just wondering how Mankind managed to survive this long when men are as dumb as stumps," marveled Donna.

"One of life's many mysteries," observed Mrs. Whipple.

Donna watched Mrs. Whipple flip the pages of the books slowly, checking for damage. Donna wondered, was it ironic or merely sad that the most fashionably daring woman in the territory was a stodgy old librarian? Secretly Donna admired Mrs. Whipple and her fashion sense.

Despite all her outward behavior that would suggest otherwise, Donna could be shy. She was working up the courage to speak, when Mrs. Whipple spoke first.

"Donna," she said.

"Hmm?" answered Donna, a little startled. Mrs. Whipple handed her a sheet of paper. "You forgot this inside your book."

"Oh!" said Donna, "Thank you, Mrs. Whipple. You're most kind to have noticed." She snatched up the paper. She hesitated, then decided it was best to catch up to George before he disappeared. She smiled briefly at Mrs. Whipple then quickly headed outside.

Mrs. Whipple saw in her ledger that the book was checked out to James Darringer, not Donna. She made a note to tell James in case Donna forgot to give the paper to him.

Donna, even if she had taken the paper with the intent to

give it to George, was not above taking a peek, and since he was no longer in front of the library, saw no harm in reading it. After all, it was just George, who never had a thought in his head she could not read off his face or wriggle out of him. She perused the words with tender amusement until she read the last line, and then her mouth dropped open. Donna was not a jealous girl by nature, but this was mainly due to the fact that she had a way of getting her way. It was obvious by the words on the paper that she ran a risk of not doing so. She nearly choked from anger and frustration. Well, we'll just see about this, she thought.

Her heels thundered against the wooden sidewalks, like church bells calling the faithful to the fold. Opal Tamsen decided she needed to close up shop that minute. She was sure she forgot something – back wherever Donna was going. She rushed to keep up with Donna.

Mabel Weatherspoon came out from her house to look for her cat. "Hello, Donna," said Mabel. "Donna, I said, 'Hello!'"

Donna proceeded full steam ahead. Oh, this is going to be good, thought Mabel, opening up her garden gate, and waddling quickly after Donna. Mabel smiled and waved at Opal, who was crossing the road to Mabel's side. Together, they hurried to keep up with Donna. Opal's calico dress hung loose on her skinny frame, which contrasted sharply against Mabel's pleasingly plump figure.

Inside her house, Ruthie McCoy heard the rumbling of Donna's heals. She was suddenly filled with a strong desire to sweep her front porch. She said nothing to Donna when she came out, but she did wave to Mabel and Opal. She motioned to them to come on through the gate and up to her porch for a better view. The ladies of the Gossip Brigade had developed a strong instinct of drama, formed through decades of prying. This particular pot had been slow to boil. The curtains were finally going to rise on this long anticipated show!

Donna fulfilled their every expectation.

The staccato rhythm of her heels sang with outrage as Donna pounded up the steps and across the porch of the Widow

Kibler's boarding house, where Ida Sue worked. Donna's rapping shook the door. Ida Sue had heard Donna coming from quite a ways off, but she was in the midst of getting a pie out of the oven and putting it to cool, so the door would have to wait. Donna sounded hot herself and Ida Sue thought it might do her friend some good to have time to cool as well.

Normally, one of Ida Sue's younger siblings, Dillon or Irene, would have answered the door, but they were off visiting their mother's Uncle Yancy. Donna rapped again. She paced. She eyed the Gossip Brigade gathered on Ruthie McCoy's newly swept porch. She came close to telling them all to 'Shoo, go on,' like one would to unwanted animals. Instead, she greeted them kindly.

"Good morning, Mrs. Weatherspoon. Good morning, Mrs. Tamsen. Good morning, Mrs. McCoy," she cooed. "Beautiful day isn't it?"

"Good morning, Donna," they all chirped back.

"Donna," said Mabel, "you wouldn't by any chance have Mr. Tom-tom over there would you?"

"I don't," said Donna, "but there's no telling what sort of thing Ida Sue might get up to."

To Donna's pleasure, her comment raised a few eyebrows. All these years, everyone thought Ida Sue was so sweet. Shows to go you, you never can tell, thought Donna.

Along with cooking, baking, and cleaning, Ida Sue also did all the laundry for the boarding house as well as take some in. She had to keep a tight schedule if she was going to get it all done. She had intended to let Donna stew a little longer, but after hearing the exchange, she decided she better go out to the porch before Donna could do much more damage. Ida Sue opened her door and stepped onto the porch. She was slender and less curvaceous than Donna, but there was something serenely sweet about her. She still had her apron around her waist.

"Good morning, Donna," she said sweetly, then seeing the ladies in the next door yard, called, "Good morning Mrs. Weatherspoon. Good morning, Mrs. Tamsen. Good morning,

Mrs. McCoy."

"Good morning, Ida Sue," they answered in turn.

"Ida Sue," called Mabel, "have you seen my Mr. Tom-tom this morning?"

"No, I haven't, Mrs. Weatherspoon, but I can help you look for him later this afternoon if you'd like," offered Ida Sue.

"Thank you, Ida Sue, that is kind of you to offer," cooed Mabel, pleased that at least Ida Sue had the good manners to offer – something Donna could learn.

Opal smiled sincerely at Donna from across the way and called, "Donna, you're a right lucky girl to have such a thoughtful friend."

"Friend?" choked Donna, "I wouldn't call a black-heart Jezebel a friend."

"Donna Tucker, what has gotten into you?" asked a shocked Ida Sue.

"This," cried Donna, shoving the paper at Ida Sue. "Read it."

Ida Sue took the paper from Donna. Her eyes scanned the page.

"Out loud," demanded Donna. She could see the women on the neighboring porch made no attempt to pretend they were minding their own business. They would be on her side soon enough.

"Oh, now Donna, really, I…," started Ida Sue.

"Fine. Then I'll read it," declared Donna and she snatched it back from Ida Sue. She cleared her throat and began to recite the poem on the paper in a loud, clear voice for the benefit of her audience.

"Meadows dance when she walks by
And song birds soar where eagles fly
To cast her name upon the wind
And spread her love across the glen"

"That's nice, Donna, but what has it got to do with me?" asked Ida Sue.

"Everything," hissed Donna. She continued to recite in melodramatic tones as she walked back and forth along the porch.

> "Stars bend down to kiss her cheeks
> And ocean tides flow to her creek
> To boast they once washed past her door
> Before receding to the moor"

"That's right pretty," called Mabel. "I didn't know you knew how to write poetry, Donna."

"I don't," snapped Donna, "George McGillicutty wrote it."
"Well land of notions!" gasped Mabel.
"Is there more?" asked Opal in a hopeful tone.

"There is, if y'all would let me finish," snapped Donna.
"Well, go on, don't let us stop you," said Mabel.
Donna continued in a theatrical tone.

> "Let fools fight o'er sea and land
> Let me humbly place upon her hand
> A ring to bind her heart to mine
> To let our lives intertwine
>
> For what sun could rise
> What earth could move
> What life could I, in faith pursue
> Without the love of Ida Sue!"

The peanut gallery gasped.
"Oh, now, for heaven's sake, Donna, you can't possibly

think…" started Ida Sue.

"I can think what I like," snorted Donna.

"That's fine, Donna, I wasn't telling you what to think, I was just wondering what makes you think George wrote that?" asked Ida Sue.

"I found it in his library book," snapped Donna.

"But that doesn't mean he wrote it," protested Ida Sue, "I mean, it doesn't sound like the George we all know."

"George McGillicutty may not be a James Darringer," thundered Donna, "but that doesn't mean he's an idiot."

"I didn't say he was," countered Ida Sue. "But even if he wrote it, who's to say it's about me?"

"You're the only Ida Sue in three counties," Donna retorted. "I lend you George for the Harvest Dance."

"Lend me?" asked Ida Sue.

"That's right," snapped Donna. "Lend you. You don't think for one small moment George would ask you over me if I hadn't told him to, do you?"

The three ladies in Ruthie's yard were soaking this all up. This promised to be the best gossip they had had since Mick Turner's murder trial.

"But, Donna," stammered Ida Sue, "why on earth would you do such a thing?"

"To prod that hopeless James Darringer out of his shell and make him take note of you, that's why. I didn't want my best friend to grow up an old maid, but apparently, you don't care if I suffer that fate!" Donna wept.

"Oh, now, Donna, please," said Ida Sue as she tried to comfort Donna. She was unsure how many of Donna's tears were genuine and how many were for the benefit of the ladies across the way, but Ida Sue was tender at heart and it pained her to see Donna upset.

"And now I've lost George," wailed Donna wiping her eyes. She had not meant to actually tear up, but she had, and now her makeup was ruined.

"Now, don't be silly," assured Ida Sue.

"Silly? Silly? That's easy for you to say, you, you, you,

homewrecker!" fumed Donna.

Homewrecker? The Gossip Brigade gasped. This was better than the murder trial! Ida Sue? A homewrecker? They knew in their hearts, it was not true, but since when did truth have anything to do with juicy gossip?

Suddenly, Ida Sue switched tactics, and she said dreamily, "Ida Sue McGillicutty. Has a poetic ring to it, don't *you* think so, Mrs. Tamsen?"

Opal was leaning over Ruthie McCoy's side porch railing in order to hear better and nearly toppled over the railing from surprise. Mabel was quick to catch her and pull her back. "Why, yes," replied a startled Opal, "I do believe it does."

Donna reeled and her nostrils flared. "You watch yourself, Ida Sue Williams. I gave you George McGillicutty and I can just as easily take him back!"

She turned on her heels and stormed down the steps, down the walk, out the gate, down the street with her head held high and her shoulders squared back.

"Well, I never," declared Ruthie.

"No, but I bet you wished you had!" smirked Opal.

The three women did their best to suppress their delight behind a thin veil of indignation, but a tinge of a smile crept through the faces of all three of them.

Wordlessly, Ida Sue turned and stepped back into the boarding house.

Chapter Fourteen: What a Man Won't Do

Throughout the following week, through no fault of his own, George found himself in a maelstrom of gossip. He was the rope in a tug of war between two determined women. Overwhelmed and confused, George sought the aid of Sheriff Dole. Sheriff Dole was old by George's reckoning – thirty, thirty-five maybe – he did not rightly know. He did know the sheriff had managed to avoid matrimony. Since maintaining his bachelorhood was of vital importance to George, Sheriff Dole seemed the best person to approach for advice.

George stood before the sheriff's door, poised to knock, unsure of what he would say. He looked over his shoulder and saw the Gossip Brigade stationed outside the grocery store. He was relieved that their eyes were cast in the opposite direction. He tapped lightly on the door. The first knock went unanswered. He knocked again.

"It ain't locked, you're welcomed to come in," called the sheriff. It was a slow day, as most days were, and he had his feet up on a stool in his "thinking" position. He was expecting the caller to be Sam Beckett, the grocer, come for a friendly game of chess. He raised half an eye to see George walk through the door. George was a good fella, not the brightest perhaps, but in these parts, a strong back and willing attitude were more important. He reckoned George would do fine.

"Good morning, Sheriff," said George.

"Morning, George," said Sheriff Dole.

Sheriff Dole's bloodhound, Crooner, was lounging on a small blanket by the wood stove that stood in the corner close to the small cupboards and counter. The stove was as cold as the day was warm, and the coffee in the pot had long been drunk.

The knocking had interrupted Crooner's nap. The bloodhound watched the young man with mild interest.

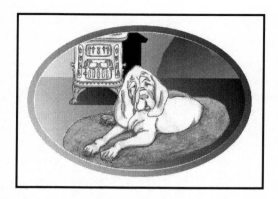

"Good morning, Crooner," said George. He walked over to the dog and rubbed his ears. Crooner snuffed a "Good morning" back. He sniffed George a bit, but as the young man had neither jerky nor bacon, the old dog put his head down to resume his nap."Good boy," said George.

Sheriff Dole hemmed and cleared his throat. George gave Crooner a final rub then stood up, and ran his fingers through his hair. He walked around the room and wrung his hands a bit. George noted, for a bachelor, Sheriff Dole was fairly well kept. His uniform was well starched and his boots polished, and his hair well groomed. George took heart; it was proof that a man could be self-sufficient.

The sheriff's hat rested on the desk close to his feet. George could feel the sheriff's eyes fixed on him and he looked away. George was doing his best to look interested in the sparse room. The holding cell was empty. While it spent most of its time that way, it had recently, albeit briefly, been the home of Henryetta's most famous out-law, Stumpy Gilbert.

"Must be quiet without Stumpy," observed George.

"Yeah, I reckon it is," agreed Sheriff Dole. He was watching George, wondering how long it would take him to get to the point, if he had one.

George studied the sole poster on the wall. It was one of several Cate Darringer had made and was circulating. Except for the angelic and wise expression, it was a fair likeness of

Stumpy. Cate is a pretty good artist, thought George, even though it was not the Stumpy face most folks knew. Truth was, Sheriff Dole had gone to great effort to have Stumpy clean-shaven for his trail, and Cate had chosen this new, clean look for the posters because a beard was too messy to draw. She also hoped that a clean-shaven face had nothing to hide and therefore, was innocent.

"Cate sure believes in his innocence," remarked George.

"Her and most the town," added Sheriff Dole.

"What do you reckon?" asked George.

"I reckon if he did shoot Mick Turner, at the least, it was an accident," replied the sheriff.

"And at most?" asked George.

The Sherriff looked thoughtfully at George. "At most, it was self-defense," surmised Sherriff Dole. He leaned back a little more in his chair. "Mick was never what you would call 'kind' to Stumpy."

"You ever wonder what Stumpy might say in his defense if he could talk?" George asked.

"Not tough to figure." The Sherriff shrugged. "Maybe something along the lines of, 'The s.o.b. deserved it.' Can't imagine there'd be too many willing to let Stumpy swing for Mick Turner if they knew the whole story."

George nodded. He was not paying much attention to the conversation, being lost in his own woes. He looked around the room. His eyes fell onto a Bible that was resting on a shelf that was anchored near the ceiling. Sheriff Dole eyed George eyeing the Bible.

Sheriff Dole was not a tall man, which he considered to be a trait in his favor as it made him a smaller target. It also meant folks liked to "remind" him of his limited stature. Someone, he was unsure as to who, had anchored a shelf near the ceiling and placed the Bible atop it as a prank. Any other book and he would have just gotten a stick and knocked it down. He was not a particularly religious man, but when it came to God and his word, he reckoned it best to err on the polite side. He was determined that Bible would live on that shelf until he figured out a way to get it down without getting out a ladder and without asking someone else to get it down for him.

Sheriff Dole decided to prod George. "Son, is there something I can do for you?"

George wrung his hands some more. "I was wondering, if a man wanted to stay hid for awhile, not long, just long enough for some trouble to blow over, where would he go to do it?"

"That depends," the sheriff said thoughtfully, "on what kind of trouble he's in. There something you want to tell me?"

George struggled for words. He was mystified by his current predicament.

Sheriff Dole placed his feet on the floor and leaned forward. "George," he asked, his eyes narrowing, "are you in some kind of trouble?"

"Yes, sir" confessed George.

"Well, go on, spit it out," urged Sheriff Dole. Good confessions made his work easier.

"I got females fighting over me," George blurted out at last.

Sheriff Dole's eyes widened. He had heard the gossip, naturally, who hadn't? But he was not one to believe everything he heard, particularly far-fetched tales of romance. Well, gosh durn, who would have thunk it?

"Women trouble?" asked Sheriff Dole. "How did you manage that?"

"I don't know," admitted George shaking his head slowly.

"The Lord doth work in mysterious ways," observed the sheriff. "Well, son, you have my sympathies."

"I was hoping for more than that," pleaded George. "I was hoping you'd hide me a spell."

The sheriff's voice took on a foreboding tone, "George, I'm sorry, but there is no hiding from a woman. A woman is like a bloodhound. She can smell fear."

"So what am I supposed to do?" pleaded George.

"Pick one and be done with it," advised Sheriff Dole. He eased back into his thinking position and folded his hands across his stomach.

"But what if I pick wrong?" asked George.

"And what if you do?" asked the sheriff. "Marriage only lasts a lifetime, there ain't nothing in the Bible that says a woman owns a man in the hereafter."

George shivered. "Put that way, I don't see I should marry either of them."

"Suit yourself, tain't against the law for a man to live and die alone," the sheriff said flatly.

"Ah, now, you ain't helping at all. All I want is some time to think things through without one or the other of them making cow eyes at me." George was hoping for more help than this. "You're single, I figured you'd know how to keep the women at bay."

Sheriff Dole sighed. "It helps that I get shot at for a living. Women tend to prefer men alive. At least, to start off with."

"That's it!" cried George.

"What's it?" asked Sheriff Dole.

"You can make me your deputy," beamed George.

"Deputy?" pondered the sheriff. "You mean you'd risk being shot at to avoid women trouble?"

"Wouldn't you?" asked George his face riffed with consternation.

Sheriff Dole studied George a moment. Maybe the young man was not as thick as he appeared. Still, there was not enough going on in town to keep a Sheriff busy, let alone keep a deputy out of trouble.

"George, don't Willy Hoffman keep you busy enough?" asked Sheriff Dole.

"He only needs me four days a week," answered George.

"Well, what about Malcolm Mitchell?" asked the sheriff. "He could use a strong back like yours."

George paled. "Ever since this crazy madness hit, two of his daughters have been shining up to me and the third is thinking on it. Last time I walked passed his place, he made a point of showing me his rifle," winced George.

"Them, too?" Sheriff Dole gave a whistle. It was the first he had heard of that particular detail. Having sisters fighting over a man could get downright ugly. This was madness indeed. It was

96

enough to make one wonder if someone was spiking the well water.

"Well?" begged George.

Sheriff Dole shook his head, "Son, being a deputy is serious business. I can't deputize every fella who gets himself in a jam with a woman."

"Oh, please, Sheriff. I swear I won't be any trouble at all. You won't even have to pay me."

"Couldn't pay you even if I wanted to." He looked at George's eager, hopeful face. It would be like saying no to a puppy. Sheriff Dole had a soft spot for puppies. Crooner had recently sired a litter. The sheriff would ride to Okmulgee soon to have his pick. He wondered what George would look like if he were a puppy and how trainable he would be. Only one way to find out.

"Well, you know I would, son, but it's like this," he explained with great sincerity. "I went and left my Bible at home this morning and I..."

"No, you didn't Sheriff!" George interrupted. "It's right here!" George easily reached the top shelf and brought down the Bible.

The sheriff smiled inwardly. "So it is!" he said with a touch of surprise.

George attempted to hand the Bible over to Sheriff Dole.

"George," scolded the sheriff indignantly, eyeing the thick coat of dust on the cover, "are you planning on swearing an oath on a dusty Bible?"

"No, sir," answered an embarrassed George.

"Well, then, you best do something about it," declared the sheriff.

George started to take a deep breath to blow the dust off, but the sheriff stopped him.

"Not in here," the sheriff reprimanded, "Go outside to dust it off."

George reluctantly took the Bible outside. He looked down the dirt road towards the grocery store. The Gossip Brigade seemed busy with their needle point. He blew the dust off and rushed back inside as quickly as he could.

Sheriff Dole took the Bible and asked George to place his left hand over it. George did. The sheriff raised his right hand, and George did the same. The sheriff studied George.

"Do you swear," the sheriff began.

"Oh, yes, sir, I sure do," agreed George.

"Not yet, son, let me finish," said the sheriff.

"Oh, right, sorry, you go ahead," George apologized.

"Thank you. Now, do you swear to uphold the law and peace of this town and do everything I tell you to do, so help you God?" asked the sheriff.

"Yes, sir, I do," nodded George.

"Then, I hereby deputize you for the period of one week," affirmed the sheriff. He lay the Bible on his desk and shook George by the hand. "Congratulations, you can start by cleaning the stable."

"A week?" complained George, "That ain't long enough."

"It's all you get. Make the most out of it," the sheriff advised.

"Yes, sir, I will sir, and I'm much obliged, sir," said a grateful George as he headed for the door. "And don't worry none, I'll have that stable so clean, ol' Phoenix and Daisy will think Hercules has run the Mississippi through it."

"That's fine, George, just so long as you get 'er done," nodded the sheriff.

A few minutes passed. The sheriff heard voices. He strode over and looked out the window. Over in the stable Donna Tucker was chatting up George. Half an eye could see she looked good in her dress. George slung manure into a wooden wheelbarrow with a pitchfork. A little splattered hazardously close to Donna's pretty shoes. Gotta hand it to Donna, she stuck it out longer than Sheriff Dole thought she would. It took five or six near misses to make her decide she would catch up with George later. George waved Donna goodbye, then continued his work, whistling a Scottish tune. The sheriff had never seen anyone so happy to be shoveling out a stable. What a man won't do to avoid a woman, he thought.

Chapter Fifteen: The Plans of Ninnies

It was short work for Frank to find the accomplices needed to bust Stumpy out of jail. Gullible nitwits were in high supply and low demand. He picked these ninnies over the others because it was fairly obvious no one would miss them once they had served their purpose. One was a balding fella, who called himself Howie, and the other was a moron named Eddy that was better known as One-Eye.

As luck would have it, he had also easily acquired the horses he needed. Some men should just never drink. Bending their elbows had a way of dislodging their brains and setting their tongues to wagging. Horse wrestlers boasting about the horses they stole and their whereabouts did not deserve to keep them. It was that plain and simple. If and when they managed to sober up, what would they do? Call the sheriff to complain that someone stole the horses they stole?

Frank had talked the two numnuts he met the night before into busting Stumpy out of jail without him. Always best to get others to do the dirty work for you. While they risked their necks, he was at the barber's getting the first shave he had had in years. He knew shaving was premature. The jailbreak could fail. Fact was, he had seen his face and his beard on a poster in the post office that morning and he considered the shave to be the lesser of two evils. Better to be thought innocent than guilty.

"You clean up nice," said the barber as he finished toweling Frank's face. "Get yourself a few flowers and you could go a-courting!"

Frank smirked. He knew the man was only looking for a decent tip, and he gave him one. He rose from the chair, and nodded a "Good day." He slipped out the door without fanfare.

Frank strolled into the telegraph office just as quietly. He sent a telegram to his half-brother, Travis. They had kept up semi-regular communication. To the unknowing soul, the words were just harmless chit chat between family members. To those who knew the code, it was much more than that. He was telling Travis where to meet him, what time, what bank they were heisting and, just as important, that he had found a patsy to take the blame. This, too, was premature, but he reckoned, once they busted Stumpy out of jail, lingering around town would not be on the agenda. If the bust failed, he could send a second telegram canceling the first. Travis understood the pattern.

A few minutes later, Frank was walking down the street towards the appointed meeting place. The half-wits had had plenty of time. Frank expected to find them waiting along with Stumpy.

A flea-bitten cat came out of nowhere and tried to weave its way between Frank's legs, caterwauling in an off-key screech. Frank hated cats of all kinds, shapes and sizes. A cat in heat tripping him up could rely on a boot to the ribs. The cat howled and ran ahead of him. Frank should have seen right then that it was an omen of the day to come.

As he strode closer to the arranged meeting place, he could see something was wrong. There were the two accomplices, but only three of the four horses, and no Stumpy.

One-Eye grabbed his balding accomplice by the arm and shouted, "There he is!" He pointed down the road towards Frank.

"Are you sure?" asked Howie. He pushed his bedraggled hat back to scratch his balding pate.

"Sure, I'm sure, who else would he be?" insisted One-Eye

"He ain't wearing the same clothes," observed the Howie.

"So, some folks have more than one suit to wear," One-Eye explained.

"How'd he get off the horse?" asked Howie.

"Who cares? Let's get him back on one 'fore Frank gets back," said One-Eye. The two would-be kidnappers crouched slightly and walked cautiously towards Frank with their arms outstretched like they had an invisible net to toss over him.

"Now, Stumpy, don't be afraid son, we're not going to hurt you none," said Howie, softly..

"Fools!" snapped Frank, "I'm Frank."

The two men stood up and looked dumbfounded. If they had been any smarter, the two patsies might have made a run for it. No one had given them instructions to run for it if something went wrong and so they were in a quandary as to what to do.

"What happened to your beard?" asked the balding accomplice.

"The same thing that might happen to you, if you aren't careful – a close shave," snapped Frank. "Where's the other horse?"

"With Stumpy," answered One-Eye.

"Which is where, exactly?" asked Frank.

The two men stood silent for a moment.

"With the horse?" asked One-Eye.

"You lost him?" Frank rubbed his shaven face in disgust.

Frank became more and more annoyed as he listened to the explanation. Everything was initially going according to plan, starting with the guard being distracted by the fancy woman Frank had hired to chat him up. She was mighty pretty and he was still busy with her as far as they knew. They found the spare key where Frank said it would be. They held out a small puppy out for Stumpy to pet, just like Frank told them to, and he followed just like Frank said he would. It was all going slicker than snake oil, 'til it came to the horse.

This was more work than one might imagine. It meant taking the puppy away. Pulling the puppy away brought on a severe reaction from Stumpy, as he was more than determined to keep it. During the struggle, the puppy ran off and Stumpy chased after him. It took both men to catch him and drag him back to the horse. They decided the best way to get him on the horse was to throw his cuffed hands around its neck, and then hoist the rest of him up and over the back of the horse.

It was an epic battle, but they managed to shove him up onto the horse. To make sure he stayed put they grabbed a rope and used it to lash him securely onto the horse. They tied first one foot, then tossed the rope beneath the underbelly of the horse and tied the other foot to the other end of the rope.

Which would have been fine, except that the rope they used was the one that tethered the horse to the hitching post. Even then, things might have been okay, except once Stumpy was on the horse's back, he lost all fear and he and the horse took off like greased lightning.

Franks temples throbbed. He considered shooting the both of them. He reached into his pockets and caressed the smooth river rocks he kept to sooth his mind. He could not well go rob a bank if he did not know where his patsy was. The fool could find a dozen eyewitnesses to protect him.

He rubbed his temples and wished he had been more temperate with his drinking the night before. The cat continued to try to vine itself around his legs. Another boot to the ribs only sent it across the lane where it continued its lamentful screech.

Well, the simpleton could not have gone too far, thought Frank. Where did those rustlers say they stole them horses? He was fairly sure they said a ranch outside Henryetta. A horse likes to return to the barn. Good possibility that's where the horse would be taking his rider, whether he liked it or not.

Frank looked the horses over thoroughly a second time. He had been careful in selecting them. It was important to him that they were devoid of any characteristics that made them readily recognizable. It could be awkward to learn a horse had a mouth tattoo only *after* running into the real owners. He looked inside their mouths, but did not find anything of concern. They looked as ordinary as any horses he had ever seen. He favored the bay horse. He'd seen a lot of bays of late and he reckoned it would blend in well.

Howie was whispering to One-Eye. They must have mistaken Frank for an old deaf fool. He did not much care for some of the implications the would-be double-crossers were coming up with.

The mangy cat was scratching its claws deep into the hitching post. As far as Frank was concerned, it might as well have been digging them into his brain. Frank called to the men, "There's something y'all need to know about me."

"Yeah?" asked Howie. "And what's that?"

Frank pulled a rock from his pocket and hurled it across the lane. Zing. Thud. The caterwauling stopped in mid-note and a lifeless pile of fur lay on the ground. "I never miss," he stated dryly.

Frank saddled up on the best horse, and rode down the alley and onto the main road as the two abandoned would-be kidnappers watched in stunned silence.

After a moment, One-Eye asked, "He never misses what?"

"How should I know?" snipped Howie.

Frank's motion had been so swift and subtle, it had gone unseen by either man.

"Well, are we supposed to follow him?" asked One-Eye.

"I suppose so, if we want to get paid," answered Howie.

They quickly saddled up and rode to catch up.

Over in Fort Smith, Travis Merrill, half-brother to Frank Merrill and full-time telegraph office employee when he was not off robbing banks, read the coded telegram he received. The telegram filled him with dread.

Travis had not heard from his half-brother since Mick showed up dead. He had an inkling from the start Frank was somehow mixed up in Mick's death. He had taken particular interest in the trial proceedings since Judge Parker rode over to Henryetta for the murder trial.

Since then, some lunatic girl had been the steam behind a full-on campaign worthy of a presidential candidate running for election. She insisted an elk button would prove the man on trial innocent. It was a detail the judge had managed to keep out of the papers, but Travis knew it.

No matter where Frank sent him telegrams from, there were a limited number of places Travis could send a response. One of those places was Henryetta, where his friend Mick Turner used to live.

Travis never liked sending uncoded messages, but they did not have a code set-up for this particular situation.

He sent the following message to Frank's alias, Mark Fennell, in care of the Henryetta Post Office.

"Lose the elk button."

Chapter Sixteen: Not for Some

The Gossip Brigade had entrenched themselves on the bench outside the grocery store. The ladies would have been more comfortable in one of their own homes, but none of them wanted to miss the action. Fresh gossip was at its juicy-best when witnessed firsthand.

They were in clear view to see George knock on Sheriff Dole's door. And they watched from the corner of their eyes when George came out to blow dust off the Bible. Oh, wouldn't a certain somebody be annoyed to learn that Sheriff Dole got that Bible down after all this time!

They saw George come out a few minutes later and walk to the stables, which is how they knew to tell Donna where he was when she came by in that pretty dress of hers pretending she was taking a casual stroll for fresh air.

And they took note when she strutted back in those pretty shoes of hers. They watched Ida Sue walk by later with a dewberry pie. Then they watched as she walked by again, only this time without the pie. Ida Sue was only the first gal walking by with baked goods that morning. Margaret Anne came by with fresh cinnamon buns, then came Debra Louise with crumb cake, and after her came Imogene with sweet iced tea. Who would have believed George McGillicutty could raise such a ruckus?

Ian Darringer came riding into town on his supply wagon with Cate riding shotgun sans the shotgun. Just because Ian had taught Cate how to use a firearm did not mean she was allowed to carry one with her wherever she went.

Cate, Ruthie, Mabel and Opal were a mutual appreciation society. The ladies appreciated Cate for her ability to create gossip, and Cate appreciated the ladies for their ability to spread it. Cate waved enthusiastically to the three ladies the moment they came into view. She was eager to catch up on the latest news.

It had been more than a week since she had set her little plan in motion and she was certain if the gossip was juicy, it would all center around a certain love poem "discovered" in a certain book by a certain botanist. Surely, with James on his way up the matrimony aisle, Cate would be the obvious choice for going to Nigeria.

Ian took a dim view of gossip, being the center of much of it since testifying in the murder trial. The last thing he wanted was to have his daughter's eager ears and willing mouth come into contact with the Gossip Brigade's eager mouths and willing ears.

"Good morning, ladies," Ian said, tipping his hat. He marveled at how three women who looked so different from each other could make such a complementary set.

"Good morning, Ian," chirped Mabel gaily.

"It certainly is for some," smiled Ruthie wickedly.

"But not for others," smirked Opal.

The three women tittered.

Cate leapt down from the supply wagon while Ian tethered the horses. "Oh?" quizzed Cate. "Who ain't having a good morning?"

"Cate," her father ordered, "Get your books and be quick about it, or next time I'll be leaving you at home." Town women have too much time on their hands, thought Ian, for the umpteenth time. He had been meaning to speak to the reverend to see if he could come up with something for them to do to keep them too busy to spread gossip. Ian had no idea what that something might be. Ordinarily, child-rearing kept a woman too busy for tongue wagging, but these women were past that stage of life.

"Yes, Papa," nodded Cate, but she stood stock still, hoping to out-wait him. The three women also were hoping to out-wait him. Their mouths quivered with anticipation, but they held their tongues. It was more fun to gossip when there was no disapproving man around to dampen the fun.

Ian assessed the situation. He was none too pleased that Cate was still standing firmly in place. His eyes bored a hole in the back of her head until she realized he meant business. Quickly, she turned and rushed to the library. She was not overly concerned. Papa always took longer than he thought he would. She could get her books and be back for the gossip half an age before he even began to shop for his wares.

Ian watched Cate open the library doors and go inside. He turned to the ladies with a stern look on his face. The thought occurred to him that if there was gossip, it was best he hear it before Cate, strictly for her benefit, of course. If he knew what was rattling around in her mind, he might be able to counter it. So, merely for Cate's sake, he smiled and said, "Not a bad day for anyone I know, I hope."

The ladies giggled joyfully as he sat down beside them.

108

Chapter Seventeen: *Darringeri carnivouri mani*

Cate flung open the library door. Mrs. Whipple looked up from her desk briefly and smiled. Cate quickly approached the desk in the hopes she could peer over the top to see what her librarian friend was working on. Mrs. Whipple gave Cate a knowing look, then covered her work with blotting paper to shield it from curious eyes.

"Good morning, Mrs. Whipple," beamed Cate, handing her a piece of paper.

Mrs. Whipple took the paper and examined it.

"Well, good morning, Cate. What have you got there?" Mrs. Whipple asked. She could see Cate could hardly contain her pride.

Cate leaned against the desk and whispered, "It's a drawing of 'Darringeri carnivouri mani.'"

"I see," said Mrs. Whipple. She arched her brow and moved the paper closer to the light. She always found Cate's attempts at Latin and other foreign languages amusing, but did her best to hide her smile.

"It's the man-eating flower I'm going to discover when I go to Nigeria," continued Cate.

"Goodness," said Mrs. Whipple. What would Cate think of next? She pointed to a protrusion and asked, "What's that sticking out of it?"

"A right leg," replied Cate. "Another botanist was about to discover it first, but he stuck his snoopy nose inside to have a look, and now it's eating him."

"How unfortunate," commented Mrs. Whipple. She could tell from Cate's expression that Cate thought it a fate well deserved.

"Yes," said Cate leaning closer in and pointing to the drawing. "That's the botanist, and that is his guide, who foolishly tried to rescue him, and now it's eating him, too. The poor plant will have indigestion for years to come from eating so much all at once."

"Poor, poor carnivouri mani," lamented Mrs. Whipple, sadly shaking her head. She could feel her soft bun loosening, so she took a moment to re-pin it.

"Of course, none of it would have happened if I'd been there," remarked Cate. Cate both envied Mrs. Whipple's beautiful hair and thought it nonsense to waste time on its maintenance.

"Of course," agreed Mrs. Whipple. "I'm sure you're far too clever to be eaten by a plant."

"That," agreed Cate, "and it's a man-eating plant. It doesn't eat women." Cate was pleased to state that obvious fact.

"Oh? Why is that?" asked Mrs. Whipple.

"Well, that's obvious, isn't it? It hunts by smell. Women smell like flowers, and while the plant may be carnivorous, it certainly can't be cannibalistic or it would have to eat itself."

"Ah, yes, that is obvious," agreed Mrs. Whipple. "But tell me, if women smell like flowers, what do men smell like?"

"Baboons. Darringeri carnivouri mani *loves* baboons! They are its favorite food. It's always a little disappointed to be eating a man by mistake; it doesn't much care for his shoes and it finds his socks downright disagreeable, so it will spit those out when it's finished eating the rest of him," explained Cate.

"Yes, that is understandable," agreed Mrs. Whipple. "How tragic. The poor botanist could have avoided being eaten if only he had worn perfume."

"Oh, no," explained Cate, "because you see, he has heavy footsteps. The flower would still mistake him for a baboon and eat him anyway."

"Well, then, a wise botanist would have stayed home and left it for the women to discover," stated Mrs. Whipple, fairly certain that was the point Cate had hoped to make all along.

"Yes," replied Cate, slightly indignant, "but men aren't always so wise, are they? Take Ralph for instance."

"Who?" asked Mrs. Whipple. She did not recall any ranch hands by the name of Ralph on the Darringer ranch.

"Ralph Mahoney," replied Cate. "The botanist who returned our books for us last week." Cate was surprised Mrs. Whipple could have forgotten him in such a short time.

Mrs. Whipple looked as if she had the breath squeezed out of her. Cate thought for a moment she had done something wrong. Mrs. Whipple shook her head.

"I'm sorry, Cate," corrected Mrs. Whipple, "but it was Donna Tucker who brought your books back. Which reminds me, James left a piece of paper in his book, and I gave it to Donna by mistake. If he needs it back, he'll have to talk to her about it."

Cate was perplexed. Why did Ralph give the books to Donna? It was pointless for Donna to find the poem. Donna already knew James was in love with Ida Sue, and so did Ida Sue. In fact, the whole town knew he was, it was just James who seemed to be unaware of the fact. And Ralph, the one person who needed to know it most, was the one person who left town without learning the truth. She had spent three-quarters of forever writing that poem in James's handwriting, and all for nothing.

"Cate?" asked Mrs. Whipple. "Are you alright?"

"I'm fine," replied Cate, "I just don't understand why Ralph didn't come in himself. He said he was absolutely desperate to explore the library AND catch up on his reading. Obviously, he must have gotten lost. That makes twice since he's been here. He got lost on the way to our house, too."

"I'm sure he must have had a lot on his mind," explained Mrs. Whipple. If he could choose to avoid her library, then she could choose to avoid puzzling out why he had.

"He says I'm too young to go to Africa with him without a chaperone, but frankly, I think he's the one who needs a chaperone. You don't see me getting lost, do you?" Cate asked.

"You? Never. Not while the sun shines in the day and the stars at night. You could never be lost, Cate," reassured Mrs. Whipple.

"Mother says it's cheeky for me to call him 'Ralph,' but I think, what's the point of having a first name if you're never going to use it? Unless you believe, like the Indians do, that a name holds power over a person and only trusted people can know your secret name. Do you believe that, Mrs. Whipple?"

She smiled. "I believe one should always be respectful with names."

"Have you a secret name?" asked Cate. "One only you and the Great Spirit in the sky knows?

"Well," sighed Mrs. Whipple, "if I did, then went around

telling everyone about it, it wouldn't be a secret for long, would it?"

"You trust me with books, don't you Mrs. Whipple?" asked Cate.

"Of course, Cate," replied Mrs. Whipple.

"Books are extremely special aren't they? Didn't you say we should treat them with all the respect we would a person?" she asked.

"Yes, I believe I did say that," admitted Mrs. Whipple.

Cate leaned in close and whispered conspiratorially, "Then it would make sense for you to trust me with your secret name, wouldn't it?"

"Well, how about we start off with my first name? Then, if you don't bat it around like a common flyswatter, we'll see about my secret name later," said Mrs. Whipple.

"Alright," agreed Cate. She wiped her hand against her shirt. "We'll spit on it." Cate cupped her hand in preparation.

"I think we can forego the spit for now, Cate," said Mrs. Whipple. "Your word will do. My first name is Nell."

"Oh," said Cate. "Is that short for anything?"

"Yes, it's short for Nelly," smiled Mrs. Whipple. She looked at Cate's crestfallen face. "Not exactly what you were hoping for?"

"Well, no," admitted Cate. "It isn't exotic – not like Zudora!"

"Zudora?" gasped Mrs. Whipple, a tad surprised, "Wherever did you hear that name?"

"I read it, in one of Ralph's journals," explained Cate. Mrs. Whipple looked almost near to tears, so Cate hurried to reassure her, "Oh, it's okay, he said I could. He left them for James and me to review while he's fundraising. Zudora ventures chorea, it's Latin for..."

"Graceful dancing Zudora," Mrs. Whipple murmured.

"That's right. I forgot you know Latin," said Cate. "It's what he named an orchid he discovered. Isn't that romantic? It sounds like a Greek goddess, don't you think?"

Mrs. Whipple knew Cate's expectations of her "librarian

114

knowledge" to be extremely high, but the only Zudora she actually knew was herself. Nell was cautious with her personal history, and dodged the topic. "Well, I've never read any myths about any Zudora."

"Well, then, we should make one up!" cried Cate.

Mrs. Whipple could see the cogs turning in Cate's mind. As Cate spoke, Mrs. Whipple felt herself being swept away. Cate had a way of making things come alive.

"Once upon a time, on an island in the Caspian Sea, the wind was always gentle, and the water clear and bright, and the crops grew plentiful beneath a loving sun. On this island lived a beautiful princess named Zudora. Many suitors came to woo Zudora and though they were men of wealth and prestige, she would have none of them, for she was in love with a poor village boy named..."

"Albireo," offered Mrs. Whipple.

"Albireo," gasped Cate. "Is he handsome?"

"Of course," nodded Mrs. Whipple. "And brave and clever and proud, too. It was his pride that was to cause all the misery. He wanted to marry the princess, but as we all know, a suitor seeking the hand of a princess must go on a quest. So he left the island to seek his fortune, vowing to return with the wealth of kings, so she would have servants all her days."

"But she's a princess," observed Cate. "Wouldn't she already have servants?"

"Yes, but not because of anything he had done. That was all her father's doing," explained Mrs. Whipple.

"But if she was in love, servants wouldn't matter to her, would they?" asked Cate.

"Of course, not," agreed Mrs. Whipple, "But like you said earlier, men are not always so wise. Albireo was proud, and his pride was more important to him."

"Then why did she love him?" asked Cate.

"Why does any woman love any man? Because she does," sighed Mrs. Whipple.

"So what did she do?" asked Cate, forgetting that she was the one telling the story.

"What any love crazed woman would do – she went looking for him," explained Mrs. Whipple.

"Did she have many great adventures?" asked Cate.

"Well, it is your story, what do you think?" asked Mrs. Whipple.

"Of course. She rode horses, and camels and even elephants searching for Albireo. She solved murders, and found treasure, and once, even stopped a war!"

"Goodness, she really was quite the remarkable princess," observed Mrs. Whipple.

"Yes, but she never forgot Albireo," sighed Cate. She was thinking of Ida Sue when she said it. She knew Ida Sue would never forget James.

Mrs. Whipple thought of her own lost love. "Yes," she agreed, "I'm sure she never did. So what became of her?"

Cate drummed her hands on the desk, in the wild fashion of the Indian drums she sometimes heard at night. She leaned forward and whispered, "One day, a messenger from her home island found her and told her she was needed at home. Things had gone terribly wrong for them since she left. The land had been invaded by windowahs!"

"Gracious! No! Whatever could they be?" asked Mrs. Whipple.

"Little insect men with razor sharp teeth," answered Cate. She made zzzt-zzzt-zzzt sounds mimicking the tiny insects. Her fingers flew around and around mimicking their flight path.

Then, suddenly, in unison, all the little windowahs that were her fingers pounced on the table and made gnashing noises as they consumed Mrs. Whipple's work papers. "And just like that, they devoured the harvest!"

Mrs. Whipple gasped, "Cate!"

"Oh, sorry," apologized Cate, attempting to smooth out the rumpled papers.

Mrs. Whipple sighed as she straightened out the papers and stacked them neatly out of the way. "Well, I must admit, I would be all pitchforks and torches if insect men devoured my harvest. What did they expect the princess to do?"

"Slay the Marthrax!" cried Cate, brandishing an invisible sword.

"The who?" asked Mrs. Whipple.

"The Marthrax, the evil monster that controlled the windowahs. He had once been human, but he had incurred the wrath of Aphrodite for turning his back on love, and she turned him into a horrible, ugly, selfish monster."

"Oh, yes, that sounds like something she would do. It never pays to spurn goddesses, especially Aphrodite," agreed Mrs. Whipple.

"So Zudora sailed back home as fast as she could," said Cate. "But it wasn't easy, for now the winds were no longer gentle, they tore at her sails and sent the waves crashing against her boat," Cate's arms undulated, acting out the scene. "But! She was steadfast in her duty. She tacked and turned and continued to defy the waves. Suddenly, a giant wave picked up her boat and carried it far into the land, flooding the countryside. When the water finally receded, she was a hundred feet up in a giant tree."

"A hundred feet!" gasped Mrs. Whipple. "How did she get down?"

"She made wings from the sails, and flew down like a bird," tweetered Cate. She spread her arms and illustrated how the princess glided down.

"It's a good thing she knew how to sew," smiled Mrs. Whipple.

Cate stopped gliding and frowned. That sounded exactly like something her mother would say. Wings were infinitely more interesting and worthwhile than the hem on a table cloth. Cate was sure she would be able to sew wings from sails, if the occasion were to arise.

Mrs. Whipple could see she had said the wrong thing, so she asked, "Did she find the Marthrax?"

"Yes," answered Cate, "and just in time, for he was dying."

"Oh?" asked Mrs. Whipple a little puzzled, "That would make it easier to slay him, one would think."

"But she didn't want to slay him," explained Cate, "The moment she saw him, she felt a great pity for him, for she knew what it was like to suffer without love. Instead of poisoning him with a magic dart, she shooed away the windowahs, and held him close. She gave him some water to drink as the tiny insects buzzed overhead, watching. The water revived the Marthrax enough so that he could speak."

"What did he say?" asked Mrs. Whipple.

"He said, 'Zudora, dance for me.' So she did." Cate danced around the room.

Mrs. Whipple found herself swept away, and she sang soft notes to accompany Cate's dancing. "She danced and danced and danced," said Cate. "All the while, the Marthrax became stronger and stronger and stronger, until finally, he was strong enough to dance with her. As they danced, the windowahs flew off and scattered across the land, and everywhere they landed they turned into beautiful flowers. Then Zudora gently kissed the Marthrax, and his ugly monster skin fell off. Underneath was Albireo!"

"She found him!" cheered Mrs. Whipple.

"She did, and they lived happily ever after in Nigeria," said Cate.

"Nigeria?" asked Mrs. Whipple.

"Of course," replied Cate, "she'd want to see the flower he named for her, wouldn't she? I wouldn't want to settle for a pencil sketch."

"Yes, I suppose so," agreed Mrs. Whipple. "Except, your

name isn't Zudora."

"Maybe it's my secret name," said Cate.

"Oh, you trust me with your secret name, do you?" asked Mrs. Whipple.

"I said, 'maybe.' Ralph doesn't know it yet, but I'm going to go with him" said Cate.

"But Cate, the town needs you. Stumpy Gilbert needs you," reminded Mrs. Whipple. "Who will clear his name once you leave?"

"That is a good point," Cate conceded. "So I'll just have to free him before I leave."

"How do you plan to do that?" asked Mrs. Whipple.

"I'll find the real killer and get him to confess," Cate said in a matter of fact manner.

"You haven't had a decent lead yet," Mrs. Whipple pointed out.

"Yes, but now that Stumpy's been convicted, don't you think the real killer will get lazy? His guard will be down, and he's more apt to make a mistake," Cate reasoned.

"There's just one thing wrong with that," remarked Mrs. Whipple. "In order for you to hear this confession, you'd have to be in the company of highly undesirable characters, so unless you suddenly take up hard living, I don't suspect the occasion will arise."

"I'll think of something," said Cate.

Mrs. Whipple was sure Cate would. She was equally sure that there was not a thing she could do to prevent her.

Chapter Eighteen: When Nerves Are Shot

Ian Darringer burst open the library door and called brusquely "Cate, time to go."

Cate was startled. They never came to town without spending some time. "But I haven't gotten a book yet," she whined.

"Not my problem," her father stated. "We need to get back to the ranch. I didn't want to worry you none, earlier, Cate, but one of the reasons we came to town was to file a report with Sheriff Dole."

"A report? About what?" asked Cate.

"A few horses went missing last night," confessed Ian.

"They what? From where?" Cate asked frantically.

"Just a few, from the stable," he admitted sheepishly.

"It's your fault for making me sleep inside!" fumed Cate. "If I had been in the stable like I should have been..."

"You might have gotten kidnapped along with the horses," snapped Ian. "You're a person, not a horse. You belong in the house at night!"

"But I could have stopped them!" insisted Cate.

"You don't know that," fumed Ian.

"You drag me away from Kiwi," accused Cate.

"As I recall, you insisted on coming to town," said Ian.

"How do we know the rustlers aren't right there this minute coming back for the ones they missed?" Cate cried in a panic. "Kiwi could be in danger!"

"Calm down," he said. "If they were going to take her, they'd have done it last night."

"It was too dark to see her last night, but she'll stand out in the daylight," said Cate. "Come on, what are you waiting for? Let's get moving."

"Go load up," said Ian, "I'll be right behind you."

Cate ran out the door and hopped on the supply wagon. She was sitting ramrod straight and as good as he had ever seen her.

Ian eyed the Gossip Brigade. They seemed busy with their stitching as if nothing else in the world mattered. Cautiously, he turned to Mrs. Whipple and whispered, "While I was talking with Sheriff Dole, a wire came in. Stumpy's broke out of jail and is on the run."

Cate sailed back into the library "We need to go find him!" she blurted out. She grabbed onto her father to drag him outside. "Some bounty-hungry hunter might shoot him! He could be on the side of the road bleeding to death!"

Ian held his ground, pulling her hands off him. How on earth had she heard him? "There's no bounty on him, at least not yet," said Ian. "Now let me finish. Mrs. Whipple, I know I speak for Ann, I'd like to invite you to the ranch."

"The ranch?" asked a puzzled Mrs. Whipple.

"You'd be safer. More men to stand guard," explained Ian.

"But Stumpy's the most innocent, simple creature on this green earth," defended Mrs. Whipple.

"Being simple didn't stop him from shooting Mick Turner," said Ian.

"And I'm sure a sober, decent person who knows how to treat someone with kindness will fare a great deal better," said Mrs. Whipple.

"But..." Cate started.

"No buts, Cate," said Mrs. Whipple. "Stumpy Gilbert didn't break out of jail to come here and terrorize the town library." She turned to Ian, "If he was going to hurt anybody, which I much doubt, it would be to hurt you, Ian. You're the one who testified against him."

"I told you, Pa," Cate started, but then Ian cut her a look that stopped her in her tracks.

Ian felt a surge of frustration, why could no one understand why he had to testify? "Listen, you live out of the way," he started to say.

"For a reason," said Mrs. Whipple, "so I don't have to be part of this sort of nonsense."

"It's for your own safety," he pressed.

"Tell that to your stolen horses," she quipped.

"Ann won't be happy I left you alone," he tried again.

"Pa, I could stay with Mrs. Whipple," offered Cate.

Ian looked at his daughter. The more angelic she looked, the more trouble she was brewing. You could almost see the halo glowing over her head. While it was easy to tell *that* she was up to something, there was never any knowing *what* that something might be. Whatever she was scheming, he was not about to let her have her way with a convicted murderer on the loose. "Alright," he said, "I guess I can ask one of the men to tend to Kiwi."

"No! I'm coming home," she said, "I'll just ride to Mrs. Whipple's after."

"You'll do no such thing," declared Ian. He had had enough. Ian quickly escorted his daughter to the door. Cate glowered, but knew it would be of no use to press on.

It ruffled Nell's feather to hear them disregard her thoughts, but since they had worked it out her way, she said nothing.

Ian turned and tipped his hat to Mrs. Whipple. "I can send James down to check on you if you'd like," he said.

"No need, I'll be fine," insisted Mrs. Whipple.

"Alright, then, we'll be seeing you," said Ian. The two disappeared like smoke in the wind.

Nell Whipple was in a mire puzzling out how a great, big, strong man like Ian Darringer could possibly be afraid of a simple man like Stumpy Gilbert. Stumpy had never harmed a soul, up until the night he allegedly shot Mick Turner. Every breathing person had dreamt of shooting that ill-mannered sot themselves one time or another, including Ian Darringer! Why Ian had to testify against Stumpy was beyond her. Sometimes justice is better served when folks keep their mouths shut, she thought.

Sheriff Dole came to check in on her, and he told her what Ian had not, not in front of Cate. Stumpy was not who they were worried about. It was the men who busted Stumpy out that concerned them: they were armed and dangerous. Mrs. Whipple immediately understood: if Cate knew Stumpy was in the company of desperadoes, she would be running off to rescue him. No wonder Ian was in a hurry to get out of town.

What none of them knew – not the sheriff – not Ian – and certainly not Mrs. Whipple – was the jailbreak news was full of erroneous information. The guard had swept his shame under the rug. He failed to mention he was absent during the jailbreak. Much of his testimony was falsified. He reckoned that with Stumpy's face plastered all over the territories, the escapee would be recognized quick enough and whoever found Stumpy would find his would-be rescuers close by. A self-inflicted "concussion" could explain away any discrepancies that might show up later.

Despite the sheriff's concern, Mrs. Whipple still reckoned she was safe. After all, she led a simple life. She did not have anything someone else would want to steal. Sheriff Dole disagreed. "Your house is out-of-the-way and would make a good hideout," Sheriff Dole pointed out.

I also have a double-barreled Smith & Wesson that would stop them dead in their tracks, she thought, but did not say. She preferred others remained ignorant of her skill with firearms. It would tarnish her librarian image. Besides the rifle at home, she also kept a .45 in her purse at all times. She would just be sure to load it before heading out tonight, she thought.

"I refuse to join in the mass hysteria. I can take care of myself," Mrs. Whipple stated firmly.

"Suit yourself," he quipped. He tipped his hat and strode out to catch up to Cate.

Sheriff Dole had plenty of other women in the town to worry about, but none of them could cook like Nell. He had been half-hoping he could wrangle a proper home-cooked meal out of her. In a quiet town like this, it was easy to under-appreciate the lawman and he had to take advantage of the opportunities as they arose. Well, maybe if I show up around breakfast time, he thought to himself.

The walk home should have been uneventful, but for all her talk, Mrs. Whipple was feeling a little uneasy. Stumpy was in the company of rough men. Rough men made poor company. Thinking on it made her tense. She knew how to shoot. She had lay low many a tin can, and every tumbleweed within a thirty mile radius shivered to see her take aim at it. That said, she had never put a bead on a living being. The possibility bunched knots in her stomach. Every noise on the way home rattled her. The wind blew ominously. Animals rustled the bushes incessantly. She pulled her .45 out from her purse and held it at the ready as she walked cautiously down the trail.

Something flew at her suddenly. Her reaction was automatic. The gun roared! A pheasant lay lifeless on the ground. Mrs. Whipple felt terrible, especially when she realized that it could have been a person, but there was nothing for it now. The slug from a .45 at short range will decimate its victim. Mrs. Whipple plucked a few of the tail feathers and left the rest for the coyotes. She pushed aside the brush and found a nest of eggs, eight all told. She put the eggs into her purse. She had hens brooding at home, and she reckoned they would not mind setting on a few more. The librarian felt responsible for rearing those eggs now. She unloaded her gun and put it in her purse, too. She had shot enough things for one day.

She breathed a sigh of relief when her home was in sight, until she saw the door was blowing open and shut with the wind. Even from a ways off, one could hear the movements of someone inside. She set down her purse, and reloaded her weapon. Leaving the purse behind, she tiptoed quietly to the door. Someone was ransacking the kitchen. She cocked her gun and held it with shaking hands. "Stumpy," she called, "if that's you, say something. You know I won't hurt you."

She knew Stumpy could not talk plain like other folk, but he could make sounds that occasionally passed for talk. Something crashed in the kitchen and she heard someone skittering across the room. The intruder's breathing was laborious.

"Stumpy? If that's you, you ought to say-so," she warned, tiptoeing closer to the kitchen. The daylight was fading. The eerie shadows of the approaching darkness gave her the heebie jeebies. She lowered her gun and took a breath. Slowly she counted to ten, then bravely entered the kitchen. Her scream was muted by the roar of a gun.

Chapter Nineteen: Alone With Manly Thoughts

Cate's silence ate at Ian. Pouting or plotting, he could not tell which, but she was clammed up the entire way home. Most of the time he was proud of her independent ways. Times like these, he wished he could rely on her doing as she was told. He knew he ought to have told her the whole truth about the horses and Stumpy's escape, but he just could not talk to her like he used to. His testimony in the murder trail had hammered a wedge between father and daughter. Cate no longer saw him as infallible. Cate refused to believe Stumpy shot Mick.

Ian had to agree. If he had not been the first to arrive, and it was somebody else telling him what had happened, he would not have believed it either. But he had been. He was late coming home that evening, and was passing by when the shot rang out. He almost ignored the report. He did not give a plugged nickel for Mick and a shot all by itself was not something to fret over. After the shot came screaming. He turned Cinder around and raced to Mick's shack. Just as Ian rode up, Stumpy came out and startled Cinder. Cinder jumped and snorted, which frightened Stumpy. Ian had called out to him to wait, "Hey, Stumpy! It's just me, stay calm." Instead, Stumpy rushed off like a man on fire.

Ian settled Cinder down, and cautiously stepped inside Mick's hovel. He found Mick slumped back in a chair. Without much effort, he would have fallen out and onto the floor. He had been shot in the stomach. The blood flowed freely from his wound and covered the room. Mick was trying to staunch the flow with his fist but was losing the battle. The gun that shot him was on the floor.

Upon seeing Ian, Mick's first request was to ask him to "Get Stumpy." His second was for more whiskey.

Mick had been drinking, and between the alcohol and the pain, he was half-delirious. He alternated between asking for liquor, and begging Ian to "get" Stumpy. Ian had no doubt in his mind that Mick was bent on restitution.

Ian removed the shirt he wore and pressed it up against the wound to slow down the blood loss. He wanted to go home and get Ann. She was better with healing and maybe she would have a more merciful remedy for the pain, but Mick had gotten a death grip on Ian's arm. Even after Mick passed out, it was a chore to free himself from his grasp. Ian removed his belt and wrapped it tight around Mick's waist to hold the shirt in place and keep pressure on the wound.

As quick as he could, Ian headed for help. He gave Cinder his head and the horse carried them through the dark night.

Once at home, James tended to Cinder and saddled fresh horses for his father, while Ian and Anne prepared for the ride back. She loaded up the medicines while he swallowed dinner as fast as he could. Cate wanted to go, but Ian refused her. A man bleeding to death was not an image he wanted indelibly imprinted in his daughter's mind.

Sometimes, he regretted the decision to leave Cate behind. Maybe if she had seen the pain Mick was in, she would have understood why there had to be a trial. Other times, the grim fact that she loathed Mick Turner and might have taken delight in his suffering reassured Ian he did right.

The way back to Mick's was laborious. They rode by lantern light. When they arrived, the house was silent. Only ragged curtains fluttering in the wind gave any signs of life. In the dim light, they thought they were too late. Ann lay a sheet over their lifeless neighbor. The weight of the sheet jolted Mick enough for a raspy breath to escape. Ian sat Mick up as Ann poured a home-made tonic down his throat. His breathing became more even and he slipped back out of consciousness.

They had seen stomach wounds before. If Mick had been a horse, they would have put a bullet through his brain to end the suffering. Instead, all they could do was ease the pain as best they could.

In the morning, Ian fetched the doctor. He agreed the only thing left to do was to plan the funeral. Occasionally, Mick would talk deliriously, always something about getting Stumpy.

A bullet to the gut is an agonizingly slow way to go, but it gets a person in the end. Two days later Mick was gone.

Ian had often wished he had just kept his mouth shut, but when he went looking for Stumpy, he found him in his old tattered gray coat, which was soaked with blood. He was certain Stumpy was clueless over what he had done, but that was what concerned Ian the most. If he did it once, without malice or intent, what was to prevent him from doing it again just as carelessly? Ian testified to protect the people he loved, and yet Cate spurned the notion that it was the right thing to do.

Nor did he have any way to explain to her that the trial had run afoul. Before it even began, Ian had sat down and worked a deal out with the local judge. They had reached an understanding before Ian took pen to paper and wrote his affidavit. When Stumpy was found guilty, the judge would show leniency and have him put in a home where his simple ways could be tended to, where he could not wander and get into things.

How was he to know the judge would take ill before the trial? How was he to know Judge Isaac Parker would fill in? The Hanging Judge did not cotton to private agreements preceding the law. If a man was guilty of murder, he hanged. It was a hard blow to Ian, but what could he do? There was his sworn statement.

It was only at the behest of the town, largely due to Cate's insistence, that the judge was willing to delay the hanging and permit time for a retrial. The Judge had also decided, due to the bias of the town, that Stumpy would be moved to Okmulgee. How was Ian to predict all that?

Ian looked over at his daughter and wondered how do you explain to someone who believes you can move the sun, the moon and the stars, that you are not infallible? Or more to the point, how do you explain to someone who has finally realized you're human, that being human ain't your fault? She still loved him, but there was a distance between them now that was as wide as the Grand Canyon.

When Ian slowed the wagon, Cate was quick to jump off before it even came to a full stop. She rushed to find Kiwi. She had half a mind to ride straight back into town and send a telegram to the sheriff of Okmulgee, telling him to call off the manhunt. She stewed to think on how she had been banned from the telegraph office. Her father had gone to great pains to make sure that the entire town, not just the clerk, knew she was not to set foot inside that building.

Ian stood at the door of the stable and looked in at his daughter. "If you care about your family even half as much you do that horse, you'll stay put tonight," he stated.

Cate said nothing.

"You hear me?" he asked.

"I heard you," she answered. She did not agreed with him, but she did hear him.

Ian watched her awhile then he set about his business. He checked on Ann and James. They were fine, so he found and spoke with the hired hands. Most of them were single, and it was an easy matter to get several to agree to stay the night and take watch. In part, it was to watch over the horses, and in part, it was to make sure his daughter did not get any fancy notions of going off on her own. Between cattle, horses and Cate, he had too much at risk to be losing it all in a night.

With ranch business attended to, his mind wandered back to James. For the first time that he could recall, Ian was anxious over his son. James had always been as easy as Cate was difficult, finding his way through life just fine without any help from anyone. It had never occurred to him before that he would need to have a father-son talk. Now that Ian was thinking on it, he was at a lost for words. Ian believed half the nonsense the Gossip Brigade was spinning was hog's wallow. All the same, it had to be based on something. Given the way James had been acting this week, he must have gotten wind of it via the ranch hands. Not one of them thought to say a word to Ian.

If felt awkward sticking his nose in uninvited. If James was old enough to travel the world, Ian reckoned he was old enough to decide matters for his own heart. Still, worried nagged him.

Ian wanted to keep his son from making a mistake he would regret the rest of his life. If James did not talk straight with Ida Sue about his expectations, his hopes and dreams, he needed to face the reality that another fella might take his place. Ian doubted James could face that disappointment with dignity.

Ian waited in the stable next to James where they would be spending the night waiting, hoping that nothing would come from the waiting, but waiting all the same. In the darkness, he felt a flood of concern for his son wash over him. He wondered if this was how Ann felt about Cate all the time. If so, how did she stand it? He struggled inwardly looking for the right words until finally, he spoke. "James, is there anything you'd like to talk about?" he asked respectfully.

After a short silence James responded. "Nothing special comes to mind."

"Okay, then, wake me up if you hear anything." Well, thought Ian, at least I tried.

"Okay, Pa," said James. Presently, he heard the restful breathing of his father asleep on the haystack next to him. Outwardly, the long night passed uneventfully. Inwardly, regrets ran treadmills through his heart.

Chapter Twenty: Missing

First thing in the morning, Sheriff Dole went round to Mrs. Whipple's place. He was not one to admit these sorts of things, but he had a soft spot for Mrs. Whipple and he worried some over her. The day had yet to warm up and he appreciated the bottom heat he was getting from riding Phoenix. George was alongside him on Daisy.

He had asked George to come along for three reasons. For one, the young man had proven himself to be useful. Not only had he done a good job cleaning the stable, he also had done a good job informing the town about the jailbreak. George was calm and matter of fact, and he left folk feeling like they were in capable hands. There was no denying that people were somehow more impressed with George now that he had women after him – one woman in particular. If he was a contender for Ida Sue's heart over James Darringer, well then, there must be more to him than they had previously reckoned.

For two, having every available woman in a thirty-mile radius vying for the same man's attention was unhealthy. Contrary to popular belief, a man can only consume so much, and the sheriff was pretty sure George would split a gut if he had one more bite of pie. The boy needed to get out and work some of it off, which brought the sheriff to reason number three: The horses needed the exercise, too.

Crooner loped lazily behind the horses, stopping to check out the smells beneath every weed and bush. Besides being the best nose in these parts, Crooner was also one of the better looking of his breed. Sheriff Dole took a lot of pride in Crooner's auburn coat and strong legs. Crooner could run for hours and never tire. A breeder over in Okmulgee had talked Sheriff Dole into pairing Crooner with his show dog, Angel, who had a liver and tan saddle.

Sheriff Dole had been skeptical as to whether Crooner

would go for a high breed female, when his own breeding was of questionable background, but it was love at first sight. Angel was now the proud mama of nine pups.

He and the breeder had agreed the sheriff would get the pick of the litter as soon as the pups were weaned. The sheriff had been up checking on his litter a few weeks back, and the breeder had offered him a second pup, a runt from another unrelated litter.

The breeder had handed him the whelp apologizing,"If you don't want this mangy cur, then I'll likely feed him to the hogs. He won't be good for much else."

 Both men knew that was a big fib. This was just the breeder's left handed way of seeing the pup had a good home. Being a runt himself, the sheriff had a softness for the little fella as soon as he saw him. He knew Crooner's fatherly instincts would kick in and the dog would be pleased to teach both whelps.

As they turned up the trail to Mrs. Whipple's place, they noticed horseshoe tracks in the soft dirt. George commented that it looked like the horse had been in a hurry. Sheriff Dole agreed. He did not believe Mrs. Whipple had a horse and he commented that maybe a neighbor had come to check on her.

Further along the trail, Crooner sniffed out the shattered remains of what the men guessed might have been a pheasant. Both men agreed it was a shame to have such a delicious bird go to a coyote. They discussed various hunting stories as Crooner sniffed around and found the dead bird's nest. The men were disappointed to find the nest was empty.

As they neared the house, Crooner ran ahead. The bloodhound gave a tongue to let the men know he had found something of interest. The men rode up and recognized Mrs. Whipple's purse immediately. Sheriff Dole asked George to dismount and take a look. George walked cautiously over to the bag, opened it, and remarked, "Looks like she found the pheasant eggs."

Both men grew quiet, listening for tell-tale sounds of activity. Her hens were squawking, suggesting they were still in the coup. They should have been let them out hours ago. The front door of the house swung eerily in the breeze.

Sheriff Dole dismounted and told George to stay with the horses. The sheriff gingerly walked to the house with his pistol drawn and ready. He listened. No footsteps, no voices. Nothing to suggest people around.

He tip-toed through the front door, into the parlor. Something caught his eye and he slowly inched towards it. A spent shell had rolled under her favorite chair, the one where she loved to sit and knit. He listened intently as he looked around. A strong breeze blew through the open doorway that lead to the kitchen. Something was causing clanking sounds. The sheriff slowly moved across the floor, regretting every squeaky floorboard as he closed in on the intruder.

Everything was in a bloody shambles. A gaping hole in the exterior wall had invited numerous wildlife to enter the house, adding to the mess and laying tracks on top of other tracks. He shooed a few doves and they fluttered through the hole in the wall. A raccoon eating from broken mason jars, knocked down from a pantry shelf, hissed at him. The sheriff hissed back and the furry bandit clamored away, irritated, dragging some food with it.

Nothing inside was where it ought to have been. Blood smeared on the floor suggested a struggle between a man and a woman. The story was hard to discern as the shoe prints mingled and were trampled over by animal prints. The sheriff's stomach knotted. He saw a .45 lying on the floor. He picked it up and sniffed. A hint of gun powder lingered. He opened up the bullet chamber and saw four bullets remained. He closed up the gun and holstered it.

The sheriff looked around, but saw no bullet holes in the room. The bullet must have been carried out along with the victim. He stepped through the hole in the wall and followed the bloody tracks that led away from the house. The sheriff examined the ground outside. Shoe prints led to horse tracks, the same horse tracks they had seen on the trail to the house. At this point, the shoe prints disappeared. The horse continued on, following the direction of the blood trail. The lawman thought on it some, then walked back to his own horses and George.

George read the worry on the sheriff's face as he came around the house. Sheriff Dole held out the .45 for George to take, saying, "I'm assuming you know how to handle one of these."

"Yes, sir, I do," admitted George quietly. He took the gun and inspected it. It looked to be in good shape. He snapped the chamber closed and tucked the gun under his belt. When George signed up as deputy, he had considered the odds of actually being shot at to be fanciful. Now that the possibility existed, he faced the reality with dignity.

"Good," said Sheriff Dole. "You just might need to. Looks like she was taken by either a man or a bear, or possibly both. Crooner, come here, boy."

Crooner stopped sniffing around the edge of the road and loped over to his friend. Sheriff Dole dug his fingers into the bloodhound's loose skin and rubbed vigorously. "George, put those pheasant eggs from her purse under her setting hens. The flock is going to need water and feed. No telling how long we'll be. When you're done, I want you to catch up with me and Crooner. There's a blood trail around the back of the house and Crooner and I are going to follow that trail to wherever it leads."

"Yes, sir," said George, 'but if you're hunting bear, shouldn't you wait for me to come along?"

"You swore an oath, son," said Sheriff Dole, "to do as you're told. I suggest you get busy doing it."

The sheriff had hunted many a bear just fine without George and it was not the bear he was worried about. A bear generally did not drag a body far, but there was never any knowing what a man might do.

Sheriff Dole took Phoenix by the reins and walked him over to where the horse tracks met up with the bloody bear tracks. Crooner followed. The bloodhound sniffed in a wide circle as the lawman climbed into his horse's saddle. The sheriff always allowed his dog to take his time. Bloodhounds were sensitive creatures and needed to be treated with respect. The dog continued to rub his nose in the dirt. Then, as if struck with an epiphany, the bloodhound took off at full speed.

Man and dog followed the trail until the trail split. Crooner bounded along following the bear tracks, but the man stopped. He looked back for George, but the young man was no where tin view. The dog continued to sniff nearby.

Sheriff Dole got down from his horse and called Crooner over. The dog stopped sniffing and loped up to him. The sheriff rubbed him and praised him for being a good dog. He gave his loyal friend a strip of deer jerky. The dog wolfed it down while the man considered the scene and waited for George.

When George rode up on Daisy, he asked, "Which way?"

"We follow the horse," answered the lawman. The sheriff walked Crooner down the new trail. Crooner sniffed around a bit. He would have preferred to go back and hunt the bear, but if the man with the food wanted horse, that was fine, too. Just so long as they were hunting something, the dog was happy.

Sheriff Dole climbed back onto Phoenix and they all took up the trail again. They followed Crooner as far as Tarnahand's tobacco field. The sheriff was quick to call Crooner back. A nose full of tobacco could overload even the best sniffer, rendering a dog useless for hours.

"Durn nuisance," fumed the sheriff. Complications made the unpleasant downright difficult. "George, how 'bout you go round to the Darringer ranch and see if Ian doesn't have a few hands to spare. The sooner we find Mrs. Whipple the better. While you're doing that, I'll run to town and see who's available to help search. We'll meet up back here."

"Yes, sir," replied George.

"And George," warned the sheriff, "Don't say anything to the womenfolk about the bear. They'll be sick enough with worry just knowing she's missing."

George nodded and headed over the hill. He was glad Daisy was surefooted as they rode over the rough, rocky terrain. The indigo bush painting the hillside in vibrant shades of blue and purple, went unnoticed as he sped to his destination.

Chapter Twenty-one: Search Parties

The sight of George riding up to the ranch filled Ian with a sense of foreboding. Ian hoped things would remain peaceful. Nothing could ruin a friendship as quickly as a dispute over a woman. It would be a shame to see their friendship end that way, especially here in front of Cate and Ann. When George explained why he had come, Ian thought the truth was worse than his fears.

Most of the ranch hands were out feeding and watering the cattle. Only a few had stayed back to do the odd chore for Ann. Ian gathered them up as quickly and quietly as he could.

Cate could see the men huddling together. She ran over to investigate.

"Go on, Cate, git," ordered James.

Git? He was telling her to git? Like she was a dog or something? Oh! She cut him a look and he knew he would be paying for the slight. Hard look aside, the men waited for her to walk off before they circled like wagons to keep out the enemy and whispered in hushed tones. When they were done talking, they walked off to their prospective assignments.

How dumb did they think I am? thought Cate. James broke from the group and headed into the gun room. She snuck in after him. "So where do you think you're going?" she asked.

"Lightning Ridge," replied James. He had never seen the point in keeping secrets from Cate and it slipped out before he had a chance to think on it.

"Why?" asked Cate.

James wanted to tell her, "Because the blood trail leads that way," but he knew better. "Listen, Cate," he sighed, looking straight at her, "We need to find Stumpy, if nothing else, for his own safety." It felt wrong to lie, yet they had agreed to keep Cate in the dark over Mrs. Whipple's disappearance.

"Sending him to prison was for 'his own safety,'" snapped

Cate. "Offhand, I can't say I'm impressed with logic that says hanging a man keeps him safe from harm."

"Cate, you'll understand better when you're older," said James.

"I hope not," sulked Cate, "I'd hate to think my brains will fall out when I get older." She squared up her shoulders and walked out with her head held high.

James was relieved that she left. If he hurried, he might be saddled and down the road before she found her second wind. He checked the rifle to make sure it was clean, grabbed a box of bullets and headed for the door. He was by his horse, getting ready to saddle up, when she caught up with him. She handed him a package. "I would not waste my time with Lightning Ridge, leastways, not if I was looking for Stumpy," she told him.

"What's this for?" he asked her.

"It's bacon," she answered, "generally speaking it's for eating."

"I know that," he snipped, "but what do you expect me to do with it?"

"I expect you to ride out to Gup's Bend, slap it on a skillet and cook it," she snapped.

"Cate, I do not think we'll be taking the time to cook," he said, handing the package back to her.

"Fine," she said taking the package back and folding her arms. "Waste your time looking in all the wrong places. You know as well as I do where Stumpy's dog is buried. You know as well as I do that's where he goes when he's scared and lonely. You think the desperadoes who busted Stumpy out are going to feed him? You slap that bacon on a skillet and he'll come to you."

"What makes you think desperadoes busted him out?" James asked.

"Because I didn't do it," proclaimed Cate, annoyed. She knew plenty of folks thought her too dumb to work things out on her own. It hurt when James was one of them. "Only desperadoes do jailbreaks. Now will you please take this and go find him?" She pushed the bacon back into his hands.

"You forgot the skillet," James smiled, taking the package.

"Did not," she refuted, "There's one sitting just inside the abandoned shaft, alongside a tinder box."

"Since when?" he asked her.

"Since the summer I went to Peru," she said.

Interesting way to put it, he thought. It occurred to him, if Gup's Bend was Peru, they could take her just outside Okmulgee and call that Africa and she would be none the wiser. Maybe when this was over they would do just that.

"That little stunt of yours aged Ma a few decades," he reminded her.

"Not my fault she doesn't have more faith in me," said Cate.

"It isn't you she doesn't have faith in. I wish you'd learn to accept that," said James.

"Ha! She's been watching me like a hawk ever since," Cate pouted.

"Can you blame her?" he asked.

"No, I don't blame her. I blame you," Cate said.

"Me?" asked James. "How do you reckon that?"

"You're always so perfect, never do anything wrong. Couldn't you just mess up once in awhile to take the heat off of me? You're the oldest, it was your job to break her in," she declared.

"Break her in?" James shook his head, "Ma isn't a mustang. You can't toss a lead on her and expect her to follow. Maybe if you just tried acting like a girl once in awhile."

Cate's eyes narrowed and her face hardened. "You know what James Edker? If Stumpy is up there, I hope you're the one to find him. I'd hate to see George McGillicutty get the best of you twice before leaving."

"You can nettle me all you want Cate, you ain't going to Nigeria." He spoke calmly, but he could feel the heat rising to his cheeks. The thought of losing Ida Sue to anyone knotted him up, but he still couldn't bring himself to say-so.

"Not nettling," denied Cate, "just saying if everything I wanted was in my own back yard, I'd be sore to leave it behind."

"And just what is it you want?" asked James.

"To go to Africa," she exclaimed.

"This week. Next week it'll be somewhere else, doing something else," he said.

"Next week I'll be crying my eyes out over missing you," she blurted.

"I'll miss you, too," he conceded.

"Then take me with you," she cried. Why people had to ignore the obvious solution was beyond her.

"It isn't up to me," he answered.

"If it was?" she asked, her face full of suspicion.

"I'd take you over sunshine," he said, bending down to kiss her on the forehead. It was a true enough sentiment, but she showed no sign of softening.

Ian called from across the yard, "James, what's taking you so long?"

"I'm coming Pa," he responded. He turned and whispered softly to his sister, "Don't worry none, I'll do you proud."

Cate sullenly watched him saddle up and ride over to the other men.

Ann strode across the yard, broom in hand, and stood next to Cate. Cate was unsure which was more annoying: being left behind, again, or the fact that her mother was carrying around a stupid broom. A manhunt going on and The Warden is worried about spiders. Cate glowered, thinking, does she honestly believe she can sweep the whole world?

Mother and daughter watched the men ride off over the hill. As the last horse turned out of sight, Ann turned to Cate. The sun bouncing off her mother's white hair glowed like a halo, but Cate knew, she was far from angelic. "Alright young lady, where is he?" interrogated The Warden.

"Where's who?" asked Cate.

"Don't play coy with me, you know exactly who I mean," The Warden's tone was clear.

"I had nothing to do with busting him out," Cate swore, "Honest, I didn't."

"You never believed he was guilty. Your posters are plastered from here to Kansas announcing to the whole world you don't believe your own father. Do you have any idea how humiliating that is?" Ann was sick and tired of the whole mess.

"An innocent man's life is worth a little humiliation," Cate asserted.

Ann abhorred physical punishments, but there were times when Cate tested her resolve. "Your father heard the shot. He saw Stumpy leaving," Ann stated firmly.

"Papa only saw someone wearing an old, shabby, gray coat stumbling from the place. Half the South wears coats just like it," Cate countered.

"Stumpy's coat was soaked in blood when they found him, and that's why they sent him to jail" said Ann.

"And I'm telling you, that wasn't Stumpy's coat," said Cate.

"Cate," her mother sighed with exhaustion, "just because the button you sewed on for him wasn't on that coat doesn't mean it wasn't his. You know you don't sew well. It probably fell off."

"It didn't fall off because that wasn't his coat," insisted Cate.

"Your father heard Mick's dying words," Ann stated.

"Mick Turner was a miserable old sot who was meaner than an acre of snakes. What makes anyone think he'd waste his last breath on the truth?" spewed Cate.

"Cate," Ann tried to interrupt, but her daughter continued, full steam ahead.

"He was as meaner than *two* acres of snakes," declared Cate, "and he loved nothing better than to torment Stumpy. He's probably happier in his grave than a dead pig in sunshine, laughing his fool head off like Brer Fox 'cause he finally got the best of Stumpy."

Ann had to take a breath to calm down. She was appalled by Cate's colorful language, and livid with her daughter taking a stance against her own father.

Ann counted to ten and then she asked again, "Where is he?" Cate stood as still as stone. "Don't clam up on me," Ann ordered. "The whole Territory knows you wanted Stumpy free.

You may not have turned the key, but you dropped a word, you planted a seed, or gave someone the tools to do it for you."

"I had nothing to do with it," spat Cate. "But it ain't Stumpy we should be worried about. Whoever busted Stumpy out did it to use him as a diversion. It's them we should be rounding up."

Ann sighed. "I suppose you have ideas on that?"

"I do," said Cate. "We need to get to town to send a telegram."

"To who?" asked Ann suspiciously.

"The sheriff of Oklahoma City, of course," said Cate. "There's going to be a bank robbery and he should know about it." Cate hoped that sounded plausible. Fact was, what she really wanted was to send a telegram to the Okmulgee Sheriff to get him to call off the manhunt, and remind him that Stumpy was an innocent victim, not a desperado. Cate had seen the men ride out armed. While she trusted the ranch hands not to shoot Stumpy, she feared a bounty hunter would consider him target practice.

Cate was forbidden against sending any more telegrams and she was certain The Warden would hold her to that ban. However, she figured, if she could walk into the telegraph office with her mother, the clerk might think her lifetime ban from sending telegrams had been lifted. Then, once her mother decided to visit the Widow Kibler, as she surely would, Cate could sneak back and send the real telegram.

Ann took a hard look at her daughter. She wanted to point out that one day was as good as the next when it came to robbing banks and Cate had no solid evidence that anyone with any sense would listen to. Ann thought on it some. If placating Cate's crazy ideas kept Ann's mind off Nell Whipple, Ann was all for it. Anything was better than sitting at home waiting for the men to come back.

Ann was fairly sure Cate knew nothing about Mrs. Whipple being missing, because if she had, her daughter would have insisted on being part of the search. Ann understood that desire. She herself had a strong urge to keep moving. It was only her loyalty to her daughter that kept Ann from joining the search party. Ann considered.

"Alright, Cate," said her mother, "Let's get the horses."

Cate was thrilled, but she put on her best Southern face and kept her emotions to herself. "We'll need ropes and guns, too," she stated, hoping she wasn't pressing her luck too far..

"What for?" asked her mother.

"In case we come across bank robbers," answered Cate. I mean, why else would we need them, she thought.

"Cate," Ann started to say, but she stopped. It made absolutely no sense to her that men looking to rob a bank in Oklahoma City would come riding into a small town like Henryetta. The town barely had a telegraph office, let alone money. But then, it made no sense that Nell had gone missing, either. She sighed.

"Alright, Cate," she agreed, "I'll get the guns, you get the horses and ropes ready."

144

Chapter Twenty-two: A Slab of Bacon

Along the trail, the search party rode in silence. Despite the fair weather, the day carried an ominous weight. James barely acknowledged George. George was normally talkative around James, but now was clammed up tight. Ian wondered if they would be better off if he simply asked them for their weapons and let the two fight it out with their fists. It was a relief when James rode up to him and told him what Cate had said.

Ian thought a moment and decided that finding Stumpy was almost as important as finding Mrs. Whipple. He agreed to let James split from the group and go to Gup's Bend. In truth, he was more than a little pleased to have a reasonable excuse to keep James out of the way of possible harm. Ian was sore to admit it, but he wanted his son to stay just as much as the women did.

James arrived at the old mine shaft quickly. He tied his horse to a tree and she immediately started to chew on the brush within reach. That horse has four hollow legs, thought James.

He looked around near the entrance to the shaft and found the skillet and the tinder. The skillet was a little rusty. He was a little light with the elbow grease when it came to scraping it clean. He had never known Stumpy to be too fussy when it came to food. Soon James was sitting on an old weathered log, with bacon sizzling over the fire.

A light wind carried the wood smoke into the surrounding scrub. James hoped it would carry far enough to be of some good, else he would look like a fool cooking bacon when he should be off helping the others. It was a leap of faith to be cooking by a campfire, but James doubted Cate realized that. She was always so sure of herself. When he heard footsteps approaching through the bush, he smiled.

"Hello, Stumpy," he said without looking.

"Hello, James," said Ida Sue.

The hair on his neck rose, and his heart quickened. He turned to look at her. The sun was filtering through the trees and she looked so delicate, her smile so serene. She was carrying a pail full of dewberries, so she must have been picking nearby. She wore a dress sewn together from flour sacks. It was well made, but simple. All her clothes were like that. She did not seem to mind: leastways, she never said she wanted more. But James wanted more for her... so much more.

"What brings you here?" he asked. Cate had sent him here looking for Stumpy. Now that Ida Sue was here, he wondered if that had been Cate's plan all along.

"My nose," she answered. "Last time I smelled cooking from Gup's Bend was when Cate was playing warrior princess. I thought maybe she would be here. Would you like some berries?" she asked, offering him the pail.

"Sure," said James. He patted the log he was sitting on. "Have a seat." She sat down next to him. Her skin brushed softly against his. He scooted away a little. He felt he would burst with emotion if she drew any closer.

"No Cate?" asked Ida Sue, offering him the pail of dewberries.

"Sorry to disappoint you, but she stayed home this time," explained James. He reached into the pail and took a few berries. He thought about how there would be no dew berries in Nigeria. He thought about how there would be no Ida Sue smiling sweetly at him. It was hard enough thinking about all he would miss, but now, with Ida Sue here, so close, it was harder still.

"I'm not disappointed in finding you here," Ida Sue said softly. James loved the softness of her voice. In a harsh world it was soothing to find a little softness. "Why did you think I'd be Stumpy?" asked Ida Sue.

"He busted out of jail. Cate thought, that is, I thought so, too, that he might be hiding near here and if I'd slab on the bacon, he might come out of hiding."

She was quiet a moment, then asked, "So, do you think it'll work?"

"Well, it brought you here, didn't it?" he tried to smile. He wanted to hold her, to tell her all the things he knew he should have years ago. The quiet between them held a tension.

Ida Sue's mother had died shortly before her father moved the family to Henryetta, and her father had run off shortly after. He knew how she felt about being left behind, and now he was fixing to do the same. It was so hard to face telling her he was leaving, yet how could he leave without saying goodbye? "Ida Sue, I know I should have told you sooner, but I'll be leaving soon," he stammered.

"I wondered how long it would take you to tell me. I was beginning to think you wouldn't until you were safe at sea." Ida Sue tried to smile, but it hurt to have heard it from Mrs. Weatherspoon. She had been waiting nearly two months to hear it from him. They fell quiet a moment. Then she asked, "Why are you going?"

"Well, it's Africa, isn't it? It's an adventure, everyone wants adventure in their lives, don't they?" he asked.

"The grandest adventure I've ever had was seeing a two-story building in Oklahoma City just before our Pa left us here," she reflected.

James could feel the shame sweep over him. He knew she knew he lived in a two-story house, and in all the years he had known her, had never once asked her to come see it. He wondered how many other oversights she had endured?

"He didn't leave you, Ida Sue," said James, trying to be reassuring. He hoped she would understand a person could leave a place, and leave his heart behind. He felt ashamed for not telling her sooner that he was going. He worried that she felt he was abandoning her, too.

"Yes, he did," she said quietly. "Oh, he wrote at first, even sent money once in awhile. But a father is more than an income. Leastways, he ought to be, way I see it. You know, he's no more real to me than the tooth fairy, and I stopped believing in that a long time ago."

"I know," said James.

"I know you know," said Ida Sue, "You know everything

there is to know about me."

James smiled. "I know you like okra in the spring and turnips in the fall. I know the way the wind plays with your hair and..." His voice trailed off. He had not meant to talk such ways.

"Do you know that meadows dance when I walk by?" she smiled.

He felt the heat rise to his cheeks. He had heard that George had written her a poem, but he had not actually heard what it said. He supposed he would have to get used to it, the idea that other men would find her attractive, but he wished she had not mentioned it. Ida Sue saw from his face that he thought what everyone else thought, that George had written it.

"You know, don't you, that it was Cate who left that poem in your book?" asked Ida Sue.

"My book?" James asked, perplexed.

"According to Mrs. Whipple, Donna returned your library book, thinking it was George's. When Mrs. Whipple found a piece of paper in it, she thought it was Donna's. She gave it to her before she realized it was your book. By the time she knew the mistake, Donna had already walked out, read the poem and was charging her way to the boarding house," Ida Sue explained. "You can ask Mrs. Whipple if you like." Ida Sue took a stick and pulled a strip of bacon from the skillet. "Bacon's done," she said. She fished out the pieces and placed them on the package paper to cool.

A relief spread over James, but was it gone as quickly as it had arrived. "But you and George..." He struggled for words.

"You took two months to tell me what everyone else knew right off. How long do you expect me to wait for you?" she asked. James could hear the hurt in her voice. It was a hurt he never wanted her to feel.

"I know I don't have a right to ask you to wait for me, that's why I haven't." He nearly choked on the words.

"I want a man who will stay by me and be content with his own backyard." She tried to hide the hurt, but it consumed her every pore.

James felt like he was back where he started.

"I know you do, and I'm sure you and George..." he stammered.

"George only asked me to the dance to make Donna happy, and I'm only going with him to make her realize she shouldn't take him for granted," Ida Sue explained. She placed a few more bacon strips in the pan. "Some folk don't know what they've got 'til it's gone."

"I know what I've got," said James. "I don't want to lose it. It's just, Aunt Muriel was a long time dying. I want to help people be a long time living. Sometimes a man's gotta serve a greater cause."

"A greater cause than love?" she asked.

To James, she embodied the essence of love. He had never seen anyone more beautiful. "There is no greater cause than love," he whispered. He felt awkward, divided, wanting to stand by his objective and wanting to reach out and hold her. "It's just, sometimes, the love of Mankind trumps everything else and there isn't room for one's own needs." It sounded all so noble, and yet, the thought of losing her seemed too steep a price. "I might not be gone that long – a year, maybe two."

"That's what my Pa said and we haven't seen him in near a decade," said Ida Sue. "A woman can't spend her days on hold waiting for permission to live while a man goes about his days doing as he sees fit."

It was a truth he could not argue against, and yet, could she not see how much she meant to him? Could she not see, he'd be waiting, too? He quietly prayed to God to help him find a way out of the awkward silence. God answered him, just not in the way James had hoped. Right then, Stumpy came crashing through the underbrush on a horse.

Chapter Twenty-three: A Happy Reunion

Both Stumpy and the horse looked a little worn. Stumpy was babbling nonsense. The horse sputtered from exhaustion. James jumped up in a flash. "Whoa, Ginger!" he said softly, reaching for the horse's neck to soothe it. "Settle down, girl. It's alright."

Ginger was happy to see a familiar face and feel a soothing hand against her neck. She settled down quickly while James continued to calm her. James's own horse, Timber, walked over and nuzzled Ginger. Ida Sue jumped up and joined James in soothing Ginger. "What sort of person ties a man onto a horse?" she wondered as she inspected the tether that held Stumpy firmly onto the horse.

"Don't know," said James, "But I don't plan to keep him tied." James pulled out his knife and cut Stumpy free. As soon as he could move his legs, Stumpy slithered down off the horse and James helped free him from the horse's neck. Stumpy's appreciation flowed like the Mississippi.

James tried to shush him. "Stumpy, be quiet," he said. He wanted to listen and see if he could hear anyone coming in pursuit.

"Stumpy," whispered Ida Sue, walking back towards the fire, "Come and have some bacon." She did not need to ask twice. He sat down next to Ida Sue and started grabbing up the bacon. James scanned the area and listened as best he could.

"Careful, don't burn yourself," Ida Sue said softly. She held Stumpy's arm and blew softly on the bacon to cool it down. Stumpy smiled and blew on the bacon, then swallowed it nearly whole. Ida Sue examined Stumpy's wrists. "How are we going to get those handcuffs off him?"

James shrugged. "Don't know, a rock maybe?"

"You might smash his hands," said Ida Sue. She thought a moment, then took some of the fat off an uncooked bacon slab and slathered it on Stumpy's wrists. The grease might have worked if his wrists had not been so swollen from the rough ride. She thought a minute longer, then pulled a hair pin from her hair. It was hard to get Stumpy to hold still. James helped by feeding him more bacon while Ida Sue fiddled with the lock.

"Why anyone would harm someone like this." Ida Sue shook her head sadly. "It does not bear thinking."

Finally, the lock swung open. One cuff came off, but his other wrist was too swollen and the unlocked cuff stayed on. Ida Sue continued to grease his wrist while Stumpy blabbered on between bites. Whatever he was saying, he certainly considered it important.

"We've got pliers at the ranch," offered James.

"It just might have to wait until then," Ida Sue conceded. "What kind of person would do such a thing?"

"No idea," admitted James. "We're all just hoping Cate had nothing to do with it."

"Cate would never have allowed Stumpy to be hurt like this," Ida Sue pointed out.

"No, no, she wouldn't," agreed James. "There's something else. This morning, Sheriff went around Mrs. Whipple's place, and she's missing. The men are out looking for her right now."

Ida Sue was thunderstruck. "We should go help them."

"I will," said James. "But I need to take care of Stumpy, first, and well, now that's he's here, I don't know what to do with him."

Ida Sue looked over at Stumpy. If you overlooked the swollen wrists, he was actually looking fairly good. Whoever ran the prison seemed to have taken care of him. He looked clean and better fed, although you would not guess it the way he was wolfing down the bacon. He nudged Ida Sue as he pointed to the bacon in the pan. She obediently turned it to cook it on the other side. "Stumpy, you're just going to have to wait some," she smiled at him. He laughed to see her smile. "Why don't you go play with the horses while you're waiting?" she suggested.

That may have seemed an odd proposal, as he had just spent

several hours in terror tied to Ginger, but Stumpy was quick to forget most things. Grabbing some dewberries from the pail, he leapt up and ran over to the horses. Previously, no one had ever succeeded in getting Stumpy on a horse willingly or otherwise, but he had no fear of them. He loved them and thought nothing of putting his hands inside one's mouth and messaging its gums. He was like a plover bird cleaning the horse's teeth. He gleefully patted the horse and hugged it, jabbering away in his own special language.

"Hard to believe he'd do anything to hurt anybody," said Ida Sue. "We should take him back to your place. Cate will be happy to see him. Who knows? Maybe she'll even cook for him, like she did when she lived in 'Peru.'"

James smiled, "I'm unsure he'd consider that much of a treat. She hasn't improved much since then." They both laughed. Cate's cooking was infamous. "We shouldn't stay here long," said James, "in case whoever tied Stumpy to Ginger is out this way looking for him."

"If you don't mind, I'd like to come with you," said Ida Sue. "I'd hate to run into them on my own."

"I don't mind," said James. He wondered, who will look after her when I'm away?

When the bacon was cooked, Stumpy fed, and the camp site cleaned, the three of them strode alongside the horses, headed towards the Darringer ranch. Along the way, Stumpy stopped to pick some wild flowers and pocket a few rocks. James and Ida Sue did the same. Stumpy took Ida Sue by the hand and led her down a side trail. "You know," said Ida Sue, "for someone who can't talk, he's pretty good at getting his point across."

"Yeah, I suppose he is," said James. James envied Stumpy for that. He wished he could get away without talking.

James and Ida Sue knew where Stumpy was going and no man-made obstacle could stop him. In a meadow by a brook, just a little ways down the trail, was Gup's grave. It was distinguished by a large cairn made with nearby stones. James smiled. Things seemed to be falling into place. It gave him heart. If he could find Stumpy and one of the horses, then maybe the search party would find Mrs. Whipple.

The horses sputtered and whinnied.

Stumpy placed the flowers atop the cairn and closed his eyes. James and Ida Sue added their flowers and closed their eyes, too, while they listened to Stumpy burble. Several years had passed since Gup died. It had been a hard loss for Stumpy. Gup must have weighed eighty pounds, but Stumpy managed to carry him around for several days after he died, holding on to hope his friend would wake up.

Pappy Michaels finally persuaded Stumpy that Gup needed to be buried, and he helped Stumpy pick a place near the Bend where Gup loved to hunt and play. It seemed like the right spot for such a fine dog. Whenever the fish were rising, Pappy would tell Stumpy that the trout had come to pay Gup their respects.

Ian had made the casket. Gup was wrapped in the first blanket Cate had ever sewn. Most of the town knew Stumpy, and came to Gup's funeral. Each person who came placed a stone on the grave, in part to say they remembered Gup and in part to keep Stumpy from digging him backup. Stumpy had taken to adding stones each time he came to visit and the cairn had grown with time.

"Think he'll ever forget about Gup?" Ida Sue asked James.

"A man never forgets who he gives his heart to," James answered and he softly took her hand. It felt good to hold her hand.

She smiled warmly at him.

Stumpy looked at the two and grinned foolishly. Since that was Stumpy's normal reaction to everything, James did not take exception to it.

Stumpy cupped his hands together and made a whistling noise. James sighed. "Figures he'd do it now when I don't have my duck gun with me."

"You know he'd never call them if you did," said Ida Sue.

Stumpy could mimic a wide range of birds and animals, but he would never do it when you wanted him to. He was known for spoiling a hunt by sounding alarms at all the wrong times. Many a hunter thought he was hot on the trail of some mighty tasty game only to learn it was Stumpy. Somehow Stumpy always knew when to give up the charade before getting shot.

Stumpy continued to whistle. Soon, a small flock of black-bellied whistling ducks swam up the crick and steered straight to shore. They waddled over to Stumpy and whistled with expectation. Stumpy pulled out bits of bacon from his pocket and offered the fatty morsels to the ducks.

"Half-starved and he still saves some to give away," Ida Sue mused.

James smiled. If he had known tossing bacon fat at ducks would have won her approval, he would have done it years ago.

Still, his mouth watered to look at the black-bellied ducks. They were small, two pounds at most, but he had never eaten a duck he did not enjoy so size was unimportant.

James looked over at the gun strapped on his horse. Maybe it was a duck gun after all. He looked over at the ducks. The ducks were just waiting to be eaten. Succulent, tender, moist. He looked at his gun. Fully loaded. He looked at the ducks, just as unafraid as any bird could be.

Ida Sue watched James's eyes swing back and forth between his rifle and the ducks. "Do you suppose they have ducks in Africa?" she asked. The thought surprised him. "I don't rightly know," he admitted. "I never thought to ask."

"Don't you think you ought to?" she smiled.

"It don't matter now," he said. He looked down at the hand he was holding. He knew when the time came to leave, he couldn't let go of her. "Ida Sue, you're my home. I don't ever want to go someplace without you. If that means staying put, then I'll stay put."

"A foolish girl might mistake that for a proposal," she blushed.

He leaned over and kissed her. "Might a foolish girl also say, 'yes'?"

By way of reply, she kissed him back.

But as is often the case, love was interrupted. The ducks began making a ruckus, and flapping their wings. Stumpy began doing the same. Ida Sue laughed. James just shook his head.

Eventually, pleasure turned to guilt and James decided it was time to head home.

"Stumpy, why don't you come on home now. We have biscuits and jam at the house that'll go to waste if you don't come along and eat them."

Stumpy may have been a simple man, but biscuits and jam was something he understood. He stopped whistling to the ducks and started trotting down the trail. James and Ida Sue had to run after him to catch up. They felt hopeful and light-hearted, but if they thought they would reach the ranch without a hitch, they were in for a surprise.

Chapter Twenty-four: A Golden Opportunity

Frank was experienced at tracking men. He might have been a bounty hunter if he had managed to stay out of trouble. Frank reckoned catching up to a simpleton would be easy work. He would be five, ten minutes at the most.

To Frank's frustration, Stumpy was nowhere to be seen. The only "finding" was done by the two numnuts who somehow managed to catch up to him. He had hoped they would have gotten scared off. Or, better yet, bickered between themselves until they killed each other.

Instead, the unwanted appendages were trailing along, interfering with his thought machinery, yapping when they should be quiet, riding ahead when they should stay behind, all in all, just being nuisances. Darkness fell before anyone had a clue where the simple man might be. Even Frank's eagle eyes could miss clues in the dark.

Cursed cat, thought Frank. Brought on bad luck rubbing up on me like that. Where's a bear when you need one? A bear, a coyote, a cougar, I don't care. God send me some kind of animal that wants to eat a pair of dim-witted sots.

Frank was used to sleeping out under the stars, preferred it, in fact, to any bed he had ever known. The problem was, the one fool snored and the other fool talked in his sleep.

Frank tossed and turned. He considered sneaking off, even now, in the dead of night. Forget about Stumpy altogether, just head for the Arbuckle Mountains. Unfortunately, he and his 'borrowed' horse were strangers. Mutual respect between horse and rider was needed for night riding. It reduced the margin of error.

Daylight took its time showing up. Frank hit the trail at the first hint of light, certain he would leave the snoring, babbling cretins behind. He had barely swung his leg over the saddle when the simpletons woke refreshed and ready to follow. He cussed under his breath. Well, I'll find Stumpy soon enough, he thought.

As they neared Henryetta, the more difficult the work became. A number of folk were out and about. Search parties, to be sure, but searching for what? Or for whom? Not Stumpy. Anyone with a lick of sense would know he would show up at the sheriff's door the first time his stomach growled. Then for whom? Whomever it was, he intended to avoid them. Posses in these numbers were reserved for the worst of them.

Frank was good at holding still, at being unseen, and could evade posses all day, but the bumbling oafs trailing along were liabilities. He had to go to great lengths to keep them out of harm's way. If he had been alone, he would have headed for Mick Turner's old place. It was out of the way and made a good hideout. He could have lay low, dug up some liquor from Mick's hidden stash, and waited out the commotion. Mick's was the kind of place you did not share with idiots prone to blurting out privileged information. He had to ditch the fools.

Frank decided getting his compadres liquored up was the best way to lose them. The three men were on their way to the nearest saloon when they noticed the whole town was headed for the church atop the hill. The why was inconsequential to Frank. What mattered was, the town looked to be empty. An empty town waiting to be robbed was a golden opportunity.

Chapter Twenty-five: A Willful Horse

Kiwi's heart leapt to see Cate walk into the barn with that look on her face. She whinnied as Cate threw the riding blanket across her back. That seemed odd given the time of year, but, what the hay, it still meant they were going for a run.

Her girl did something totally unexpected. She tossed a saddle on Kiwi's back. A saddle? Has she gone mad? And now, a bit? Of all the insults!

Kiwi rose above the indignation, and strutted with her head held high as Cate led her to the door.

Lep, the only other horse in the barn, nickered.

Son of a three-eyed toad, thought Kiwi. Oh well, at least I'm getting out of the barn. That blotted half-bred mule can stay here and eat moldy oats for all I care. Hog's breath, nickered Kiwi. Pigeon-hoofed nanny goat, responded Lep.

Cate loaded ropes onto Kiwi's saddle. The end of one of the ropes was twisted into a new-fangled knob Cate hoped would someday be known as the "Darringer knot." It was elaborate and difficult to tie. In fact, she could not remember how she had tied it, which is why it was still taking up a sizable portion of the end of her rope. She hoped to find a good use for it and there was no time like the present.

Cate grabbed Kiwi by the reins. Lep sputtered. Kiwi curled her upper lip to show her teeth. She took great delight in knowing that sad sack excuse of a horse was being left behind. Serves him right, calling me names.

Cate tethered Kiwi to the post outside and returned to the barn. Kiwi was at a lost thinking on what her girl could have forgotten. They were both wild and carefree spirits. All they ever needed to be happy was themselves.

Kiwi watched in stunned silence as Cate walked out with a bareback smug looking Lep. It was bad enough to tolerate him in the barn, but on the trail? We'll see about that, thought Kiwi.

Lep enjoyed the fury on Kiwi's face. He spat out a raspberry. Uppity mare, he thought.

Kiwi kept her thoughts to herself. Which, if Lep had known anything about them, would have sent him packing.

Out in the strong sunshine, Cate felt a little remorseful for having thrown a saddle on Kiwi. The bulky leather hid the beauty of the cinnamon that danced inside her dark coat. Kiwi always looked sad when she was saddled.

But some things can't be helped. All the world knew that Cate was the better rider and Kiwi the more reliable horse, and so it made sense she would be saddled up for Cate's mother.

Ann was surprised and also relieved. Her daughter's act of devotion may have clouded Ann's judgment. If she had been thinking more clearly, she would have insisted they double up on Kiwi and leave Lep in the barn. Lep was proving to be an unreliable horse.

Ann strapped the shotgun on to the saddle next to the ropes and climbed onto Kiwi. Cate spoke softly to Lep. Kiwi fumed silently. That was her girl! What had she done to make Cate forget about her like this, toss her over for that ugly, ill-mannered beast?

If this girl thinks she can tame me with a few soft words, thought Lep, she has another think coming. He looked over at Kiwi. Silly mare, always chasing butterflies in the meadow, always putting on airs like she's special. I'll show her.

Cate walked over to Kiwi. That's better, thought Kiwi. "Kiwi," whispered Cate, "we're going to town. You're the lead horse, so go as fast as you like, just take care of Mother." Kiwi nodded. Town, eh? She knew at least five ways to town and that hairy, mottled, flea-brained, bag of bones did not know a single one. Let's just see him try to keep up.

Cate climbed onto to Lep's back and dug her hands deep into his mane. Lep stood surprisingly still.

So, you think you can ride me, he snorted, we'll see about that.

"Ready when you are," Cate said to her mother.

Ann grasped the reins firmly and called, "Yaw!" Kiwi

bolted like a racehorse at the Kentucky Derby. Lep can just eat my dust, thought Kiwi.

Lep reared up and thrashed his front legs. He had every intention of showing that silly mare what he was made of, but first, he had to get rid of his rider. He bucked and twisted, but Cate knew how to hang on. He was not the first horse to try to throw her. With her hands deeply entrenched in his mane, he could not shake her. He bowed his head down low, hoping she would flip off him like a pancake from a greased skillet. She held on.

"You're letting her get away, you foolish mule," said Cate.

Lep looked up. Kiwi had a clear lead. He made a few more attempts to lose Cate, and then charged after Kiwi.

Ann's heart raced. She had never ridden a horse this fast, this smooth. The thrill of the ride overtook her and she felt young again. No wonder Cate rode Kiwi so much.

Ann felt like a young girl. Only the wind and her heart and the horse beneath her existed.

Lep put on a burst of speed. The earth below his hooves rushed to get out of his way. Kiwi was following the road, but he took a more direct route across the meadow. Cate gave him his head. She wanted to catch up as much as he did. The grass brushed against her feet, whipping closed behind them.

They cleared the meadow and found the road. Kiwi was just ahead, swiftly passing the Lightning Tree. That snooty mare ain't about to make a fool of me, snorted Lep. He put on speed. He brushed against the Lightning Tree in an attempt to lose his rider. Much to his regret, Cate was privy to such tricks. She had pulled her legs up high and all Lep earned was a belly scratch. The abrasion angered him. He raced on.

When he was within reach of Kiwi's flanks, Lep stretched his neck and bared his teeth. Suddenly, Cate pulled his head away. Lep faltered. Kiwi broke away from them and took a clear lead. Lep was furious. No half-pint girl was going to stop him! He sped up. He reached out his neck a second time. Suddenly, the girl yanked on his mane and pulled his head back. He reared up. How dare she! He tried again to shake off his rider. Cate held on.

Kiwi snorted. She could hear she was putting distance between her and tomorrow's glue. Fool, she thought, letting his anger do his thinking. Kiwi left the road and made her own trail. She flew over logs, brambles and creeks. Each time they went airborne, Ann felt sure they would rise to heaven. She marveled at how smoothly they landed. She had never felt so free!

While Ann felt like she rode on the wings of an angel, Cate considered her horse to be an equine demon. Lep was furious he had let Kiwi get ahead. He gave up trying to lose Cate and charged in after Kiwi.

Kiwi raced through narrow gaps between trees. Lep chased right behind. He narrowed the gap between him and Kiwi. Cate thought he was trying to take the lead, but then he stretched his neck again and bared his teeth.

No horse *I* ride is going to bite another horse, thought Cate, especially not Kiwi. She pulled Lep's neck back hard.

He reared and tried to shake her. When those efforts failed, he tried to race after Kiwi, who was rapidly moving away. Again, Cate stopped him. He bucked and spun in small circles. Cate held on. He was not taking one more step forward until she could trust him to keep his teeth to himself.

Cate regretted tying all the ropes to her mother's saddle. She would just have to make do. She continued to hang on to Lep's mane and control his neck. She loathed bossing about a horse, but some horses gave you no choice, and Lep, obviously, was one of them.

Kiwi disappeared from view. Then the sound of her thundering hooves softened into the far distance. Lep sputtered and spewed curses only a horse would understand. He blamed the miserable runt of a girl on his back. There is more than one way to lose a rider, he thought. He lay down and attempted to roll Cate off. He was to learn to his frustration just how quick that runt of a girl could be.

Meanwhile, Kiwi continued to carry Ann on the best ride of her life. As they neared town, Kiwi slowed down. She had proven her point. Ann reached down and hugged her neck. "Land of notions," cried Ann, "you are a wonder!"

For the first time since the ride began, Ann looked back. Where was Cate? Ann wanted to turn around and look for her daughter. It dawned on Ann that Kiwi had taken an unfamiliar way into town and she did not know which way to go back, the way they had come, or the way she knew. What a fool she was to have taken the lead. For all she knew, that was Cate's way of losing her and going off on her own. Ann was overcome with humiliation mixed with a tinge of worry.

Kiwi instinctively walked to the Kibler Boarding house. She had delivered Cate to these doors many a time to visit Dalene. Despite the few years' age difference between Cate and Dalene, the two girls got along well. They often would visit Mrs. McCoy to get the lowdown on the latest gossip.

Kiwi found human events boring, but she appreciated the watering trough and feed behind the boarding house.

Ann climbed off Kiwi, then tethered her to a post by the trough. She grabbed a hunk of hay and tossed it into the feed trough.

Ann walked up to the back door and knocked. No one answered. She knocked again. Again, no answer. Ann peered into the windows and saw no signs of life.

Ann left Kiwi where she was and walked over to the next house to see Mrs. McCoy. The pride of the Gossip Brigade also was not home. In fact, no one seemed to be home in the whole town. Ann looked up and down the empty streets. Ann pressed her nose against Opal's shop window. It was dark inside and all she could see was her own reflection. Mercy, I look old, thought Ann. She missed her chestnut hair and carefree days.

A tumbleweed blew across the silent dirt road that divided the town. It was as if the entire population of Henryetta had turned to dust and had blown away in the wind.

What Ann had no way of knowing was that when word of Mrs. Whipple's mysterious disappearance spread, nearly all the men joined in the manhunt. Few women could cook like Nell Whipple. By God, her disappearance angered many an appreciative stomach. A few men stayed behind to protect the women and children, all of whom had gone to the church on the knoll to pray for the missing librarian.

A horse whinnied and Ann thought for a moment Cate had made it to town, but then she heard strange voices. She pressed tightly against the building wall and peered around the corner. Two men were arguing over the best way to calm the team of horses hitched to a supply wagon. To add insult to injury, Ann recognized the horses as two of the ones stolen from her ranch: Brugger and Buttercup. The wagon belonged to Sam Beckett, the grocer.

She did not see the man behind the oak tree, but he spotted her. The wind had caught Ann's billowing skirts and Frank had seen the hem flutter out from the building edge like a flag on the train tracks.

Frank stepped back into the shadows. He bristled to see an old busybody sticking her nose where it was uninvited. He watched her watching the men. Just what sort of trouble might she be? he wondered.

My gun, thought Ann. She had left it strapped to Kiwi. Quietly, she tiptoed back to the Kibler Boarding House.

She'll be back, thought Frank. He bent down and began filling his pockets with rocks.

Chapter Twenty-six: Caught!

Ann was relieved to find her gun right where she had left it. If Cate or someone else had come across it while she was gone, her shame would know no end. She held the shotgun open and looked down the barrel. She had never actually loaded a gun before. It did looked simple enough but she had a superstitious nature. She knew a poorly loaded gun could backfire. She believed better safe than sorry.

Still, she was a woman who did what needed to be done. No one would ever brand her a coward. She was in a quandary over the loading when Cate came riding up with Lep, prancing like he was a show horse. Well, leave it to Cate to teach that brute a few manners, thought Ann.

Lep snorted at Kiwi in passing. Kiwi ignored his existence. She continued to eat the hay beside her. Over-sized skunk, thought Kiwi. Serves him right.

Holding her gun in one hand and a rope in the other, Ann walked over to Cate.

Cate took the rope from her mother and placed it around Lep's neck. Cate tied him as far away from Kiwi, the water and the food as she could. He could eat later. For now, he could learn to behave. Kiwi waited until Lep was fully secured to nicker at him. He snorted viciously at her.

"Stop it, the both of you," said Cate.

"Ssssh!" whispered Ann.

Cate looked at her mother. Ann handed Cate the shotgun and the ammo. Cate's eyes grew wide. "I get the gun?" she whispered.

"No, I need you to load it for me," whispered Ann.

Good Lord, thought Cate, and they think *I* need a chaperone? Cate took the gun and loaded the shot and handed it back.

Ann whispered, "Much obliged. There's a robbery going on.

Follow me."

Cate could feel the tension in her mother's movements. She grabbed the ropes and followed. They quietly made their way down the street to the back of the saloon, which was next to the grocer.

The sight of her family's horses hitched to Sam Beckett's wagon infuriated Cate. She almost called out, but her mother shushed her. Cate mouthed, Brugger and Buttercup. Ann mouthed back, I know. Be quiet. Cate nodded. Two men were leaning up against the back window peering in.

"You ain't supposed to be here," the man in the hat whispered loudly. He gave his partner a shove. "Get to the front and keep a lookout."

"Why?" asked the other man. "T'aint nobody around. Thought that was the whole idea of robbing the place now."

"In case somebody wanders in, that's why," snapped the first man.

"Why are you whispering?" asked the second man. Seemed a stupid thing to do when the town was empty.

The first man groaned and rubbed his face, "Tell you what, since you're here, why don't you break the window, crawl in and open the door."

"Why should I?" asked his partner. "That's your job."

The man in the hat grabbed his partner's hand and shoved it through the window pane. Shards of blood-splattered glass exploded into the storage room.

"There," said the man in the hat, "Now hurry it up. Who knows when they'll be back."

"That hurt," cried his partner. The man grasped his bloody hand and danced around in circles. As he turned towards them, Cate saw he had only one good eye.

"Of course it did. But it don't hurt as much as your head will if I have to use it as a battering ram," said the man with the hat. "Now crawl through the window and open the door."

"I don't see why I got to do it," said One-Eye, picking a shard from his hand. He put his mouth over the cut to suck up the blood.

"Listen, you half-blind orangutan, you're already bleeding. What's another cut?" said the man with the hat.

"Still don't seem right," protested One-Eye.

"Alright, then it's because I'm prettier than you," sneered Hat Man. "No one wants to see *me* get cut up. Now get a move on."

That hurt. One-Eye considered his partner, Howie, fairly ugly and he hated to think he was uglier. True, he had only one good eye, but that eye was a pretty clear blue. Back when his name was Eddie, the ladies used to really go for his pair of blue eyes. His hair may be long and greasy now, but at least he had hair. Howie had a handful of strands he liked to comb over his pate, but half the time, the strands would fall out of place unless he pasted them down, which is why he kept the pathetic do covered up with a hat. Ugly hat at that, thought One-Eye. Who was Howie to be judging looks?

One-Eye knocked more of the glass out of the frame and crawled through, grumbling to himself. His boots crunched the glass shards scattered on the floor. He walked over to the back door and opened it. Howie walked through. One-Eye stepped outside and looked down the alley.

"Now you want to look?" asked Howie. "I already checked everywhere. Unlike some people, I actually have all the eyes I was born with."

"I thought I heard something," said One-Eye.

Howie glanced back through the door. "Just the horses, you paranoid cyclops. Always imagining things, I don't know why I put up with you. Come on, we don't have all day."

Cate and Ann were so focused on the two men, the third continued to hide in the shadows unnoticed by them.

Frank was surprised how quickly the old granny had returned, and amused that her choice of backup was her pint-size grandson. He studied the child again. No, not a boy, a hoyden, a girl in boy's clothing. An old biddy and her sawed-off granddaughter, now don't that just take the cake?

Frank listened to his incompetent accomplices squabble. That Stumpy fella they busted out had more smarts than the both of them put together. Leastways, Stumpy had managed to escape. Which was exactly what Frank would be doing if this heist ran south. He liked his neck too much to waste it on inept fools.

He knew the babbling blitherers were both armed, but he had doubts either of them knew how to use the blunt knives they were so proud to own. Wield a knife poorly and you would end up with a witness who was bent on revenge.

Despite their squabbling, the two idiots had managed to get inside the saloon warehouse. Frank watched as the woman tip-toed across the dirt road. Pretty spry for an old biddy, thought Frank. The hoyden trailed so close behind her it was a wonder she did not trip the both of them. The girl carried a rope with a noose at the end. He smirked. Now, just what did she think she could do with that?

The two half-wits walked out, arms loaded with heavy crates of bottles. "Now what's the matter?" asked Howie as One-Eye halted in his steps, causing Howie to run into him.

"I thought you said you checked everywhere," said One-Eye.

"I did," said Howie.

"Then how do you explain those two hussies?" asked One-Eye, looking at the approaching women.

"What hussies?" Howie asked. He turned and looked where One-Eye was pointing and saw what looked to be an old biddy and her granddaughter. The old biddy had a double-barreled shotgun pointed at Howie, and the little girlie was lazily playing with her rope.

Frank ignored the rope, it was just an empty threat far as he could tell, not much more than a toy, but the shotgun was another matter. He bristled. He thought it ought to be against the law for women to carry guns. A gun evened the playing field a little too much, made women believe they were equal to men, or worse, made them think they were superior. He despised uppity women.

The white-haired granny spoke calmly, "I can get the both of you before you can turn the other cheek, so why don't y'all be gentlemen and let Cate here tie you up without a fuss."

"I told you I heard something," snipped One-Eye and he gave Howie a dirty look before readdressing Ann. "Well, ma'am," said One-Eye, "We'd like to but as you can see, our hands are full."

"Put the crates down slowly," said Anne. "Then get your hands up."

They put the crates on the wagon. One-Eye kept his knife in his boot, a stupid place for a knife in Howie's mind as you couldn't reach it when you needed it.

Howie reached for the knife by his side, but it did him no good. He did not see the rope coming, but he sure enough felt it. A sudden jerk sent his hat flying in the air and the rest of him falling towards the dirt.

Cate had him lassoed and trussed up like a turkey in less than eight seconds. Eight seconds was not her personal best, but he smelled worse than most livestock and it threw her for a second. "Dang it, get her off me!" Howie shouted, as he struggled.

One-Eye sneered. "You told me you were a bare knuckle champion. Some fighter you turned out to be." He was slow on the draw or he might have tried to do something. Instead, he just watched in fascination. Howie would have responded, but Cate now had pulled a kerchief from her pocket and had him gagged. She tossed his knife aside, stood up and prepared a second rope.

"I suggest you go quiet-like," Ann said to One-Eye. "It'll be easier on you in the long run."

One-Eye flashed what was once his charming smile. Before his teeth became targets for fists, his toothy grin worked wonders on the women. It took a moment for the cogs to turn and make him realize, he would be next. He made a run for it. He found himself face down in the dirt, hogtied.

"Another knife," said Cate, pulling it from his boot.

"Hey," he cried, "that's mmmmmmmmmm." The rest of what he was going to say was muted by a handkerchief.

In the shadow of the tree, Frank was filled with disgust. He had a deep-seated hatred for women. Any man that could be bested by the weaker sex deserved to be whipped. Next thing you know, the uppity females are going to want to vote. No woman would be telling him what to do. Their little triumph over those undeserving morons was going to cost those females more than just their pride. Frank reached into his pockets and felt around for a nice small rock and waited.

The white-haired woman was vigilante watching over the tied up men. She was a watchful thing, that one. Good she hadn't been the guard in charge of the simpleton they busted out, or they wouldn't have pulled it off.

Ann eyed the men. "What do you think, Cate?" she asked, "Think these fellas are the ones who busted Stumpy out?"

Cate leaned in to get a better look. First she peered at the culprit with a hat, then she studied the man with the one eye. She had to admit, she had been hoping for better. Stumpy deserved to be busted out by famous outlaws, not these no-namers. Neither of them looked smart enough. Which gave her an uneasy feeling. If they weren't smart enough, whose orders were they following?

"No," she said dryly. Her eyes slowly scanned the surroundings, looking for something out of place. They came to rest on the tree. It took a moment for the shadow behind the tree to register as a man.

Chapter Twenty-seven: A True Confession

"Duck!" cried Cate.

The hoyden jumped behind the wagon. The white-haired granny was slower on the draw. She let out a satisfyingly loud gasp of pain and fell to the ground, dropping her shotgun. Frank smiled. If stoning was good enough for the Bible, it was good enough for him.

Cate looked from behind the wagon. Blood trickled down her mother's forehead. "Mama!" cried Cate. She scrambled away from the safety of the wagon and rushed to her mother's side. Ann was doing her best to hold back the sobs from the goose egg swelling up on her noggin, but it had been so long since Cate had called her Mama, she let loose a flood of tears.

"What happened?" asked a confused Ann.

"I happened," said Frank in a soft, threatening whisper. He had come out from behind the tree and was carrying a rifle slung low. With the granny and her gun out of commission, he considered the girl easy pickings, particularly since his pockets were bulging with rocks.

"She'll be alright, it was a small rock," he assured Cate with a smug air. "I'd prefer not to have to use this thing," he continued, indicating the rifle. "It can be a little on the loud side, but give me any trouble and I will."

Cate looked at the man with such rage, the average person would have gone packing. Frank was used to staring down wild cats and this half-pint girl weren't nothing to fret over.

Cate stared intensely at the man. He had the same build as Stumpy and similar features. Cate could see how they might be mistaken for each other in dimming light. This was the man she had been hoping to find, but in her thoughts, the scene was played out differently.

Frank strolled over casually to look at the trussed men struggling on the ground. Durn fools. He was half-tempted to leave them tied and be quit of them. They deserved their humiliation. Still, Frank had something to prove to those uppity females.

"That's pretty handy packaging you did there, girlie. I'm sore to ask you to undo it, but I need these yahoos to get to work. I need you to get up real slow."

Cate reached for the trigger end of Ann's shotgun instead, and her hand was pelted with a rock. He was faster than she had reckoned on. She swallowed a gasp.

"I said, get up," Frank said calmly. His hand was in his pocket, wrapped around another rock.

"Please, Cate," her mother implored, "just do as you're told."

Cate was too angry to speak. Ambushed by a low-down thief, it just weren't right, no matter how you looked at it. It is amazing just how much hatred can be squeezed into one small body, and Cate was nearing the saturation point. Slowly, she rose to her feet.

"Good, now untie them," Frank said flatly.

Molasses on a cold winter morning moved quicker than Cate as she stepped over the closest man and made her way to the furthest. Frank made a mental note of the small act of defiance. He allowed it to pass as it made no difference to him which one she untied, just that she hurry it up some.

"You might put a little fire under that kettle," said Frank. He pulled a rock from his pocket and began tossing it in the air and catching it again, with his eyes fixed on her.

Cate seethed. "You want that I should un-gag him first?" she asked, barely able to hold in her rage.

"I'm in no hurry for that part of him. Just need his arms, legs and back moving the goods is all," he answered matter-of-factly.

Cate knelt down next to the one-eyed man. His bad eye faced her and his good eye was down in the dirt. She wondered how he had lost his eye. She pulled roughly at the already tight rope causing One-Eye to groan.

"Suck it up, you miserable excuse," said Frank, "you

deserve it for letting a little filly like that truss you up."

Cate's eyes stayed glued to this third man. He was wearing Stumpy's coat and she knew it. She had made the top button herself out of elk antler.

"Nobody blames you for killing Mick Turner," she said hotly.

"Good to know, seeing how I didn't kill Mick," Frank answered evenly.

"But you were there," Cate pressed. "It was you Papa saw running from Mick's shack."

Frank eyed Cate carefully. "Well, now, that would make you Ian Darringer's precocious, darling girl who's been wallpapering the county with Stumpy's posters. I obliged to you for that, gave me the idea of freeing him myself."

"Why?" asked Cate.

"Oh, a sharp little thing like you can figure that one out, can't you darling?" he sneered.

Cate's cheeks burned.

"You figured Stumpy took the heat for you last time, he could do it again," she reasoned.

"Give the girl a wooden nickel," said Frank.

She felt a twinge of guilt. She had often wished she had a twin sister she could put the blame on when her plans went wrong.

Frank eyed her as she continued to saw roughly at the ropes. "You sure are taking your time on those knots," he observed. "Didn't anyone ever teach you how to do a slipknot?" he said, hoping to spur her to move a little faster.

"A Chinaman taught me this knot and it tightens the more a person struggles," explained Cate as she wrestled with the ropes. "It ain't my fault he fought the ropes so hard."

"So use the knife you took from him," Frank said dully. Cate had been hoping he had forgotten she had it.

One-Eye squirmed and protested. That was his knife! No sawed-off female was going to be using his knife!

"Stop squealing you durn fool," Frank snorted.

For the briefest moment, Cate considered flinging the knife

into her captor, but even she had to admit her knife throwing skills were lacking. She pulled out the knife and held it in a threatening manner near the man's throat. Frank smirked. "I think we both know you're smarter than that."

"You'd risk his life?" she asked.

"Not much of a risk," he said, "it ain't my throat."

One-Eye squealed and even his sagging eyelid attempted to open. The sweat was starting to pour from his forehead as she rolled him a bit and started sawing the rope. She deliberately chose to cut in the thickest part of the knot.

"This knife is as dull as he is," complained Cate, and she sawed as slowly and as roughly as she dared. She was hoping he would squirm, to make it harder, but One-Eye showed no outward movement. Inside, he was fuming, and his mind was racing, thinking about all he would do to her when turnabout was fair play.

Cate continued to puzzle out the events, "You freed Stumpy because you figured everyone would blame me for it, and certainly, there are those who do." Cate eyed her mother, and immediately was sorry for the barb. Ann's hands were up against her head, as if she had to hold her skull together or it would split apart. Cate could see even more blood running from the cut. It mingled with her mother's silent tears. In all her life, Cate had never seen her mother cry, though plenty of people had said she had while Cate was off in Peru. With a newfound sense of guilt, Cate looked back at the man waiting for an answer, but Frank said nothing. He just kept tossing his rock up into the air and catching it again, his eyes never leaving her.

"Did you argue with Mick that night?" she asked.

His eyes narrowed. He was tempted to pelt her with another rock and be done with it, but he was sore to damage merchandise. He spoke slowly and deliberately to get the point across, "I ain't telling you a third time. I didn't kill Mick."

"Who did?" Cate asked.

"Mick shot Mick," said Frank, glad to get the truth out. "He was drunk and blathering on about who knows what, a dingo I think."

"A what?" asked Cate.

"Some wild dog he had in Australia," explained Frank. "Always yammering on about it whenever he got drunk. Anyway, a centipede crawled out across his stomach and he tried to brush it off with his gun. I think you can figure out how well that worked out for him."

"If you were innocent, why'd you run?" she asked.

A twisted smile slithered across his face. "Let's see, I'm wanted in three counties, and my clothes are soaked in the blood of a dying man, and there's someone on a horse riding up. Seemed like the sensible thing to do. I stumbled out of there as fast as a drunk could run. Amazing how fast you can sober up with the right incentive."

The events started to make sense. Stumpy had a disjointed way of walking, similar a drunkard. She could forgive her father his mistake. "The town could forgive you for killing Mick," Cate started.

Frank smirked. "The pious town decides which life is worth hanging for and which one ain't. How almighty of them."

Cate's nostrils flared and the heat in her tone rose. "But not for pinning it on Stumpy. Why'd you do that?"

"Weren't intentional," he said with an air of innocence, "I found a coat laying in the bushes. I took this coat and left the other one in trade. Seemed fair at the time."

Cate weighed this claim with suspicion.

"Cate," croaked her mother, her voice was thin and frightened. "You've asked the gentlemen enough."

"Your Mama is a wise woman, Cate. You should listen to her," affirmed Frank. "Got that rope cut yet?" he asked, impatiently.

"Almost," said Cate. The knife busted through the rope and the rope loosened, but One-Eye remained still firmly wrapped. "I must have cut in the wrong place."

"Sorry to hear that," Frank said. He reached into his pocket and pulled out a rock. He caught her mother unaware, but Cate was wise to him now. She kept an eye on his hand, and offered as little a target as she could, keeping One-Eye between them.

176

Cate could almost make out the singing going on in the church far up on the hill. It caught her attention for only a second, but that was all he needed. The motion was quick and subtle. She managed to avoid taking the full force of the hit, but it still grazed her shoulder.

"Ow!" she cried, tears flooding down her face. It stung some, but she exaggerated the pain because she wanted him to think she was hurt more than she was.

"I'll give you ten seconds to find the right place and cut through it." His tone was low and threatening. Cate sawed furiously while he counted down. "Ten, nine, eight,"

"You're supposed to say 'Mississippi' between the numbers," Cate protested.

"Of all the people here today, I ain't the one you should be telling what I is 'supposed' to do," he mocked.

"Cate, please, listen to the man," her mother pleaded.

"But even Miss Barris says so," whispered Cate.

"Miss Barris?" asked Frank. "That your school marm?"

"Yes, sir," replied Cate, with immediate regret. She hated for him knowing something about the town because of her say-so.

Frank smiled. He had to appreciate this girl's spunk. A gun to her head and she's quoting her school marm like she's standing in front of the chalk board. "Well, I can't say I'm overly fond of Mississippi," he drawled. Mississippi wanted to hang him, provided of course, someone did not shoot him first. "But out of respect for Miss Barris, how about we compromise? I'll say Utah instead."

"Utah's not a state," pronounced Cate.

"Neither is this territory," Frank reminded her. "Now cut. Seven Utah... six Utah... five Utah."

Cate nodded and worked quickly as Frank continued, "Four Utah... three Utah... two Utah"

"There," said Cate, "your man's free." In the short time One-Eye had been tied, he felt his arms go numb and he frantically struggled to pull the ropes off. Finally free, One-Eye turned to grab Cate. Quick as lightning, she scrambled out of reach and held the knife out in a threatening manner.

"Your boss won't care if I run you full of holes," taunted Cate. She clung on tight to the weapon. He would regret any attempts to harm her.

"Leave her alone," warned Frank. "A girl with that much spunk is worth a fair piece."

Ann gasped, and tried to stand. For a moment, Cate thought she might, but then she collapsed back down to the ground. Mama is truly hurt, thought Cate.

"There's a better knife in my boot," Frank said to One-Eye, "Come get it and untie your partner." One-Eye stumbled over to Frank. His clumsy attempts to fumble inside the boot annoyed Frank. "Get off, you moron," he said, shoving One-Eye, who stumbled backwards.

Keeping his eyes on Cate, Frank pocketed the rock. "I'm even faster with a knife than I am a rock, so don't try anything."

Cate watched as he lifted his knee to his chest to reach his boot knife. Man has amazing balance for a drunk, she thought. Of course, he was sober at the moment. He pulled the knife out, flicked it into the air and caught it, all the while staring her down. Frank held the knife out for One-Eye to take.

One-Eye walked over and grabbed for it. Cate could tell from the way One-Eye winced when he grabbed the knife by the blade that this knife was considerably sharper than the one she held in her hand. One-Eye cut his gag off, slightly slicing his cheek in the process. "See what you made me do?" One-Eye spewed. He took half a step towards Cate only to feel the sting of a rock on his back side.

"I said leave her alone," Frank snapped. "Now get him untied. You have work to do."

Howie had been tied with a slipknot and if One-Eye had known the first thing about it, he could have just pulled on it. Instead, he cut it. Ruined a perfectly good rope and made it too short to tie up their hostages. Howie cut his own gag off and glared at Cate. He walked over and picked up his hat and rammed it back onto his head.

Howie had seen how revenge attempts had gone for his

friend, so he kept his desires to himself and made no move to harm the women. Frank was glad the buffoon seemed able to show restraint.

"Hand me that knot," said Frank, pointing to a cut piece of rope.

"You mean this?" asked Howie picking up the remnant of rope.

"Yeah, I mean that," answered Frank.

"Kind of useless," said Howie.

"My daughter does not tie useless knots!" fumed Ann.

Frank smirked, taking the short piece of rope with the knot in it. "Well, then, we'll just have to find a good use for it. Now, ladies, if you'd kindly get up, I think it best if we moved y'all to inside for the time being."

Cate helped her mother up. Ann leaned heavily against her daughter. They entered the saloon warehouse with Frank behind them. Howie grabbed the shotgun the white-haired woman had dropped on the ground. He clumsily followed behind. Frank felt the barrel of the shotgun against his arm. "Do you mind?" snapped Frank.

"But," Howie started.

"No, buts," said Frank, "Put it down and get to work."

"Put it where?" asked Howie.

"Somewhere out of the way," said Frank. Next time, he was getting smarter thieves. It was too much work to explain every step.

Frank kept his eyes on his captives as he moved them through the storage room toward the saloon. He had no idea Howie placed the shotgun against the wood stove, which was still warm from the morning fire.

Chapter Twenty-eight: Slider Johnson's Red Mash

Inside the saloon, Cate immediately rushed around to the back of the bar and found a clean cloth. Frank watched her as she plunged into a pail of water, wrung it and dabbed it on her mother's forehead. Frank smirked, "As touching as that is, we don't have time for sentiment. I want you ladies loading up the liquor."

"Into what?" snapped Cate, "There's nothing to put the bottles in."

Frank looked around and, not seeing what he wanted, shouted, "Hey, Eddy, or whatever your name is, bring an empty crate in here. I'd like the ladies to load up the liquor behind the bar."

One-Eye was still rubbing the numbness from his arms, but he found an empty crate and brought it into the front room and placed it on the bar. He gave Cate a sick and twisted smile. "That's enough of that," snarled Frank. "Quit leering and get to work."

One-Eye shuffled back to the storage room and he and Howie set to work clearing out the supplies and loading them onto the wagon outside. One-Eye grumbled to Howie that he could see better with just the one eye than Howie could with two. Howie countered that at least he would have known how to loosen a slipknot without ruining the rope.

Frank placed a few rocks on a tabletop, then sat down and made himself comfortable as he studied Ann. She was a pretty thing, probably younger than her snow white hair made her out to be. He wondered if she knew how to cook. He would not trust her to fix his own food, but he was sure he could find a camp of men who would be willing to give it a try.

Cate bristled over the way the man was looking at her mother. "Indians or Mexicans?" Cate asked.

Frank smirked. She wanted to know who he would be

selling them to. Slavery may have been banned, but to an outlaw that only means the price jumps. He would sell the woman to the first camp of men who would take her, but the girl was special. She was worth a trip to El Paso. "Why don't we just keep that a surprise?" he smiled, exposing a mouthful of rotted teeth.

Ann was horrified by implication this man was making. Her head throbbed. She kept an eye open for an opportunity to turn the tide. Ann lifted a bottle. Her vision was slightly blurred. She decided against throwing it at her captor's head. She adopted Cate's slow pace.

Cate set to uncorking the bottles. She had found a funnel, which she was using to pour liquid from one bottle to another.

Frank played with the rope. "So this knot of yours. Looks like a Gordian puzzle."

"It's a Darringer knot," snipped Cate. "And it ain't useless, it's for catching *chupacabras.*"

Frank snorted. "Of course it is! It takes a mythical knot to catch a mythical creature."

"They ain't mythical. I've seen them," Cate attested.

"I see." Frank smiled. "So tell me darling, how do you catch a *chupacabra* with this knot?"

Cate squared her shoulders and lifted her chin. "You soak it in tar, then you roll it in tamarind powder. Then you hang it up in a tree. When the *chupacabra* comes prowling in the night, he mistakes it for a tamarind fruit. He bites into and gets glue-trapped on it. The first rays of light burn him to ash so the only way you know for sure you caught one is by the ash pile beneath the knot."

Frank snickered. Muddle-headed superstitious female. "Well, that is a right handy knot." He studied Cate's movements. Finally, he asked,"What are you doing, girlie-girl?"

"I'm consolidating," snipped Cate.

"You're what?" He knew what she meant, he just found it amusing a two-bit girl would know a ten-dollar word.

"I'm putting partial bottles together so they take up less space on the wagon," said Cate. "You ought to thank me for thinking of it."

Frank snorted. "Don't pay to mix liquors in the bottle. That's what stomachs are for." He stood up and came closer to the bar. He brought the rope remnant with him. He had other uses for it, if need be. "So what have you there?" he asked, sitting down at the bar.

"Slider Johnson's Red Mash," said Cate, mixing one bottle of red liquid into another one.

"Imagine a sweet, innocent, little peach like you knowing a thing like that," he mused.

"Ain't hard to reckon. It's red, it's liquid, and I found it in a saloon," she snapped.

"I've heard a lot about that Red Mash, why don't you just hand it over and I'll save you the trouble of packing it," he smiled. Cate put the bottle on the bar. He stood up. Leaving the rifle on the table, he walked over to the bar, picked up the bottle and took a swig. He made a face and shuddered. "Dang, that's some potent stuff," he lied, sitting heavily on a bar stool. The mash drew up short of its reputation. He'd play along for awhile.

"Wouldn't think it would bother an experienced drinker," said Cate.

He eyed her carefully. She was thinking she could get him drunk and turn the tables on him. He snickered. He rolled a rock around in his fingers. "It don't. It takes a whole lot more liquor than what's here in this bottle to get me three sheets to the wind," he boasted. With the next gulp, he drained the bottle and belched. "Excuse me," he said with faked sincerity, "I didn't mean to offend you fine ladies."

Suddenly, Ann just couldn't stand it any more and she blurted out, "What'd you do with Nell?"

"Who?" Frank asked. He was genuinely perplexed.

"Nell Whipple, the librarian you kidnapped last night," Ann said accusingly.

"Tarnation, I gotta get me a new coat. I'm getting tired of being mistaken for every fool in this Territory," he grumbled. He picked up the bottle before he remembered it was empty.

Cate was thunderstruck. "Why am I just now hearing this?" She was hurt and confused.

"We were afraid you'd have run off looking for her and get hurt," Ann answered.

"I can take care of myself," asserted Cate.

"Says the girl who's about to get sold into slavery," replied her mother.

"Well, ain't the two of you just having a tender moment," Frank sneered.

"Be quiet," they shouted at him in unison.

Normally, Frank would have slung a rock at one or the other, or both of them, but his stomach was rebelling. He had drunk bad liquor before, but nothing like this. He stumbled off of his bar stool and began retching on the floor.

"Good Lord," cried Ann, "That smell is hellacious. What on earth has that man been eating?"

"Don't know about that," said Cate, "but the Red Mash mixed with the syrup of ipecac he just drank might be an influence."

"Catherine Mariah," her mother started to scold, then stopped. In a softer voice, she said, "That was mighty clever thinking."

Cate beamed. "Thank you. I do what I can."

Cate jumped on the bar and swung her legs over. She looked down at Frank. She was wishing now she had boots on. He was on his hands and knees, resembling a spring board. She leapt down, planting both feet on the small of his back and sprung off him, landing a few feet away.

Frank's arms buckled, and collapsed to the floor groaning.

"Hmmph," snorted Cate. "Not much bounce to him."

He tried to grab her by the legs, but another convulsion stopped him. Cate sauntered over to the table and picked up the rifle. Lifting it to her shoulder she pointed the gun at the retching man. "Take that coat off," she demanded. "It isn't yours."

He continued to retch.

Ann walked around the bar to take a look. "Don't think he

can, Cate," she noted.

Frank surprised Ann by latching onto her ankles. Ann stumbled forward. She grabbed the rope and smacked Frank on the head with the now-famous Darringer knot.

Smacking Frank on each syllable, Ann shouted,"I told you, my daughter doesn't tie useless knots."

Frank let go. He had other urges to attend to.

Ann stepped away and turned to Cate. "You keep that gun on him, I'm going to go check on the other two." She dropped the rope on the table and picked up the rocks.

As Cate watched over Frank's heaving body, Ann slipped quietly down the hall and peered into the storage room. She saw the men outside bickering. She spied her shotgun leaning against the wood stove. What fool idiot leaves a loaded and cocked shotgun leaning against a heat source? She wondered how long it had been since Sam had cooked breakfast and if the stove had any heat left in it. Ann could hear Frank retching in the saloon behind her as she watched the men outside by the wagon. Apparently, they could hear Frank, too.

"You hear something?" asked Howie. "Sounds like Frank is losing a gut."

"Why should I care about his gut?" shrugged One-Eye tossing another crate on the wagon. "He don't care if I get poked full of holes." One-Eye would be licking that wound for a month of Sundays.

"If Frank's retching, who's holding the gun on those two hussies?" pondered Howie.

One-Eye stopped for a moment. "What'd you do with the shotgun?" he asked nervously.

"Me? I'm not the one who picked it up," countered Howie.

"You did, too," insisted One-Eye.

"Yeah, but he hollered at me to put it down and get busy, remember? I was supposed to load up the crates. I can't hold a shotgun and load loot at the same time," wailed Howie.

"Oh, and you think I can? What's the matter with you?" griped One-Eye.

"Idiot," fumed Howie.

"Well at least I had the smarts to cut the rope up so she can't tie us up again," One-Eye boasted.

"Well, la-de-da. They can still shoot us, you flea brain!"

Suddenly, One-Eye bolted through the storage room door, heading for the shotgun.

"You idjet," screamed Howie in a harsh whisper, "don't go in there. Get on the wagon and let's get out of here."

It was too late. One-Eye grabbed the shotgun by the barrel.

His scream scattered crows for miles around. He dropped the shotgun with a thud. It fired, sending a spray of shot over a wide area. One shot nicked Howie's hat, taking it clean off, exposing his nearly bald pate.

Howie screamed, "You durn near killed me, you fool!"

"I burned my hand," moaned One-Eye. He was near weeping.

"You got three seconds to get your fool hide in this wagon, or it's leaving without you," Howie ordered. "Now let's git."

The two men started for the wagon. Howie climbed onto the wagon first and took the driver's seat. One-Eye climbed into the back with the supplies.

Ann strode out and stood on the boardwalk, throwing arm at the ready.

Howie was a slow thinker in the best of times, but fear had a way of locking up the cogs in his mind. He sat stock still, mouth gaping, staring at Ann.

"What are you waiting for?" asked One-Eye.

Howie bent over to reach for the reins.

Ann had to make a split second decision. She was sore to do it, but with blood trickling into her eyes, she had to go for the biggest target. She threw a rock square at the flanks of the nearest horse. Brugger reared and bolted.

The jolt of the wagon suddenly lurching forward caused One-Eye to fall off instantly. Howie fell back into the load first, then rolled off the wagon entirely. The horses raced down the dirt road towards the knoll.

Terrible thing to do to a horse, thought Ann. She wondered how far they would run without a driver. She looked at the men groaning on the road. She took another rock from her pocket. Cate came outside. "Found some twine," she said as she walked over to tie the men up. "We can add it to our tab."

"I'm sure Sam won't have a problem with that," said her mother, "Just be quick about it."

"I am," protested Cate."I already done tied up the boss man. Weren't easy with him retching like that, but I think he's done now." Just then, they could hear clearly that he wasn't. "Or maybe not," said Cate.

One-Eye and Howie pushed themselves up onto their hands and knees and started crawling away.

"Cate, get these two tied up again, before they hurt themselves," The Warden ordered.

"Alright! Alright!" said Cate. She quickly tied first one man, then the other. "I suggest you fellas don't move, or hog tying will be the least of your consequences," she warned.

Cate grabbed her mother by the arm. "We should be able to find something inside. We need to get you bandaged up." Together they walked into the storage room and looked for medical supplies.

Ann sat still, like a good patient, while Cate cleaned and bandaged her wound. Both were feeling and thinking more than they were saying. Cate was furious folks treated her like a child and did not tell her that the manhunt was for Nell. She worried about the librarian, but more than that, she was scared about how close she came to losing her mother. Cate had never been this worried about another human being's safety before. She hoped the feeling was short lived. She did not her hair to turn white, too.

Chapter Twenty-nine: Like Worms on a Hook

Inside the church on the knoll, Ruthie McCoy heard the unmistakable sound of gunshot. She swung her legs around the organ bench and scurried to the church window. She pressed her nose to the window pane so hard it is a wonder it did not break. Her keen eyes scanned the hillside. Nothing but a flock of crows.

Mabel and Opal looked at Ruthie with anticipation. She turned, shook her head and glided back to the organ bench. She fiddled with the sheet music to bide her time.

The sound of horse hooves pounding toward them gave Ruthie new encouragement. She rushed back to the window for a second look. She waved to her friends and the two women gleefully joined her. The Gossip Brigade hogged the view.

"It's a team of horses," announced Mabel.
"There's no driver," gasped Ruthie.

"It's like they're being driven by ghosts!" added Opal.

"Now Opal, don't be going into hysterics. I'm sure there's a better explanation," said Sam Beckett, craning his neck to peer over the women. He cussed.

"Sam Beckett, I'll thank you to remember this is a house of the Lord," reprimanded Ruthie.

"That's *my* wagon!" roared Sam, as he lunged for the door.

Ruthie, Mabel and Opal turned to Reverend John Bethlehem.

"You know Reverend, this is the thing I've been talking to you about," said Ruthie.

"Raw language," said Mabel.

"Comes from being a bachelor," added Opal.

"That's right," agreed Mabel.

"We need to get the town men married off if you want to improve the public image of Henryetta," said Ruthie.

Reverend Bethlehem nodded his head.

Willy Hoffman and Malcolm Mitchell ran after Sam. Willy was the quickest and he overtook Sam before he reached the church gate. He called after the horses, "Whoa! Slow down down ladies!" The horses slowed and Willy leapt onto the back of the supply wagon. He walked his way to the front and grabbed the reins. He slowed them down further and turned them around to head back to town.

Willy stopped at the church to pick up Sam and Malcolm.

"Give me a sec, I'm coming with you," said Malcolm. He ran back into the church. He stepped past the Gossip Brigade, and reached under a pew for his rifle. Malcolm had been carrying his rifle with him everywhere he went since his daughters started making moon eyes at that George fella. He had been young once and knew what young fellas could be like. None of them would be going near his daughters.

Ruthie McCoy gasped. "A weapon of war does not belong on sacred ground!"

"Well, then," said Malcolm, "it's a good thing I'm taking it away from sacred ground." He ran back outside.

"Shocking!" gasped Ruthie.

"Rude, if you ask me," chimed Mabel.

"Nothing a good woman couldn't handle," observed Opal.

"That's right," nodded Mabel. "That man needs a woman to keep him out of trouble. I know just the girl."

"So do I," smiled Opal.

"Opal! Mabel! I declare!" scolded Ruthie. She considered herself to be the best matchmaker in three counties and she did not appreciate her lady friends horning in on her territory. "That man is clearly beyond a woman's scope." She already had a bride picked out and their interference was unwelcomed. "He needs the Reverend to bring him to the Lord. That's the reverend's job, isn't that right, Reverend?"

The reverend was not listening. He peered out the door at the men. The three of them made quite the sight: Sam, the long, lean, wiry grocer; Malcolm, the scarred and irritable leather tanner; and Willy, the good-natured, burly and bearded blacksmith.

Malcolm climbed onto the wagon next to Willy, while Sam rode in the back, taking inventory of his stock. Willy flicked the reins and the horses jumped forward. Three men on a mission. The reverend wished he was going with them.

"Perhaps, ladies, we should practice some hymns," he suggested.

℧

Sam was a pretty good Christian for the most part. At the moment, he was madder than a wet hen. "What kind of low-down vermin would steal my wares? Is there no decency left in this world? No sense of decorum or fair play? The skunks better hope the law catches up to them before I do," he threatened.

"My guess is they're long gone," said Willy, "Something had to have gone wrong or the horses wouldn't have run off without a driver."

Sam was still sore. "You reckon the Lord would disapprove

of breaking a man's jaw for stealing another man's livelihood?"

"Yep, I'm thinking He would," said Willy.

"Yeah, could be," grumbled Sam, "What about you, Malcolm? You think He'd disapprove?"

"Yep," agreed Malcolm, "though probably not as much as He'd disapprove of the stealing. Probably just give you a light penance."

"Like what?" asked Sam.

"Oh, I don't know, polish the pews, maybe," answered Malcolm. He wondered what the penance would be for running off prospective suitors. Probably nothing, he thought, since they did not deserve to be looking at his daughters.

Sam weighed the enjoyment of breaking the jaw of a thief against the annoyance of polishing pews. "That seems reasonable," he decided.

"Now, hold on," said Willy, "Malcolm ain't the Lord, he don't get to decide what sort of penance you get."

The three men continued this theological debate the rest of the way to town. As they approached the service road, the horse with the sore flank whined and shied. She stopped and would not go any further. The men looked down the road and were unsure what to make of the scene before them: two scruffy transients trussed up like Christmas turkeys lay in the middle of the service road, groaning and moaning. They looked like worms trying to wiggle their way off the hook.

Sam jumped off the wagon and soothed the skittish horse. He did not trust himself to go nearer. These men likely had something to do with the stealing of his wares. Yet for all his talk, he was unsure the Lord would go light on hitting a man when he was tied up.

Willy and Malcolm climbed down and walked slowly towards the struggling men. Malcolm raised his rifle and Willy pushed it gently back down. "Ain't right to shoot a man who's tied up," he observed.

"Oh, I don't know," said Malcolm. "They must have done something to have deserved it."

Howie and One-Eye were more than a little nervous to see

these men walking towards them, particularly since one seemed keen on using his rifle. Cate had not bothered to re-gag either of her captives, so they were quick to plead their case. "Help!" cried One-Eye, "We've been wrangled by hussies."

"Hush," said Howie. He whispered over to One-Eye, "Ain't you got any self-respect?" Howie wondered to himself, what fool admits to being bested by a granny and her granddaughter? He called loudly to the approaching men, "My friend here is delirious on account of being ambushed."

Willy and Malcolm stepped closer. "You want to explain how y'all got to be here the way you are?" Willy asked politely.

"Well, sir," began Howie, craning his neck to look at the men, "We're new in town and we was looking for the post office to...to..."

"Ta git directions ta the church," said One-Eye. He reckoned folks went easier on those who loved the Lord.

"Yes, sir, that's right," said Howie.

"You don't look like churchgoers to me," said Malcolm.

"Neither do you," noted Willy to Malcolm.

That hurt. Some of the tanning chemicals had left scars on his hands and face and he was none too happy with his looks. Malcolm re-considered. He ought not judge, he thought. Still, this was the closest he would come to having a plausible excuse for shooting someone. He pointed his rifle at the balding one. Willy gently lowered the barrel.

"Did y'all say something about 'hussies'?" asked Willy.

"Oh, no, sir," smiled One-Eye. "I said we was ambushed by a gang of husky dudes."

"That's right," said Howie, trying to look pitiful enough to be untied. "Big, powerful brutes. Strong as bears they were."

"Yeah! Mean-looking fellas with masks," said One-Eye, putting on his most innocent expression.

"How do you know they were mean-looking if they wore masks?" asked Malcolm.

"Well, they had ugly scars running down..." He stopped mid-sentence as he took in the tanner's face. "Well, they tied us up. That's how we knew they was mean."

"Tied us, beat us," said Howie, "and one even took a potshot at me. Check out my hat. It's lying over there with a bullet hole. Villain nearly killed me! Look at my scalp."

Willy and Malcolm took a look. Sure enough, a thin red line grazed the top of the man's head. Willy walked over to the hat and picked it up. It was peppered with holes from shot. Given the spray of a shotgun, it was a wonder he had only the one scratch. Whoever shot him either had lousy aim, or meant to miss. He looked back at Malcolm.

"So, these men, where'd they go?" asked Willy walking back with the hat.

"Not a clue," said Howie. "Far away from here, I hope."

Willy studied the situation. His gut was trying to tell him something. He looked to his friend for help. "What do you think, Malcolm? Should we undo the ropes?"

"Could we shoot them, then untie them?" asked Malcolm.

"Now," pleaded Howie, "you don't want to be doing that."

"Actually," said Malcolm, "I think that is exactly what I want to be doing."

"That's what we git for trying to be heroes!" sniffed One-Eye, sweat beading on his face.

"Heroes?" asked Willy.

"Of course," said One-Eye, "that's why they tied us up! It would bend their noses out of joint to have you set us free." He rolled over hoping they would loosen the knots. Willy bent down and had a look.

"Mighty fine knot work," noted Willy. "Malcolm, how many folks do you reckon can tie a knot like that?"

Malcolm studied the knot. "Don't know," he said, "not many I suppose."

"What difference does that make?" asked Howie. "We didn't tie ourselves! What sort of good Samaritans are you two, leaving your fellow man that done been victimized all tied up?"

Willy called over his shoulder, "Sam! Come here."

Sam hesitated. He still worried what the Lord might think.

"Sam? You coming?" prodded Willy.

Sam patted the horse one more time and walked over to

Willy and Malcolm.

"Do these guys look like victims or criminals to you?" asked Willy.

"They look like victims, but they smell like criminals," said Sam.

"We'd be happy to bathe if you'd only kindly untie us," said One-Eye, smiling his best smile. Sam shivered to see how many teeth the man was missing.

Willy thought he heard someone retching inside the building. "Excuse me a moment," he said standing up. "I'm going to go check out that noise. Don't make any hasty decisions while I'm gone."

Willy walked over to the back of the building, leaving Sam and Malcolm to mull over the two men. Inside the storage room he looked at the shattered glass on the floor and shook his head. He sniffed. The smell was awful. Someone in the saloon was groaning.

"Don't blame me," said a familiar voice, "It weren't my fault you drank so much."

Willy smiled and heaved a sigh of relief. Every person in three counties knew the young lady that voice belonged to.

"Afternoon, Cate," he said walking into the room. He stopped, surprised to see Cate tending a woman with a head bandage. "What's new?"

"Not much," said Cate. "Willy, have you met my mother?"

"No, I believe this is the first time I've had the pleasure." He smiled and extended a hand to Ann.

"Delighted," Ann said wearily, shaking his hand lightly.

On the floor, Frank groaned. Willy took a closer look at the man on the floor and asked, "What's a matter with Stumpy?"

"That's not Stumpy," said Cate. "That's the low-down vermin who busted Stumpy out of jail so he could go on a crime spree and let Stumpy take the fall."

"That *is* a low-down thing to do," noted Willy.

"Maybe we should substitute him for Stumpy and let him hang," said Cate.

"Did he kill Mick?" asked Willy.

"No," Cate reluctantly admitted, "but neither did Stumpy. Mick shot himself."

"Well, let's let Sheriff Dole work out the details," suggested Willy.

Chapter Thirty: Telegraph Secrets

The Henryetta Hotel for Wayward Men just happened to have a vacancy. No reservation needed. Sam, Willy and Malcolm tossed the three would-be robbers into the cell without fanfare – after, of course, Cate removed the coat off the one called Frank. He did not deserve to wear it, and she planned to use it as evidence.

Malcolm and Sam wanted to "interrogate" the men, but Willy had strong feelings to the contrary. "What's the point of paying a sheriff if you're going to do his job for him?" asked Willy.

"He might not know what to ask," said the grocer.

"Then you can make him a list," said Willy. "Right now, you're both too hot-headed to talk to these men."

"Wasn't planning on talking," said Malcolm.

"Which is exactly my point," Willy affirmed. He stood between the jail cell and Malcolm. "It's important that the sheriff see his face just the way it is, without any alterations. If you care about Stumpy, you'll leave him be."

"What about the other two?" asked Malcolm, leaning around Willy to have a look, "They's already bunged up. Won't matter what happens to them."

"It does to me!" protested One-Eye.

"Listen, these men have already caused enough trouble for today. You don't need to be joining them," said Willy, firmly.

Malcolm sighed. It was not often he wanted to hurt someone, but he wanted to now. He considered punching his friend in the face, then maybe Willy would toss him in with the others and he could do as he pleased with them.

Willy could see the cogs moving around in Malcolm's brain and he paled to think where they were going. He put his hand against Malcolm's chest to slow him down. "How would your girls feel if their daddy landed in a jail cell?" Willy asked in a soft tone.

Malcolm thought a moment, then headed for the door.

Willy felt a sense of relief. He had never seen his friend in such a state before. Pointing a finger hard at Malcolm, he called after him, "And you can put that gun down and quit threatening every boy in town. You got to man up to the fact your daughters are growing up."

Malcolm paused with the door open, holding the handle. He was sore to admit it, but Willy was right. Malcolm was near to weeping, thinking of his daughters. "But they's my little darlings," he sniffed.

"Yep, and someday they'll give you darling grandchildren, but not if you don't put that rifle away," Willy explained. "Now why don't the two of you get back and unload the stolen goods off that wagon."

Malcolm nodded.

"That's a good idea," Sam agreed, heading for the door, "Come on, if there isn't too much damage, I might even be able to find something pretty you can take home to the girls."

The two men walked solemnly towards their duty, Sam grumbling over his financial loss and Malcolm ruing the fact his daughters were growing up.

Inside the saloon, Ann rested with her eyes closed. She had sent Cate to the town well for water to clean the floor. Cate grumbled considerably.

"Cleopatra didn't have to clean up smelly bodily fluids," grumbled Cate.

"Cleopatra didn't give Julius Caesar syrup of ipecac," her mother replied, smiling weakly.

"How was I to know he'd drink so much?" Cate asked irritably. She stormed out the door with a bucket in hand.

Cate walked to the well, then, seeing no one was around, quickly snuck down the road to the telegraph office. The door was locked. Peering through the window, she could see no one inside. Looking around, she saw no one watching her.

She pulled out a piece of heavy gauge wire from her pocket. She had been carrying the wire around since the day she saw

Mrs. Whipple pick the library door lock with her hair pin.

Cate bent the wire just so, and wiggled and jiggled, and jiggled and wiggled. Durn it all, she thought, it looked easy when Mrs. Whipple did it.

After a few more wiggles and jiggles, the lock turned over. Cate rushed inside and closed the door. She put down her bucket and stepped behind the counter, where the telegraph machine was stationed. She sat down.

Cate had sent so many telegrams in regards to Stumpy, she knew how to do it herself just from watching the clerk. She tapped out her message.

> deer sharif muler okmulgee cull off
> serch desperado ape prehanded
> stumpy inosent yer frend shirif dole

She counted the words and determined the cost based on previous messages. She pulled out her pocket change and left what she considered to be a fair amount on the counter. She considered sending a second message, but that doubled the risk of getting caught. She hurried to the door, picked up her bucket, and was about to close the door behind her when she heard the church choir singing up on the hill. If the choir was singing on a day that was not Sunday, then it was a sign from God. She turned around and sent a second telegram, this time to Judge Isaac Parker.

> Hon jugde parker Fort smith stumpy
> cleered coat with elk buton fond stop
> fink merel imp lick cated stop him
> and to ruff men hog tied and awaitin
> yer or ders stop yers truly sher if dole
> stop stop

She counted out her money. Dang! She did not bring enough! She left a note:

198

She picked up her bucket and shut the door quietly behind her. Durn. She realized picking a lock was different from locking a door without a key. She went back in to see if it would be easier from the inside. Once inside she remembered she should check the mail in case Judge Parker had decided to respond to any of the dozens of letters she had written.

The Darringer slot was empty, but the adjacent slot held an envelope addressed to a Mark Fennell from someone in Fort Smith. It must have come as a telegram, because she recognized the handwriting belonging to the clerk. She did not know a Mark Fennell, but she knew Judge Parker was in Fort Smith. She was tempted to take it, but she knew it was a federal offense to take mail that did not belong to you. She strained her ears. Durn it. The church choir had stopped singing. Reluctantly, she put the letter back.

Over in Fort Smith, Travis Merrill read the telegram intended for Judge Parker from Sheriff Dole, or someone claiming to be Sheriff Dole. It was likely from that muddle-headed girl over in Henryetta. She had sent so many appeals, Judge Parker threatened to declare her in contempt of court if her parents did not get some control over her.

Nonetheless, Travis was supposed to see to it that any and all messages were delivered to the judge. Judge Parker would not have it said he ignored her.

Travis did not always do what he was supposed to do. For instance, just shortly after he received the message from Frank in Okmulgee, another message came through about an escaped prisoner from the same town. He had sat on that news for awhile on the chance it had something to do with Frank and he needed extra time to get away.

Now, Travis had an almost undecipherable message from Henryetta, a small town that just happened to be on the way between Okmulgee and their planned rendezvous. If the message was to be believed, Frank was likely hogtied and sitting in the Henryetta jail. Travis did not cotton to his kin swinging from the gallows because of an elk button. He had to clarify.

Cate was about to leave again when the telegraph machine started clicking. She ran back and read the message:

> Repeat back

Repeat back? Durn it all. Why can't telegraph employees learn more than one way to spell? Cate sighed. This was taking way longer than she meant. She quickly typed out a second message:

> Frnk errol out law locked up
> stumpy in o cent

She waited a moment, but received no reply. She took her note and scribbled an amendment that she owed them two bars of "saop" and was about to leave when a second telegram came in:

> Sheriff Dole Henryetta US Marshal
> on the way stop Release prisoners
> to his custody stop Wanted on
> other charges stop Judge Parker

Durn it all, thought Cate. She typed back:

> Wat a boat stumpy query

Over in Fort Smith, Travis considered a moment then typed:

> Top secret tell no one Judge Parker
> will pardon Stumpy Gilbert in
> person stop Release Frank Merrill
> to US Marshal on the way stop By
> authority of Hon Judge Isaac Parker

Cate's eyes popped to see the telegram. A pardon! From Judge Parker himself in person! Cate typed back:

> Wen queery

The Fort Smith telegraph clerk smiled. He was tempted to write back, "When hot places grow snowballs," but he wrote instead:

> Soon. Top secret tell no one stop
> Hon Judge Isaac Parker

Over in Henryetta, it was all Cate could do to not shout out "Yippee! Hurray!"

Then she remembered: Tell no one. She hid her IOU deep under a pile of paperwork, hoping it would take the clerk a few days to find it. Then she snatched up the all telegrams received. If no one was to know, she could not well tell them, not even Sheriff Dole.

She returned to locking the door without a key. It was a struggle, but she managed. She ran back to the well and started pumping. The first pump creaked something awful and she cursed her luck. She pumped a few more times and finally, water filled her bucket. She hurried back to the saloon.

"That was quick," said her mother, startled from her slumber.

"I do what I can," said Cate, as she silently gave a sigh of relief. Maybe the clonk on the head rattled her mother's brains enough to lose track of time.

After the men put the wares back where they belonged, Malcolm unhitched Brugger, who was skittish from his bruising. Ann heard what was going on and forced herself to rise from the chair.

"Let me help," said Cate, reaching for her mother's arm.

"Cate," said Ann, "Brugger's my responsibility, not yours. You go clean up the glass and make sure everything is as good as it can get."

"But..." said Cate.

"I'm not in the mood for arguments," said The Warden. "If I need help, Mr. Mitchell will run back and let you know."

Cate watched her mother make her way outside to the horse. The tanner helped steady Ann and the two of them helped moved the horse to the sheriff's stable.

Cate stomped back to the saloon. She swept and scrubbed the wood floor for the third time, "just to be sure."

ʊ

Over in Fort Smith, Travis decided his concerned "Aunt" had sent him a telegram in regards to the ailing health of his loving (and thoroughly deceased) mother. It would be a small matter to attain leave as his superior officer had recently himself buried his own mother and wished he had spent more time with her while she was still on this earth. Family was family. Frank was all he had in that department. He had no intention of letting Frank swing, not in Mississippi, not in Louisiana, and certainly not in some podunk town in a godforsaken territory.

Chapter Thirty-one: Not From My End

Back in Henryetta, Ann stood in the sheriff's stable looking for a batch of muscle salve. She had given him a fresh batch recently as a gift for all his help with Cate during the murder trial. She found the jar on a shelf, took it down, opened it and gave it a sniff. Nothing. It never ceased to amaze her that a lineament that had no odor could taste like garlic when you put it on your hands. Suppose it did not matter too much, so long as it worked. She bathed the horse's sore flank with the salve and asked Brugger to forgive her. The horse flinched a little, but seemed to be grateful for the care.

Ann was putting the lid back on the salve when a thought occurred to her. She slowly unwound her bandage, and applied the lineament to the goose egg on her head. Tenderly, she re-wrapped it.

Cate had fetched Lep from behind the Kibler Boarding House. As she came around the corner, Malcolm was helping Ann to steady against the wagon. Curious, he walked over to examine Lep.

"That's a mighty fine coat," said the tanner. "Unusual pattern, rare."

Lep felt entitled to the praise, even if it came from a lowly scarred human not worth an oat. He snorted.

"I'll sell him to you," said Ann.

"No, you won't," cried Cate, shooting her mother a stern look.

"He's my horse, I'll do as I please with him," said Ann, returning the look.

Cate cut her eyes towards the tanner and spoke with a hard tone, "I know what you do for a living."

"Wasn't going to butcher him," Malcolm assured Cate, "My daughter Amy needs a horse to ride."

"He's too wild for her," said Cate, "He needs breaking in."

204

"Looks nice enough to me," said Malcolm, studying Lep's skeletal structure. He was well-built and sturdy. His withers were a little on the high side, but if a short girl like Cate could manage him, then his tall, lanky Amy could do so, too.

Lep snorted and shook his head. He looked maliciously at the tanner. It was not so much that the man's face and hands were scarred, it was that he smelled like saddles and boots.

Lep stretched his neck and bared his teeth. Cate grabbed Lep's mane quickly and pulled him back.

"Looks can be deceiving. I'll let you know when he's ready," she said. Cate liked Lep about as much as a dog likes fleas, but she was never one to turn away from a challenge, and this polka-dotted bumpkin was just that.

"Alright," agreed the tanner. "Just don't be too long."

"I'll be as long as it takes," said Cate. "Good things can't be rushed."

"Yeah, well she needs that horse sooner than later," said the tanner. He hitched Lep next to Buttercup to complete the team.

"Cate," said her mother, "I'd like to get home. Can you catch up with us on Kiwi?"

"Will do, Mama," said Cate, and she hurried towards the Kibler Boarding House.

Willy helped Ann climb aboard. Then a thought occurred to him.

"Malcolm, why don't you come along?" Willy asked his friend.

"What for?" asked the tanner.

"Give you more time to decide if you really want that horse or not," said Willy.

Malcolm thought that weren't too bad an idea, so he climbed aboard the wagon. The three of them headed for the Darringer ranch.

ʊ

Kiwi was miffed. First, her girl threw a saddle – a saddle! – on her. Then, she rides that tick hotel to town. Now, she fetches *him* while leaving *her* still hitched to the post. What on earth was going on? The moon was a little too round, that must be it. I haven't done anything wrong, sniffed Kiwi.

Cate came around the corner. Hmph, frumped Kiwi. Cate could see she was in hot water with her horse. She put her arms around her friend and whispered softly in her ear.

Kiwi's ear perked up. At first, Cate thought she was responding to soft words. Then she realized Kiwi heard something. Cate unhitched Kiwi, climbed on and gave her her head. Kiwi rambled along a trail until they came across Tar Heel, another of the missing horses. He was a bay that looked to be wearing black socks.

Cate felt foolish. She should have known three robbers meant three horses. Since Tar Heel was the best of the three horses, Cate reckoned Frank must have tied him up here to avoid detection. She had to admit, she approved of his choice of hiding places. She hitched Tar Heel's tether to Kiwi's saddle and rode off to catch up to the wagon.

℧

Willy slowed the wagon as it passed by the church. Ruthie McCoy led the congregation out into the churchyard to learn the latest.

"Speed up," whispered Malcolm, "or we'll be here all day."

"Whoa," said Willy, bringing the wagon to a halt.

"What has gotten into you?" asked Malcolm, reaching for the reins.

"Ann is going to need someone to nurse her along," said Willy, tightening his grip, pulling the reins away. "Go pick one of those gals to come along with us."

Malcolm paled.

"Go on," said Willy, planting his boot against Malcolm's

thigh, "or I'll leave you here with the whole bunch of them."

Malcolm jumped down and in half a shake of a lamb's tail, he was helping his daughter Amy into the wagon.

"Nothing personal, Amy," said Willy, "but Ann's going to need someone with more experience."

"But…" said Malcolm, stupefied.

"No buts," said Willy. "Amy can stay home with her sisters." A confused Amy climbed out of the wagon and looked at her father, who was as confused as she was.

"Try again," said Willy, slightly disgusted. The churchyard was littered with available females. Did he have to spell it out for the widower?

A smug smile spread across Ruthie McCoy's face as she gave Fanny Fredrick a knowing nudge forward.

Opal Tamsen leapt into action and brushed past both women. "I'll go!" she piped up. Lickety split, she was hoisting up her calico skirts and running to the wagon.

Ruthie McCoy's mouth scraped the ground. If Fanny had been carrying a feather, she could have knocked Ruthie over with it.

Opal hopped into the wagon as nimbly as a cricket and sat by Ann before either Ruthie or Willy could think of a reasonable excuse to turn her away. "Don't you worry yourself none," Opal said, patting Ann's hand, "I'll take good care of you."

Malcolm climbed back into his seat next to Willy. He looked at the bemused faces of the women nearby and felt flushed, although he was not a hundred percent sure why. He stretched his neck a little and loosened his collar. He looked at Willy and said. "Well, what are you waiting for? We got a nursemaid, now let's go."

Idiot, thought Willy. At this rate, you'll never remarry.

Willy set the horses back in motion while Opal held Ann's hand and chatted lightly, sharing all manner of idle thoughts.

Cate caught up to the wagon. She was happy to see Opal had joined the party. Opal was lively and entertaining.

Meanwhile, the horses were entertaining thoughts of their

own.

Ox, mule, beast of burden, nickered Kiwi.

Uppity mare, snorted Lep. Think your farts don't smell.

Kiwi held her head high, trotted up in front of Lep, raised her tail and let one rip, loud and long. They don't, from my end, nickered Kiwi.

Lep snorted and sputtered and swung his head from side to side. Tar Heel gave Kiwi as wide a berth as his tether allowed.

"Good, Lord, Cate," gasped Willy Hoffman, "What are you feeding that animal?"

"Timothy hay, why?" asked Cate.

"Well, stop it," ordered Willy.

After that, Cate kept Kiwi to the rear of the caravan.

When they reached the ranch, they found Stumpy sitting on the porch, helping himself to bread and blueberry jam. His wrists were badly swollen, but other than that, he looked to be fine.

Chapter Thirty-two: Company

Cate was thrilled to see Stumpy. She ran to the porch and clanged the triangle in the "get here quick" pattern, sure her brother would turn up soon. When he did not, she searched the barn and stable looking for him. When she discovered the buckboard wagon was missing, she worried that the thieves had returned.

Willy and Malcolm decided to stay put with the women until the search party returned. Opal talked Willy into going out to the garden for greens and Malcolm into peeling the potatoes while she started cooking the rest of the meal.

Willy came in with the greens and near dropped them at the sight of Malcolm wearing a frilly apron. This was not what Willy had in mind when he stopped at the church. "What are you doing in an apron?" Willy fumed.

"I always wear an apron when I work," said Malcolm flatly. He looked at the furrows on Willy's face and added, "And so do you."

"I do not," protested Willy.

"You do, too," argued Malcolm. "I know you do, 'cause I made it for you."

"Wearing a man's leather apron to work hot metal is different from wearing a frilly yard of cloth to peel potatoes," declared Willy.

"That you don't care about your clothes is your own look out," said Malcolm, and he continued to peel the spuds.

Willy shook his head and looked at Opal. An enormous smile had stretched out the mass of wrinkles that lived on her face. For a moment, Willy forgot that Opal was past her prime. Well, it's none of my business, he stewed quietly to himself.

Cate busied herself with drawing a map of the surrounding countryside, plotting out possible places Mrs. Whipple could have been taken. She desperately wanted to go to Nell's place and see the blood trail for herself, but she wanted to stay near her mother more. Her mother might need her.

Stumpy burbled over the map with enthusiasm. He pulled a piece of paper from his pocket and tried to smooth it out with his fingers. It was one of Cate's posters of him. You could see he was pleased with it.

Eventually, the sun set and the worry rose as the men did not come home. When they finally did, it was well past midnight. Guided by the full moon, they rode home empty handed and discouraged. They rode in quietly.

Ian saw light shining through the window from the kerosene lamp. Ann, no doubt.

He left the tending of the horses to the men, and strode towards the house. He had no more stuck his nose through the front door of his house when his ears were assaulted with snoring. Someone was asleep in the parlor. Whoever it was, he would find out in the morning.

Entering his room, Ian was surprised to see Opal asleep in the chair beside the bed and Cate asleep next to her mother. He woke Opal and she filled him in on how things came to be.

ʊ

Morning came bright and early, and so did Nebraska Jo. He rode straight to the barn and began getting the horses ready for a day's work. He would rather have gone fishing with his brothers, but the trouble with ranch work is that it multiplies. If you don't keep up, it only makes for more work.

Lying in bed, Ian had heard Nebraska ride up. He quietly rose. He was still dressed from the day before, so he simply tiptoed out and down the stairs. Ian closed the door of the house behind him softly. If anyone had managed to get to sleep, he just as soon they stayed that way. His feet felt heavy and he was tired from a sleepless night, but he managed to put one foot before the other as he walked to the barn.

Ian heard Neb softly singing a tribal chant to the horses. Normal routine seemed out of place when loved ones were missing. "Morning, Neb," said Ian, his voice cracking slightly.

"Morning, Ian," Neb replied. He looked over and saw Ian's eyes strained from a long, night. "What's the matter? Celebrate too much?"

"What would I have to celebrate?" Ian asked wearily.

Neb looked at Ian a moment and an awkward feeling spread over him.

"I take it the lovebirds haven't made it back yet," Neb said hesitantly, not knowing if he was supposed to spill the beans or not.

"What lovebirds?" asked Ian.

"The four of them. They said they'd be leaving you a note. I take it, they didn't," said Neb.

"What four birds would that be?" asked Ian, still groggy from worry.

"Well, for starters, Nell and that botanist fella ran off and got themselves hitched," Neb explained. "They were just leaving when I got back at the end of the day."

Nebraska Jo had been out mending fences and had no idea anyone thought the librarian was missing.

It did not make sense to Ian for two total strangers to run off with each other like that, but he had heard stranger things. "And the other two?" he asked hopefully.

Neb was glad to be telling Ian and not Ann. "Well, that would be your son and his girl. I tell you, when that boy gets an idea in his head, he doesn't waste time. They was leaving to go get hitched themselves."

Ian felt both relief and terror. How the heck was he supposed to tell Ann that her son ran off and got married without her being there? "Neb, I need you to come repeat that to Ann," he said.

"No, sir," refused Neb. "She's your wife. You do it." He weren't no dummy.

"Why, she'll be so glad to hear everyone's alive and well, she'll overlook the fact they failed to tell her anything about it," lied Ian.

"To think folks think you're an honest man," Neb said sourly. "I ain't even going to be present when she hears that."

"You will if you want to get paid this month," declared Ian.

"You could double my wage and I wouldn't do it," affirmed Neb. "You're the head of this ranch. Do it yourself."

"Do what?" asked Cate.

The two men smiled. They had not heard her come into the barn but they were sure glad to see her. Cate was not only brave enough, she seemed grateful for the opportunity to tattle on her older brother. Finally, after all these years, James was going to be in trouble with their mother.

And he was, too. As far as Ann was concerned, what they had done was unspeakable. If they were not married in a church in front of her eyes, than they were not married. When they returned, she gave them every thought her mind held. Her tirade might have gone on until this day, but Cate made the mistake of snickering. Cate found herself being sent upstairs to clean her room. Ann's stride was broken.

"James," said his mother,"you go get Dillon, Dalene and Yancy and bring them here to help with the preparations."

"Yes, Ma," said James, still holding hands with Ida Sue, too startled to move. He had never been in trouble before. He had no idea this was how it felt.

"Now!" said Ann.

"Yes, Ma," said James. He hesitated a moment, gave Ida Sue the briefest of kisses under the watchful eye of his mother, then left in a hurry. He spied Cate in the hall. His Little Peanut had neglected to go to her room upstairs, the little snoop. His recent skirmish with the harsh side of his mother's tongue left him feeling both humble and charitable. He said nothing, much to Cate's relief.

After her brother's hasty departure, Cate returned to eavesdropping.

"Ida Sue, you can stay with us until the wedding," said Ann. "In Cate's room, with Cate," she emphasized.

"Thank you Mrs. Darringer," said Ida Sue.

"Call me 'Ma,'" said Ann, near trembling.

"Yes, Ma," said Ida Sue. It had been a dozen years since she had anyone to call ma, and it felt good to say the words, even if she were in trouble with Ann. They embraced, vibrating with womanly emotions.

Cate thought now would be a good time to tiptoe out of the hall and…

"Where do you think you're going?" The Warden snapped. Cate froze. She slowly turned and faced her interrogator.

"Upstairs to clean my room?" lied Cate.

"You'll do no such thing," warned The Warden. She knew durn well Cate was up to something. "Ida Sue, I am making you personally responsible for your new sister. You are not to let her out of your sight, you hear me?"

"Yes, Ma," said Ida Sue. She was flabbergasted. Ida Sue had been the head of her family for so long, it shocked her to be bossed around again. Especially so soon. They had just now, this minute, had their first mother-daughter embrace.

"Did you hear that Cate? You are not to touch a single bed sheet in this house, is that clear?" The Warden pronounced. "Your new big sister is going to keep an eye on you. You don't want her to get in trouble with me, now, do you?"

Cate wondered how her mother knew what she was going to do. She had to be telepathic. "No, ma'am," replied Cate.

"No, what?" The surprise in Ann's voice carried a tone of hurt with it.

"No, Mama," said Cate.

"That's fine," Ann said. Good Lord, wondered Ann, am I going to have to get hit in the head with a rock every day to get that girl to call me Mama? "Cate, I want you to take a bath – with soap! And then put on your cleanest undergarments. Ida Sue here is going to make sure you do, so don't be thinking you can get away with not. Don't dally none. I need you back down here lickety split. And bring the newspapers."

"Yes, Mama!" cried Cate. Her mother was going to sew for her! Cate flew up the stairs and Ida Sue could hardly keep up.

"Ian!" Ann cried, a tad too loud.

Ian cringed. He was in spitting distance and hardly deaf, though he would be soon if she kept thundering away like that.

"Yes, my dear love?" he responded, as politely as he could.

His tone caught her attention and she spun around to look at him. His face was pointed towards her, but his eyes were straining to peer at something to one side. The corner of his mouth twitched ever so slightly on that side. Ann's gaze drifted in the direction they were pointing.

What had she been thinking? Ann had been so upset about the elopement she had forgotten Opal Tamsen, the biggest gossip is all seven Territories, including Alaska, was still freely roaming her home. Opal had snuck in sometime during Ann's tirade and had wedged her bone-skinny self between Ralph and the arm of the loveseat he was sharing with his new bride, the former Mrs. Whipple. Not that he minded much, seeing as how the two of them were snuggled up like teenagers spooning on a Saturday night, right there in Ann's own parlor. For shame!

Ann fingered her bandaged head as she worked to gain her composure. She looked at Opal and smiled politely. Opal beamed! She had not had this much fun since, well, she was not right sure, but this was awfully good. With a bowl of corn popped the way the Indians liked it, she could sit on Ann's sofa all week and be just fine.

Ann continued to smile as she slowly considered her options. As the saying goes, "Fish and house guests get a little old after three days." Ann was unsure how many days Opal had been caring for her, but more than enough came to mind. When she finally mustered up her best Southern hospitality, she spoke softly, even serenely.

"I am thinking we have imposed on Mrs. Tamsen's kind and generous nature for far too long. I think it would be only considerate of us to ask Neb to take her home."

Ian returned his wife's polite smile. He opened his mouth to speak, but Opal beat him to the punch.

"Oh, y'all are much too kind," remarked Opal. "But I believe Malcolm Mitchell will be driving me home this afternoon, soon as he gets back test-riding that spotted horse of yours. If y'all don't find me an imposition and need to be rid of me before then, that is." Opal was having the time of her life.

"No, no, not at all," smiled Ann. Dear Lord, what have I done? "It's just, haven't you a shop in town to run?"

"Oh, aren't you so kind for asking," smiled Opal. "I guess you haven't heard the news, what with you being so busy with company and all. I hired Donna Tucker to run the store for me when I'm not there."

"Why, that is absolutely delightful to hear," smiled Ann. "I am ever so glad to know your business is doing well."

Ian looked at his wife's serene facade. He knew, delighted or not, she wanted Opal's all-hearing ears removed from the premises at the earliest moment of convenience.

"Opal," Ian said cheerily, "Cate tells me you know how to play nine pins."

"I do," perked Opal, with clear enthusiasm.

"Well, since you're here, I was wondering if you'd be so good as to teach me," said Ian. "I've been thinking of setting up a lane out back of the barn a ways. I figure it could come in handy when we have picnics."

"You been thinking on it long?" she asked, with only the slightest hint of suspicion.

"I have," lied Ian. All thirty seconds worth. He stood up and offered Opal his hand. "Why don't you come with me and see if your keen eye can't help tell the men how it should be graded."

"Well, if your men don't know how to do a thing, I'm more than happy to tell them!" Opal took his hand and stood up. She walked over to Ann. "Don't you fret a minute, dear. I'll be sure to tell the whole town you're looking for help to sew up that wedding dress. These last minute weddings can be a burden on the unprepared."

Ann smiled. She waited for Opal to leave the room before allowing her face to shake with fury.

216

Chapter Thirty-three: Crawdads

After Cate had washed up and put on clean clothes, she ran back downstairs with Ida Sue trailing after her. Cate enthusiastically lay down on top of the Oklahoma Herald newsprint spread out on the floor.

"Don't move," ordered her mother. Ann traced Cate's outline on the newsprint with chalk to create a pattern. Cate snickered to herself. She wondered what President Harrison would think to know his image was on her bloomer's pattern?

Ida Sue's pattern came next. Ida Sue's sister, Dalene, usually was the one to chalk her. Dalene's lines tended to wobble and needed a fair amount of correction. Ida Sue was glad Ann had a steady hand and worked quickly.

When the patterns were cut, Ann brought out the fabrics.

"Ida Sue, I want you to help Cate pick something pretty," ordered Ann.

"Yes, Ma," replied Ida Sue.

"I'm sorry that I won't be giving you the same considerations, but I picked out the fabrics for your dress over a year ago," and with that Ann began to weep. She had been planning this wedding for years. How could James just run off and elope like that? What was he thinking? Did she really matter so little to him?

Ida Sue found herself consoling Ann. How could her new Ma have bottled up so much emotion for so long? Ann's whole body was shaking.

What a bunch of ballyhoo, thought Cate, running her hands across the fabrics. Maybe if I let Mama make me a dress, she'll relent and make me some riding pants.

℧

Later that evening, Ida Sue came to Ann. "I hate to impose," said Ida Sue respectfully, "but I was wondering if you could show me to Cate's room."

Ann was surprised. "Hasn't Cate shown you the room?"

"Yes," admitted Ida Sue, "but there's something I was hoping you'd explain to me."

Ann puzzled on that. "Oh? What would that be?"

"Just come with me," said Ida Sue.

Ann followed Ida Sue up the stairs and down the hall to Cate's room. Ida Sue opened the door and put her hand out. Pointing to the pile of storage, she asked politely, "I was just wondering, where's the bed?"

Ann was horrified. The room wasn't this bad a few days ago, when she was looking at Cate's flower drawing. What had happened?

Cate figured the worse her room looked, the less likely her mother would be willing to help clean it. The less likely she was to help clean it, the less likely she would force the issue of finding Juliette's dress. It was Cate's hope that her own mother would start to supply the polite excuses as to why it could not be returned. Once her mother created the first excuse, Cate was home free!

Ann felt defeated and ashamed. She felt double the shame because she knew her daughter had none. Ann had neither the strength nor the time to deal with the mess now. "The two of you can share James' room until he gets back," she decided.

Cate wanted Ida Sue to stay out of trouble so she reluctantly slept in the house.

℧

By morning, Ida Sue was pretty sure she would prefer the trouble to a second night of thrashing, kicking and blanket hogging, not to mention snoring. How someone as small as Cate could produce a noise so big was beyond her. She hoped snoring was not a family trait.

A sleep-deprived Ida Sue descended the stairs and entered the kitchen to start breakfast.

By the time Cate woke up and looked out the window, the convoy of wagons filled with town women had already started to arrive. Seeing Mrs. Davenport climbing out of the wagon sent chills down Cate's spine. Mrs. Davenport was an unusually tall woman, as tall as Cate's father. She was as redheaded as that toe rag son of hers, Jimmy Davenport. On top of her towering head rested a plumed hat with a feather that stuck up like a weather vane looking to catch the wind. You could see that woman coming for miles.

This undoubtedly factored into her son's squirrelly behavior. Jimmy knew to hightail the scene of the crime long before the long arm of his mother could reach him. You needed stealth to catch vermin in action and she lacked it in abundance. Her voice was as loud as thunder and she shook the ground with every step she took. Cate's Pa always said Mrs. Davenport would make a good opera singer, if she could only carry a note.

Cate was relieved to see Jimmy had not tagged along. Instead, his sister, Juliette, had come. Cate liked Juliette just fine, but answering awkward questions regarding the whereabouts of the dress that no longer existed was low on Cate's to-do list.

Her mind raced for explanations. Maybe she could tell Juliette a cow ate the dress. Or maybe a horde of female bandits had invaded the ranch and stolen it. Maybe she could say she was wearing the dress when she came across a wild child being raised by wolves, with no clothes whatsoever. Being a kind-hearted soul, Cate was bound by her Christianity to give the child her dress. Maybe her mother would not tan her hide for telling fibs, but The Warden would find another way to get her point across. Cate loathed cowardice, but sometimes prudence was the better part of valor. She skedaddled for safer grounds.

While two score women flooded the parlor and the house, helping with preparations from sewing to cooking to baking to gossiping, Cate slipped down to the crick with a pole, some line, a hook, a knife, and a covered basket she made from a few of her mother's old sieves.

She hardly had time to wiggle a comfy seat into the dirt bank with her bottom when Stumpy stepped out of the scrub, babbling like a popinjay. She was happy to see him. Stumpy had made himself scarce when her father had returned home. Probably a wise move on Stumpy's part. Her father was prone to doing "the right thing," even if it was the wrong thing to do. Cate was sure her father would return Stumpy to custody if he found him.

Even though Cate had Stumpy's pardon in her pocket, she knew spilling top secrets was a federal offense. Even worse, it made you a blabbermouth and you would never be trusted with another secret again. Cate was still hoping to prove to Mrs. Mahoney she was worthy of secret names.

Something her father had said worried Cate. Now she was unsure what the pardon pardoned. Was Judge Parker going to pardon Stumpy for the criminal act of escaping his jail, or for the murder that was not a really a murder? It would not do for Stumpy to get off for the escape if he was still hung for murder. Nor would it be good for him to get off for the murder just to be jailed for life for the escape. She decided the pardon was best kept a secret until the time came.

She cast her eyes over at Stumpy. He had brought a hammer and a few nails with him. He also had one of her "Free Stumpy" posters, and he was babbling along like a brook.

Stumpy understood trading. He knew people would leave things when taking something else. He often would leave oak leaves, pine cones, sticks, stones, acorns or whatever else he might have in his pockets. It was Stumpy's way to pick up one thing at one house and leave it at another when he "traded" it for something else.

Every Sunday folks gathered at the church and brought the things Stumpy left them in hopes of trading them for their own missing possessions. John Bethlehem took it all in stride. The Lord worked in mysterious ways and if Stumpy was what it took to get folks to pray for their sins, who was he to argue?

Cate wondered what Stumpy had left in trade for the nails. She helped him pick out a good tree to nail his poster to. He admired it awhile, then came over to help Cate.

Stumpy lay on the bank of the crick with his hand in the water. One fish after another would swim up to investigate his fingers. When he saw one he wanted, he would pick it up by the gills and put in on the bank. He made it look so easy.

He fished out a ring-tail for Cate and she cut it up for bait. She was going fishing for crawdads. Stumpy would just pluck them out by hand, but Cate preferred using a line. It always amazed her that if you pulled the line out gently, the crawdads would hang onto the bait. They could let go and escape, but they would not. She felt justified eating them when it was their own greed that entrapped them. She stored them in the home made basket that she kept in the water to keep them calm.

ʊ

Earlier that morning in Fort Smith, Judge Parker was running late. Normally, he was as punctual as the sun but today he had a bit of a head cold and was feeling poorly. He almost decided to stay in bed altogether.

He walked into his office and greeted his secretary as usual. The young man was already busy going through the mail and other communications that had piled up.

"I'm sorry to hear you're unwell," said the young man. "You're the second person today. I hope it isn't an epidemic."

"Oh? Who else do you know is sick?" asked the judge.

"Travis Merrill's mother," the secretary answered. He continued to inspect the mail.

"I don't believe I know Travis or his mother," said Judge Parker, dabbing his nose with a handkerchief.

"He's the young man at the telegraph office who normally delivers the messages from Cate Darringer," explained the secretary. "He won't be coming in this week because he's gone to take care of his mother in Shawnee."

"Oh," said Judge Parker, "That's a good son." He sniffed. He had a sister in Shawnee he had not seen in quite some time. That was an oversight that needed correcting.

Chapter Thirty-four: Pigs in a Boubou

When James returned with Ida Sue's family, Ann sent the male members of the family to Mrs. Mahoney's to repair the damage that had been made by a small bear. James, Uncle Yancy and Dillon were glad to have an excuse to be away from the ranch, which was overrun with women.

Mrs. Mahoney took Ann aside and suggested to her that instead of a dress, perhaps she should try sewing Cate some culottes. Ann had never heard of the French term. When Nell explained, Ann replied she had no idea how to make something that was half dress and half pants, and at any rate, she already had the pattern cut.

Donna, who had long been fascinated by Mrs. Mahoney's sense of style, had been listening in. (Opal had decided to give Donna the day off because she had an inkling her gentleman caller might want to pay her a visit at the shop. She preferred to keep prying, meddling eyes away from her new romance.) Donna quickly volunteered to figure out how to add pieces to the pattern to make the alteration. The French curves Mrs. Mahoney had brought with her made pattern adjustment quick work.

In the midst of the commotion, Ann gratefully offered to plan a second wedding for Nell, too, but Nell would not have it. "It took long enough to get him to walk down the aisle for the first wedding," she wailed. "I'm not about to make him do it twice."

It turned out that she knew Ralph Albireo Mahoney from his college days back East. She had been a budding actress and he had only known her by her stage name, Zudora Kelly. They had been close then, but he was shy and bashful and never worked up the courage to ask for her hand in marriage. He had been afraid a career woman would be unsatisfied with just being his wife. They had gone their separate ways without knowing how either truly felt. Nell moved to Paris and was quite the darling of the stage for many years, but eventually gave up the spotlight and settled in Henryetta because Ralph had always spoken so well of it.

Sitting in the parlor with a room filled with curious women, Nell reveled in telling the story about how she had gone home that evening, scared out of her wits, and found a small black bear in her kitchen, tearing it to pieces. In her panic, the gun fired, injuring the bear. She screamed! It roared! Then it ran through the wall to get out.

Ralph had been on his way back to the Darringer's, but had gotten turned around and was riding down the wrong road. He heard the first shot. He headed in that direction hoping to find someone, a hunter most likely, to give him directions. He heard a woman scream as a second shot roared. He hurried to aid the unknown damsel in distress. He heard the bear crying in pain as it ran away. He leapt off Shadow, and, heart pounding, he dashed into the dark house.

Nell, still in a panic, fearing an intruder, nearly shot Ralph, too, but he called out just in time, "Are you alright?"

Hearing his voice startled her so, she could not speak, so he asked again in the darkness, "Madam? Are you alright?"

With trembling hands, she lit a lantern, and in the soft light, Ralph saw his true love. Swept up in the moment, he threw his arms around her and they embraced. The embrace turned into a slow waltz and the slow waltz turned into a baring of the souls. A flood of feelings poured out.

With a laugh and a tear, they thought they should help the bear if they could, so they went looking for it. They spent the night riding Shadow under the moonlight, and in the morning, Ralph proposed. Nell gave him no chance to think better of it. They eloped then and there. On the return trip, they bumped into James and Ida Sue. When the young lovebirds heard their story, they decided to elope, too.

Knowing how long it can take to get a man to say "I do," Nell left nothing to chance, so the newly married couple went along to bear witness.

No matter how many women sighed and said, "That is so romantic," James Edker Darringer was still in hot water with his mother.

Ʊ

Cate was banned from the sewing because she always worked the treadle too hard, causing the fabric to bunch up.

On the second day of the sewing madness, Cate was keenly aware that The Warden had no time to notice her. Cate figured if she was going to make her own boubou, it was now or never.

Cate had given up the idea of using a bed sheet, but there was that old rag of a dressing gown not worth mentioning in the bottom of her mother's drawers. Surely, her mother would not miss that!

The gown was already sewn into a loose fitting garment. All Cate needed to do was cut the bottom off to match it to her height, which she did easily. One snip, then a good tug and the bottom tore off just like that. Well, not just like that; it did tear a little unevenly. Cate made more adjustments trying to straighten out the grain. You know how it goes. She had meant for the hem to hide her ankles. Once it was above her knees, she decided it was time to stop or she would have nothing left to dye.

Cate knew well enough not to dye the gown anywhere close to the house. She chose to do it out by the pigs. Stumpy showed up and the two of them used potato slips, wood blocks, rocks, leaves, and even her hands to imprint the colors on the fragile fabric she had spread out on the ground. It came out a little muddier than she had hoped, but true art can neither be suppressed nor judged by minor imperfections. She was rather quite pleased by the effect as a whole.

While Cate and Stumpy were busy being artistic, Juliette Davenport and Dalene were getting bored and restless. Juliette wondered if it would be alright to play with Dalene's dolls. Dalene said she did not have any dolls at the ranch, but she thought Cate might. Neither girl knew where Cate kept her dolls, so they asked Mrs. Darringer. Ann did not know either, but she was not going to let them go snooping around. She strode out to the porch deck and called, "Cate!" in a loud, clear voice.

Not wishing to be discovered, Cate leapt up as quick as she could and ran for the house. She left Stumpy to clean up the mess. How was Cate to know that would be the precise moment Stumpy decided to take the pigs out for a stroll?

The pigs headed straight for the potato slips. After eating them, they rolled around on the gown, oinking in delight.

Suffice it to say, the Darringers had the only "Easter egg" pigs at the county fair that year. The dressing gown-boubou was never the same.

When Ann saw her the last of her maternity clothes muddied, shredded, and dyed every color of the rainbow, she could not stop weeping.

That woman, thought Cate, does not even know her own mind. Her mother clearly had expressed the notion that she did not care for that old dressing gown. Now she's throwing fits over its demise. Why, the way her mother carried on, one might think that tattered old thing had been the gown worn by Mary Todd Lincoln at the Inaugural Ball.

Chapter Thirty-five: Loose Lips

Travis Merrill rode through Henryetta keeping an eye open for signs folk might be privy to his ruse. A stranger in a small town riding with an extra horse was apt to warrant suspicion. No one seemed to bat an eye. Just normal town activity, as best he could reckon. He rode up to the sheriff's office and dismounted. The horses were well-trained and would wait without hitching, a trait that came in handy for quick departures.

Travis knew the sheriff by his reputation at Fort Smith. Travis had heard that the sheriff did not look like much, just a sawed-off fella, but looks can be deceiving. Travis himself looked angelic, which was how he got away with so much.

Sherriff Dole was known as a keen hunter. He bagged bear, puma, elk, you name it. He also had a bloodhound – apparently a good one. Despite his diminutive size, you did not turn your back on the sheriff.

Travis tried the door to the sheriff's office, but it was locked.

"If you're waiting for the sheriff, he'll be awhile," said a voice behind him. He turned and saw a bony old woman, as dolled up as any bony old woman he had ever seen. She wore a frilly dress and her hair was meticulously swept up into a soft bun, with little bouncy ringlets hanging in front of her droopy ears. Travis suspected she had pricked her finger and used the blood to trace red circles on her cheeks to add color. He held in his laughter.

"Oh? And why is that?" he asked her politely.

"He's entertaining guests," remarked Opal Tamsen, smiling the wrinkles out of her face. She was fairly sure Malcolm Mitchell would be calling on her this morning.

"Guests?" posed Travis, with a dull drawl. He preferred to seem politely disinterested.

"Criminals!" cried Opal enthusiastically. "Our Sheriff Dole

is a decent man. The government doesn't allot enough money to feed them proper so he's out catching fish, or maybe rabbit, so he can fatten them up like turkeys in autumn."

"Mighty fine of him," agreed Travis, although the comparison left him a tad uneasy.

"Oh, yes, him and George should be along any time now with a good catch of something. Just you wait and see!" boasted Opal.

"George?" asked Travis.

"McGillicutty," continued Opal. "Big lad, strong as they come, though not the brightest. He's the new deputy in town."

"Is that right," said Travis, attempting to sound bored by the chatter, which he was not. That Henryetta had a deputy was critical news. He had not planned on a second man to backup the sheriff. That placed the odds under a different light. He had figured he could just pretend to be a Marshal, spring Frank in an "official" capacity, and if any problems arose, clonk the sheriff on the back of the head and be gone before he awoke. Travis considered his chances of taking two armed men to be less than desirable.

Travis found himself walking along with this old wrinkled prune as she prattled. She filled him in on all the town news. Desperate men had come to Henryetta and would have stolen the town blind but a white-haired rancher's wife and her mere slip of a daughter tricked the brains of the operation into drinking syrup of ipecac. Then the daughter, Cate Darringer was her name, hogtied the other villains while the mastermind was puking his guts. Travis smiled and agreed what an amazing story that was.

The old biddy jabbered on about eloping lovebirds and their hurried circumstances. Who would have thunk it? The mother of one of the lovebirds was fit to be tied she had been left out and insisted on a big shindig wedding this Sunday. George McGillicutty would be the best man, naturally, and Sheriff Dole would have to attend to keep the peace or folks might end up having too much fun.

A wedding? thought Travis. Weddings make for good

distractions. He could wait a day or two.

Travis took a casual glance at the Furrs Mining Office as they passed by. Where there was a mine, there was dynamite. One never knew when explosives would come in handy. He hardly looked in the direction of the office when the bony little gossip began blathering on about the mine and how she wished they kept the dynamite in a safer storage place than that old rickety shed of theirs just outside of town. The lanky man suppressed a smile.

Travis continued to listen to the whirlwind of information pouring from her mouth until suddenly, she stopped in front of Opal's Boutique and Curiosity Shoppe and said, "Well, this is my place. You're welcome to come in if you want, but I expect you to buy something if you do. I ain't running the place for my health!"

Travis entered the cluttered shop and bought the cheapest thing he could find, which was some handmade soap. He thanked Opal and left.

Chapter Thirty-six: Wedding Bells

Suddenly, it was Sunday, and James found himself waiting at the altar with George as his best man. James looked positively handsome in his pressed suit and boutonnière.

George McGillicutty cut a surprisingly fine figure himself in his formal kilt and coat. He was probably a good deal more nervous than the groom. He felt like every available female in the church seemed to be looking his way. And they were. He wondered if he could get an extension on his deputy duties.

John Bethlehem stood in front of the congregation in his finest sermon clothes. He looked out across the sea of attendees and wished he could draw in that many every Sunday. It was standing room only. Even the ranch hands were duded up and scrubbed from head to toe. The packed conditions added to the already warm morning.

The reverend signaled to Ruthie McCoy. With aplomb, she pounded away on the organ as if she were driving away the devil himself.

Dillon walked down the aisle first, carrying the ring on a small pillow. Next, came Dalene, sprinkling the aisle with white rose petals, followed by Cate who in turn, tossed pink rose petals. Folks nudged and pointed, and smiled. Cate was in a dress, and her wild hair had been tamed. A few wondered aloud how long it must have taken to plait that crow's nest into cornrows. None of them suspected Cate was wearing billowy pants.

Cate endured the humiliation until she was halfway down the aisle and a spitball hit the back of her head, pasting itself neatly between two rows of plaits. Cate turned, and with the flashing eyes of an angry tiger, she stormed back a few rows and dumped the rest of the rose petals over Jimmy Davenport's carrot-top head. That mild attention-getter might have escalated into a tussle, but Donna appeared and pushed Cate down the aisle.

With a heightened sense of pride and satisfaction, Cate returned to her duty dispensing imaginary rose petals as she strode towards the altar with her head held high. Just wait, she thought, smiling to herself, I'll get the little toe rag proper. Just see if I don't.

Several eyebrows rose in appreciation as Donna adjusted her clothes and waited to promenade before the congregation. Carrying a bouquet of meadow flowers, the maid of honor took a breath then glided down the aisle. Donna was so lovely, a few folks worried she might upstage the bride.

Then, Ida Sue came into view. A unifying gasp of approval filled the church. All the hours of tatting and sewing had been well spent. The congregation rose to its feet. Folk leaned over each other and craned their necks for a better look.

By God, she was beautiful.

While the hairstyle Mrs. Mahoney had selected for Ida Sue might be considered passé in Paris now, it was fresh and alive in Henryetta, and it flattered the blushing bride most radiantly.

Ian Darringer was proud to walk Ida Sue down the aisle.

Normally, John Bethlehem would have frowned heavily on the hurried-up circumstances of the wedding, but he was fond of both Ida Sue and James. He was certain God would forgive them their trespasses, and so he should, too. The reverend spoke at length about love and commitment. Even the ranch hands had to dab their eyes.

Ann sat pensively through the entire ceremony, listening closely for the words, "I do." Their utterance assured her all would end well, but she remained tense until the minister declared clearly, in a loud and booming voice, "I now pronounce you man and wife."

Ann was finally willing to believe her James was married off to the loveliest girl in the county. It was good she was sitting, or she would have fainted from exhaustion. At the reception, George McGillicutty played the bagpipes. Not to be upstaged by a piper, Ian tuned up his banjo and Sam Beckett resined up his bow. It was a cacophony of sound. (This occasion has long been suspected as the inspiration behind the subsequent banning of dancing in those parts.)

Chapter Thirty-seven: Dynamite

Down in the empty town, Frank worried if he had to stay in the Henryetta Hotel for Wayward Men much longer, he might add two murder charges on top of his other crimes. One-Eye was blithering on about something. Frank no idea what, and he had no desire to find out. He just wanted him to stop. He considered the gruesome fact that the law could only hang him once, no matter how many men he murdered. Murdering these two would be more like justified homicide than actual murder. A good lawyer could make a case for mercy killing.

Frank reconsidered. Knowing the sheriff's lackadaisical ways, the bodies would be left to rot in the cell as evidence.

The sheriff, in his infinite wisdom, had handcuffed one hand of each man to a different cell bar to keep them out of reach of each other. They could stand, they could sit, they could even lie down. The one thing they could not do was wring each other's throats.

A rock. Frank would give his right arm for a rock.

Frank could hear the bagpipe in the distance. Even that ear-splitting noise was better than his cellmate's yammering. The fool's endless procession of meaningless words was like a woodpecker drilling into Frank's mind.

Someone inserted a key into the sheriff's office front door. Frank shifted his eyes to the door and waited. Whoever it was was all thumbs. Waiting for them to open the door was almost as bad as being stuck with the fools. When the door finally swung open, Frank was surprised to see a freshly shaved Stumpy walk in wearing a Sunday-best suit with a boutonnière. Frank rose to his feet.

"Stumpy!" he cried with hope. "You old man, how y'all doing?" He had often watched Mick Turner torment Stumpy but Frank himself had never partaken in the cruelty. He hoped Stumpy remembered him kindly.

Stumpy wandered in, leaving the key in the door lock. He babbled randomly. He had a new coat. He was looking for his button to go on it.

"Hey, Stump," said Howie.

"Hush," snapped Frank. "Don't call him that. He don't like it."

"Why not?" asked Howie.

"How should I know?" snarled Frank, "Shut up and let me do the talking."

"Howdy, Mr. Stump," Howie called. He had heard all about Stumpy the last few days of his comfortable stay as Sheriff Dole's guest. He felt he had as much right as the next person to say howdy.

Stumpy waved at Howie and proceeded to express in a language all his own.

"Hey, Mr. Stump," Howie continued, in a soft and polite tone, "I don't suppose you'd mind looking in that desk for a set of keys would you?" He rattled his handcuff against the bar. "My wrists are getting a mite sore. I'd be grateful if you'd unlock me."

Stumpy's eyes followed the man's pointing arm to the sheriff's desk and took in the black book with the gold lettering sitting atop it. What was the book doing on the desk? The whole time he had been visiting the sheriff, it had been on the shelf way up by the ceiling. Someone was obviously playing a trick on the man with the shiny badge.

Stumpy scooted the sheriff's chair over to beneath the shelf. All three pairs of eyes watched him as Stumpy picked up the Bible, climbed on the chair and put the Holy Book back in its proper place on the shelf. Stumpy took the collective groan coming from the jail guests as a sign he did the right thing. He felt good to be doing the short man a big favor.

"Mr. Gilbert, sir, would you mind looking *inside* the desk?" asked One-Eye. He tried to mimic opening the drawers and looking inside, but he felt limited with the one hand still cuffed to the bar.

Stumpy climbed down and looked around for his old gray

coat while the three men continued to vie for his attention. Where was it? It had to be here somewhere. The funny girl he liked to fish with said as much.

Over in the corner stood a coat rack. Stumpy took one coat off the rack and dropped it to the floor. He took the next and dropped it, too. The third coat was his, but he was having so much fun dropping coats he went ahead and dropped the rest of them before plucking his coat off the rack. He laughed to himself.

He laid the coat on the desk, opened the drawer and pawed through its contents. All three men were calling and pleading only confused Stumpy. He put his fingers to his lips and told them to "Sssshhh."

Stumpy rummaged around while the three men watched quietly. Stumpy removed the sheriff's scissors, needle and thread one at a time. He put the needle and thread in his pocket and brought out some acorns and left them in the sheriff's desk. He produced the sheriff's key ring from the drawer and laid it on the desk.

"That's right Stumpy," urged Frank, straining his neck, "Bring the keys over here."

"Ssssh," replied Stumpy. He snipped the elk button off the coat and stuck both the scissors and the button into his pocket. He stuffed an acorn into the pocket of the gray coat. He walked back to the coat rack and dropped his gray coat on the floor with the others.

He was about to leave when all three men started rattling their cuffs against the bars, pleading for the key. Stumpy stopped to look at the cuffs. He nodded his head. He remembered what cuffs felt like. He picked up the key ring with the handcuff and cell keys. He nodded to the men and hurried off to the stable across the road. The pretty cook at the old woman's house had greased his cuffs off with bacon fat. The funny girl sometimes left bacon fat with seeds mixed in it over at the stable so he could feed the birds.

Stumpy crossed the street to the stable. There were no seed balls this time, but he did find an apple. He bit into it. It was pretty good. He left an acorn in exchange. He took a second bite. It was not as good as the first, so he picked up the acorn and left the key ring.

Munching on the apple, Stumpy wandered out of the stable. He noticed the door lock key sticking out of the sheriff's office door. He walked over to the door. The men inside all greeted him and he waved happily to them. He shut the door and turned the key. He decided to keep the key, so he reached in to his pocket to pull out an acorn and came across his elk button.

That's right, he remembered now, he was going to have that funny girl sew it back on. He put the button and the door key back into his pocket and ran down the street.

Chapter Thirty-eight: *A Gay Reception*

Back at the gaiety, Ann had made a special wedding punch for the occasion. Ian was sure she used up all the mint in seven counties to make it. Sam Beckett had wired down to Fort Smith to get all the oranges and lemons needed shipped in fast enough. Slider Johnson swore on a stack of Bibles, right hand before God, there was not a drop of alcohol in the ginger ale he made to go in punch. Since he was not struck down by lightning for lying, Slider must have been telling the truth.

The punch had always been popular with the ladies, but for some reason it was even more popular with the men today. It was disappearing almost as fast as Imogene and Debra Louise could ladle it out. Debra Louise persuaded Margaret Ann to take Willy Hoffman a sip of punch. She felt sorry for him sitting all alone, brooding the way he was.

Willy Hoffman was brooding over how his friend Malcolm was carrying on with Opal Tamsen. She was kicking up her skirts like she was a schoolgirl, and Malcolm was do-si-do-ing with her like a moonstruck puppy. The fool. She was old enough to be his mother. She would be old enough to be his grandmother if this were the state of Kentucky. She was older than the Arbuckle Mountains. Older than sin. Older than...

Margaret Ann handed Willy the punch. He took it, muttering a thanks. He sipped it. Durn. It was pretty good. He swallowed the rest of it, grabbed Margaret Ann by the hand and stepped onto the dance floor to join the fun.

Ann took another swig of punch. Everything was going along so well. She felt blessed and carefree. She even managed to forget she was the mother of an irrepressible child.

Judge Isaac Parker was riding his horse down the road on his way to Shawnee to visit his sister. He came upon a church just this side of Henryetta. He noted the gay sounds coming from within and theorized a wedding was taking place. He loved weddings. They were a sight better than a hanging, even though he was more famous for the latter. He decided he would stop in just long enough to wish the bride and groom a happy and long life together, and perhaps have a glass or two of refreshments before going on his way. He climbed off his horse and began hitching her to a post.

Cate was outside in the midst of explaining to Jimmy Davenport, as gently as her soft feminine nature allowed, why toe rags should never, ever, under any circumstances, hurl spitballs at the backs of young ladies. Jimmy was reaching a new level of understanding when Stumpy walked up.

The simple man's chest was puffed up proud, and he held a needle and thread in one hand. His other hand held the elk button Cate had made him.

Cate gasped! How in the name of Sam Hill did he get his button out of the sheriff's office?

Stumpy was going through the sewing motions and patting his chest periodically. He wanted her to sew his old button onto his new coat. Good Lord! thought Cate. Doesn't he know that's evidence?

A stunned Cate softened her grip on Jimmy's dirt covered hair. This lapse in concentration allowed her subject to wiggle free like a greased pig and run squealing to his mother. No matter. Cate had already confiscated his best pea shooter, sling shot and a two-dollar pocket knife he got for his birthday last month. She was pretty close to being done with him anyway. For now, Cate had more important things to attend to.

"Come on, Stumpy," she coaxed. "Show me where you left your old gray coat." She had to get it back into evidence.

Stumpy was insistent that she sew the button on his new coat for him.

"I will, Stumpy," she assured him, "just as soon as I get a look at that old gray coat of yours. I need it for a pattern. So I can remember how to do it."

Stumpy did not want that old gray coat now that he had this nice newer one with the boutonnière. If the funny girl would not sew it on, he would find someone else who would. He walked towards the church.

"Stumpy Gilbert, if you don't show me where that coat is right now, I'm never going crawdad fishing with you ever again," fumed Cate.

Stumpy stopped and looked at her. He did not understand every word she said, but he understood the tone. He dropped the sheriff's needle and thread and his elk button and ran!

Cate picked up the needle and thread and the elk button and ran after him. To her astonishment, Stumpy jumped on Kiwi and took off like the wind!

Bless Donna Tucker for making her pants instead of a dress, and bless her twice for adding secret pockets. Cate put the needle, thread and button into one of her pockets, hopped onto Shadow and headed for town. She knew she'd never catch Stumpy riding Kiwi, but she could get the button back to the sheriff's office before anyone knew it was missing. Provided, of course, the coat was still in the sheriff's office.

Judge Isaac Parker was flabbergasted. Wasn't that man Stumpy Gilbert? Wasn't he supposed to be in Okmulgee awaiting arraignment? Where's he going on that horse? Suddenly, a young lady leapt on another horse and rode after the man. Judge Parker blinked. If he had not known better, he would have mistaken that young lady for Cate Darringer. No, he thought, she would never be caught in a dress.

The young lady called out as she rode down the road, "Kiwi! Slow down!" Judge Parker had no idea who Kiwi was, but that voice definitely belonged to Miss Darringer. He walked inside the church. If the local Sheriff was in attendance, it might be best if they got to the bottom of whatever was going on, sooner rather than later.

Judge Parker walked in just in time to see the bouquet toss. While he recognized many faces from the trial, most of their names escaped him. A beautiful, curvaceous woman with blonde hair was primed to catch the bouquet. Suddenly, an old widow woman all in black sprung out a hand and snatched it midair. That brought an uproar. To no one's surprise, the young men seemed to lose interest in the garter toss and an old fella had no trouble catching it. The entire room first gasped, then whispered as the old man walked over and held hands with the widow.

Willy was relieved it was the Widow Kibler and Uncle Yancy who caught the tosses. He would have kicked himself all the way home if it had been Opal and Malcolm.

Sheriff Dole was thinking, here is another example how diminutive stature pays off. No one ever expected him to win the garter toss. Bachelorhood would always be his.

Another example came to him when he spied Judge Parker in the church reception hall. He had yet to file the paperwork on the men he had in the jail house, so what the judge was a doing in Henryetta was a puzzlement. He ducked behind some of the taller fellows to watch and see how things played out.

Chapter Thirty-nine: Pretty Sparklers

In the town of Henryetta, Travis Merrill was setting up a series of small explosives borrowed from the Furrs Mining Company's rickety old shack just outside of town. He preferred small ones, less attention called to them. His idea to escort his half-brother out legally by posing as a US Marshal was stymied by the presence of an additional deputy. His idea to slip Frank the jail cell and handcuff keys he brought with him from Fort Smith also failed, as they did not fit the locks. He had considered breaking in through the front door, but every time he had walked by the previous day, the old biddy from the curio shoppe had poked her nose out her door and shouted, "Howdy," like a cuckoo on a German clock. Nothing seemed to get past her.

Travis preferred the privacy on the back side of the building. If he had come a few minutes earlier, he could have waltzed in after Stumpy. Lacking the insight of premonition, Travis was sticking to his plan to blow out the bars of the window and get his half-brother out that way. He liked blowing things up and this was as fine an excuse as any he had known in awhile.

"Hurry it up," demanded Frank, through the window. Travis hardly recognized his half-brother without his full beard.

"If you don't like the way I'm doing this, you can do it yourself," he whispered.

"You don't know what it's been like being jailed with these two prattling morons," pleaded Frank.

"I heard that," said One-Eye.

"So did I," said Howie.

"I don't care what y'all heard," snapped Frank, "hush now or I'll make your silence permanent."

One-Eye and Howie sulked. Frank was no barrel of monkeys himself.

"Come on, what's the hold up?" asked Frank, impatiently.

Frank had already admonished Travis severely for not being around when that fool Stumpy had opened the door. Travis found the continuous tongue-lashing grating.

"Dynamite is something you don't want to rush," said Travis adamantly. He wedged small sticks in the holes he had drilled in the exterior wall. "Besides, I'm waiting for the drunken singing to start."

"You think those people drink?" smirked Frank.

"They do today," smiled Travis. "Miss Darringer isn't the only person who knows how to swap out liquids in a bottle."

Frank smiled at the idea of the town getting tipsy. That was something he almost wanted to see. He wanted freedom more. Soon as he was out, he was going to shoot his cell mates dead and flee the country. Frank wondered how convoluted a route he would have to take to get to Peru while circumventing Texas.

Travis would have been perfectly happy to have a short fast-burning fuse, but that was not what was in the old rickety shed just outside of town. These were thick and long and slow to make sure everyone had time to get out of the way.

"You could cut the fuse shorter," snipped Frank.

"Bad luck to cut a fuse," stated Travis.

"Superstitious nonsense," muttered Frank.

"Lots of things is bad luck," said Howie, who was superstitious. "For instance, it's bad luck to kill a cat on a Tuesday."

"It is?" asked One-Eye.

"Then it's a good thing it was a Wednesday when I killed that cat," snorted Frank.

"Wait. The cat's dead?" asked One-Eye, horrified.

"What cat?" asked Howie.

"The one in the alley wrapping itself around his legs back in Okmulgee," said One-Eye.

"There was a cat?" Howie didn't remember seeing no cat.

"Yes! There was a cat! And yes! I killed it!" snarled Frank, "And I'm going to kill the two of you if you don't both shut up."

One-Eye and Howie cringed. "Cat killer," muttered One-Eye under his breath.

Frank glowered.

Seeing the threat was empty, Howie whispered, "That was Tuesday, not Wednesday."

Frank strained at his shackles, his grasping hands just inches from reaching his cellmate. "Travis! Give me the bolt cutters!" he ordered. "I want to kill these brainless monkeys."

Travis ignored his half-brother. He saw no reason to add abetting to murder to his currently clean record.

Suddenly, the door flew open and Cate walked in. Howie looked at her. "How did you get in?" he asked.

"Hairpin," said Cate flatly, "Don't you boys know how to use a hairpin?"

"A hairpin!" said Frank sardonically. "Imagine using a hairpin to open a lock." He hoped Travis heard him outside.

Travis was unaware someone had entered the jailhouse. He casually replied, "Of course I know how to use hairpins. I just assumed an old misogynist like you might take offense at being rescued by something as feminine as a hairpin." There was also the fact that Travis loved blowing things up.

Cate had grabbed Stumpy's old gray coat and was reckoning on how to sew the button back on when she heard Travis's response. "Durn," she muttered. "This is the wrong color thread." She put the button back into her culottes' pocket and walked out the door.

She scurried over to the sheriff's stable for some rope. She walked in and saw the ropes missing from their usual place. Durn and tarnation. She wished her father would let her carry a gun.

If this was a jail bust, then they had horses somewhere. Cate grabbed a ball of twine, a couple of lead sticks and as many carrots as she could hold from the bin by the stable door.

Shadow had been watching Cate and when she saw her come out with the carrots started walking towards her. Cate led Shadow down the road onto a smaller, narrow trail. She did not know where the jail breakers were hiding horses, but she knew

where she would hide them. She had no sooner disappeared
with Shadow when Travis, on Frank's insistence, came around
to the front to have a look-see.

His pistol was drawn and at the ready. The street was empty,
but she could be hiding in some alley or behind a tree. He had
heard all the entertaining stories of a certain Miss Cate
Darringer and he was not going to be added to her list of
accomplishments.

Frank looked out the barred window of the jail and saw
Stumpy walking up to the fuse.

Pretty sparkles, thought Stumpy. He bent down, pulled out
the scissors from his pocket and snipped the fuse. Frank paled.
Stumpy picked up the still burning snippet of fuse and re-lit the
other end of the fuse. He stood up and handed the still burning
snippet through the window to Frank.

"Much obliged, Stumpy," said Frank, unsure as to what else
he should say.

Stumpy nodded and smiled. He bent down and repeated the
action of snipping, relighting and handing Frank another lit fuse.

"That's fine, Stumpy, but I really think..." said Frank.

Stumpy beamed and did it again. The fuse was getting
shorter by the minute. He continued this pattern for a time until
a butterfly caught his eye. He chased it with the sparkling fuse
in his hand and the unlit fuse dangling against the outside of the
jailhouse wall.

Frank tried to relight the snipped fuse with the burning fuses
in his hand, but found it just outside his reach. The heat from
one of the fuses burned his fingers and he was forced to drop it.
Frank stomped on it to be sure it was out.

Travis rammed open the front door of the sheriff's office.
He holstered his pistol and walked over to the jail cell. He
removed a small pair of bolt cutters from his pocket and cut his
half-brother's cuff from the bar.

"About time," muttered Frank.

"You are most kindly welcome," Travis retorted.

Freed of the bar, Frank reached out the window and pulled
up the fuse and re-lit it with his remaining "sparkler."

"What about us?" Howie pleaded

"What about you?" asked Travis, "Don't y'all have your own kin to come rescue y'all?"

"No," pouted Howie.

"Shame," said Travis. He put the bolt cutter back into his pocket.

ʊ

Cate was pleased to find two horses waiting where she expected them, but her eyes popped to see they were Cavalry stock. She could tell by the way they were groomed that they were used to a high standard of care. There was one way to know for sure. She gave them the signal and both of them lay down immediately. Cavalry horses were trained to get down quick in the event of gun fire. What in the name of Sam Hill was the Cavalry doing mixed up in jail breaking?

She had planned on tying the training sticks to the horses and dangling carrots so they could lead themselves away from town. That would be a humiliation to horses as well-trained as these. Instead she had them roll over a bit so she could release the straps and remove the saddles. Then she had them get up and let them feed on the carrots while she tethered both horses to Shadow's saddle.

Shadow may be an old horse, but she was also a dominant one. She was used to taking the lead and training the yearlings to follow. She looked over at the two horses behind her and snorted to let them know who was in charge. They nodded and continued to eat carrots. Cate gave Shadow the last of the carrots while she talked to her.

"These two horses are new to the area," whispered Cate. "I want you to take them back to the barn to get them acquainted with the place."

"Back to the barn" were the sweetest words you could say to Shadow. She trotted down the horse trail at a lively clip, munching on the last of the carrot.

As the trio of horses disappeared, Cate heard a series of small explosions.

Cate's mind raced. Another sound grabbed her attention. She looked up into the trees and smiled. She used the longest training stick to reach up as high as she could and gently poked the large papery nest. It was heavy. A wasp came out to inspect the movement. That's all she needed to know. She placed the saddles strategically, then found a good hiding spot with a clear sight of the nest.

Chapter Forty: Very Noble

Inside the reception hall, Judge Isaac Parker congratulated the bride and groom. He firmly shook James' hand and asked the fortunate groom where he planned to take his blushing bride for their honeymoon. The Judge could tell by the look on his face, the groom had not planned that far ahead. The bride piped in, "Nigeria!" The groom's eyes grew wide. That was the first James had heard of it. "We're going there to look for a cure for cancer," she explained to the judge.

"Very noble. Very noble indeed," approved the judge.

Ida Sue smiled. She did not know how noble it was. She did know she loved her new Mama. She thought she might love her even more if she were six thousand miles away.

Debra Louise walked over and offered the judge a glass of punch. The Judge was delighted to have liquid refreshment.

"To Nigeria!" toasted the judge.

"To Nigeria!" toasted Ida Sue and James.

"To Noble Causes!" toasted the judge.

"To Noble Causes!" toasted the married couple.

Sheriff Dole decided it was safe to pay the judge a call.

Seeing the sheriff reminded the judge of his duties. He explained that he had been on his way to his sister's in Shawnee, when he happened to see Stumpy jumping on a horse. The Judge wondered aloud, what was Stumpy doing out of jail?

Sheriff Dole wished he had stayed behind the taller men, but he explained as best he could all he knew.

The Judge suggested that the two of them go to town and let the judge see this coat and its illustrious button for himself.

Just then, the newly wedded Mrs. Mahoney came out in her finest dancing costume from her days in Gay Paree, and the band started playing their version of the can-can.

The Judge decided he could see the button later. He had another sip of punch.

250

Chapter Forty-one: *Pffft - Bzzzzz*

The truth can be disappointing. As delightful as it would be to say the dynamite exploded with a big bang, it was more like a series of small, "pffts." Frank turned to Travis and cussed. "Oh great! A fat lot of good that did me."

Travis was annoyed with his half-brother's lack of faith. "Push on it," he drawled. Frank pushed on the bars and the whole window hinged out and fell to the ground. Frank smiled. He was a nimble man and he leapt through the hole like a fly in a flea circus. He was free! His joy overshadowed his feelings of revenge and he forgot about killing his cell mates.

Soon, the half-brothers were headed for their horses.

ʊ

Inside the jailhouse Howie and One-Eye felt a mixture of abandonment and relief. They would have liked to have escaped, too, but they were still handcuffed to the bars.

"Well," drawled One-Eye, "Look at the bright side. At least he won't be here to tell us to 'shut up' all the time."

Howie was feeling a tad less gracious. He looked over at his cellmate and sneered, "Shut up."

ʊ

Cate was secure in her hiding place. She heard Frank and his accomplice running up the trail. "Where are the horses?"

thundered Frank.

"They should be right here," puzzled Travis, looking about.

"You didn't take care of that meddling know-it-all hussy, did you?" accused Frank.

"I didn't see no girl, hussy or otherwise," insisted Travis.

Frank responded with vocabulary unfit for the printed page. Suffice it to say, the gentleman was displeased with the revelation.

Cate waited patiently.

"Don't get your panties in a bunch," muttered Travis. He pursed his lips and whistled.

Cate held her breath. She had not taken that into consideration. She knew horses could see with their ears. If they could hear him, they would come trotting back. She hoped they were out of hearing range.

ʊ

Up the trail a ways, all three horses heard the whistle. The two Cavalry horses turned. Shadow held steady. She was headed home and home was where she was headed. The two horses whinnied a soft protest. Shadow snorted. Shadow had a lot in common with her rider, Ann. You did not argue with either lady.

The two Cavalry horses nodded. They were not wearing their saddles and as far as they were concerned, that meant they were off-duty and could do as they liked. This mare they were following promised fresh meadows and sweet water. They continued to trudge up the hill.

ʊ

Down below, Frank was impatient. "Where are they?" he asked again.

"Quit acting like a frantic granny," scolded Travis. "They'll be here." He listened carefully for the sound of hooves.

"I ain't standing around like a fool waiting," snapped Frank. He trotted further up the trail and cussed as he nearly tripped on the saddles.

Travis came up the trail and joined him. "What kind of horse thief leaves the saddles behind?"

"Tain't no thief. It's that blasted snot-nosed, loud-mouth hoyden," cursed Frank. "I hate uppity females. Come on, let's get out of here, for I lose my temper."

"Not before we stash these saddles," insisted Travis. He bent down to pick one up.

Cate could see Frank was backing away. In a moment, he would make a run for it. The men's positions were less than ideal, but as the saying goes, "Close counts in dancing, horseshoes and wasps' nests." Using her newly acquired sling shot, Cate let a rock missile its way to the apex of the nest. It was an impressive shot, even for Cate. The nest crashed to the ground and the wasps streamed out.

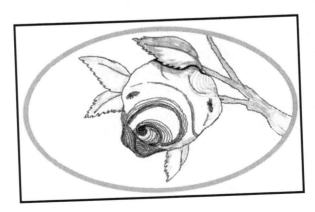

"Holy!" was all the surprise Frank could muster prior to terror overriding all other senses. He took off like a bat out of a chiming belfry.

Travis was a little slower to notice. He was bent on hiding the saddles. He took several stings like a man. Carrying the saddle, he was approaching the bush Cate was hiding in when one stung him in the face. He dropped the saddle and blurted out language that Cate had never heard before. It might have been French. He swung his arms around and danced like a scarecrow left out in the wind. Realizing he was losing the battle, he followed after the screams of his half-brother.

Cate took out her newly acquired pocket knife and started cutting lengths of trumpet vine. The rope they made was inferior, but they would have to do.

When Cate finally reckoned the wasps had done their worst, she took her vine-rope and walked up the trail, following the sound of moaning. When she neared the scene, even she took pity. With swollen eyes, they had come to rest in a cozy patch of Jimsonweed. Cate cringed. She stood at the edge of the path looking in on their predicament and wondered. What would possess anyone to take refuge among such vile smelling, evil plants?

Frank sniffed. "Did you set those morons free?" he sneered accusingly.

"No, I did not set the morons free," denied Travis.

"Then why does it smell so bad?" asked Frank.

"How should I know?" snipped Travis.

"You farted," accused Frank.

"No, I did not. And even if I had, that is no way to treat family," glowered Travis.

Cate snapped a twig underfoot. Frank bolted straight up and cocked his head. He could not see, but there was nothing wrong with his hearing. He put his hand into his pocket and felt the smooth rocks waiting to be unleashed.

"She's out there," snarled Frank in a low tone.

"Don't matter if she is," said Travis. "There's nothing we can do about it."

"Quitter," snapped Frank.

Cate took the sling shot and sent a rock hurdling towards a tree truck. Thunk. Fast as lightening, Frank hurdled a rock towards the same tree. Thunk.

"She's just playing games with you, Little Brother," said Travis.

So am I, thought Frank. She'll slip up. She's bound to get cocky and make a noise she didn't mean to, then BAM! Just desserts.

Thunk. Thunk. Thunk. Thunk. Thunk.

All the rock throwing sounded so much like woodpeckers, one showed up to see what the fuss was all about. The woodpecker started in on the trunk. Frank threw a rock, and nicked the bird's tail-feathers. The bird flew off more angry than harmed.

"That miss was deliberate," shouted Frank. "I like woodpeckers."

"No, you don't," whispered Travis.

"Be quiet," warned Frank.

Cate threw another rock, but Frank did nothing. She wondered if he was out of rocks, or just faking. She snapped a twig.

"Give me your gun," Frank whispered to Travis. "I know where she is."

"I ain't letting you shoot no little girl," said Travis.

"I said, 'Give me your gun'" snarled Frank.

"And I said, 'I ain't letting you shoot no little girl,'" repeated Travis.

"She ain't no little girl. She's a freak show midget. Now give me that gun!" roared Frank. Frank rolled over to Travis and started searching for his gun.

"What is wrong with you?" cried Travis, pushing Frank off him.

The two men had been wrestling each other since the time they could each crawl. Frank had the speed, but Travis had him on finesse.

Frank grabbed hold of the gun handle, but had come at it from the wrong angle so it snagged. Travis reached over and grabbed Frank's wrist and squeezed hard.

"Careful, you moron. You could kill someone," warned

Travis.

"That's the whole idea," agreed Frank, pulling the gun free of the holster.

Travis reached over with his other hand and clamped onto Frank's arm. With both hands firmly attached, Travis twisted Frank's arm like he was wringing out a wet towel. Frank dropped the gun. He made a fist with his free hand and boxed his last remaining family member in the ear. Travis responded with a sharp elbow to the ribs.

Frank rolled off Travis and began searching on his hands and knees for the gun. Travis wrapped Frank into an arm bar and held him firm. Frank flopped like a trout on a stream bank trying to break free.

It was hard enough to see two men sitting in a patch of Jimsonweed, but watching them crush the poisonous herbs like steamrollers, releasing all the venom. The thought of it made Cate itch.

"You can't hold me forever," snarled Frank, twisting and turning.

"Don't need to, Little Bro," said Travis, struggling to hold on to his captive. "I just need to hold you long enough for her to run away."

Cate bristled and stepped out from behind the tree. She piped up, "A Darringer has never run away from a fight in the whole history of Darringers." Just who did he think he was talking about?

"Hear that, Big Bro? She ain't running," wheezed Frank. He twisted against his half-brother's hold. "She wants to get shot!"

"I ain't letting you shoot no little girl!" growled Travis. He held his Little Bro firmly on top of him.

Frank pushed back hard and flipped his legs up over both their heads.

"Don't you dare!" threatened Travis. There were some maneuvers they were sworn not to use on each other and this was one of them.

"Then let me go!" fumed Frank. His awkward position was not doing his swollen face any favors.

"NO!" Travis attempted to rotate his legs and torso out of harm's way.

Frank took aim and snapped his legs down like a steel trap. The sudden force from Frank's body against his stomach expelled all the air out of Travis and his arms flew out to his side. He lay on the ground gasping for air.

Free of his half-brother's grasp, Frank was on his hands and knees feeling around for the gun.

"Where is it? Where's the gun?" steamed Frank.

"It's to your left," offered Cate. She would go pick it up herself if it were not for the Jimsonweed.

"Where to my left?" fumed Frank, frantically sweeping his hands across the area.

"Did I say left?" said Cate, all innocent, "I meant my other left."

"What schoolgirl doesn't know her left from her right?" spat Frank. He was brushing his hand all over the crushed, trampled, poisonous plants.

"I think it may have fallen behind that rock about five feet in front of you," Cate directed.

Travis sat up. He was regaining his fighting strength. "You dumb enough to think she'll tell you?" he wheezed.

"She's arrogant enough to think it won't matter," snarled Frank, scrambling and feeling around for the rock. He felt a sizable rock, then reached around and grabbed hold of a rattler. The rattler did not enjoy being squeezed and it whipped around and bit Frank in the face. Lucky for Frank, it was in the process of digesting and had recently used up most of its venom.

"Aaaaaaaa!" cursed Frank. He sent the rattler flying through the air. Cate noted where it landed. In the event it didn't survive, she could use the skin for a hat band.

"It must have been a different rock," observed Cate. "They all look alike after awhile."

"When I get my hands on that gun…" growled Frank.

Travis crawled over to Frank and grabbed him by his hair.

"Hey!" protested Frank, "Not the hair! You promised!"

"Yeah? And here's something else I promised never to do,"

said Travis. He reached under Frank's pants with the intention of giving him a wedgy, only to learn to his horror that his Little Bro was wearing his birthday suit underneath.

"That's a little personal," yelped Frank. He elbowed Travis in the ribs.

Travis reached under Frank's arms and up behind the back of his neck. He pushed his Little Bro's face down into the dirt. Frank could feel hard cold steel against his cheek.

"Uncle!" cried Frank in a false panic.

"You ain't never cried 'Uncle' your whole life," Travis drawled suspiciously. He tightened his hold.

"I'm saying it now!" cried Frank. "I've had enough."

"You ain't going to shoot no little girl are you?" Travis asked cautiously.

"No, I ain't going to shoot no little girl," Frank agreed. "She's gone. I heard her run off after the snake bit me."

Travis doubted his half-brother. "You still around Miss Darringer?" he called.

Cate said nothing. She was half a step from cover and was not overly concerned.

"It is to your advantage to respond if you are still out there," called Travis.

Cate said nothing. She stood motionless.

"Alright," said Travis, loud so he could be heard at a distance. "On the count of ten, I'm going to let Frank go." He whispered to Frank, "That means you don't go after her. You good with that?"

The gun pressed against Frank's cheek was starting to cut into his skin. Frank muttered his agreement. Cate said nothing.

"Okay, one ... two ..." counted Travis, slowly releasing pressure.

"You're supposed to say 'Mississippi'" corrected Cate.

"I knew it!" thundered Frank. He pushed his half-brother off him, grabbed the gun and fired. Cate ducked behind a large oak while Frank let loose a few rounds.

"You idiot!" screamed Travis. "That was right next to my ear! I won't be able to hear a thing for a week!"

Frank scrambled to his feet. With all the rolling around, he had lost his sense of direction. He was out of ammo anyway. He clicked the gun a few times cursing his luck. He threw the weapon to the ground in a rage.

Travis jabbed Frank in the back of the knees and he buckled to the ground. The wrestling started all over.

Cate watched in amazement. She had thought the wasps would have been enough for either man in one day, but they seemed bent on serving up more punishment. Cate had paid a nickel once to watch a wrestling match at a carnival show that was not near as good as the one she was watching for free. She wished she had some pralines to snack on. It looked like the men were in it for the long haul.

Cate took her lead stick and tied a length of twine to it. Then she tied on the hairpin and cast her line out, fishing for the gun. The gun was out of ammo, but it could still be useful. She tossed out the line, but the gun eluded her.

"You always thought you were better than me," fumed Frank, twisting around to get a better hold of Travis.

"Get over it," ordered Travis. "Ain't my fault my mother is prettier than yours." He wrapped his leg around Frank's leg to pin it down.

"Yours is three times meaner," snarled Frank. He was wishing he had thought to get his knife from the sheriff's desk drawer. He reached up and started smacking Travis in the face.

Travis tilted his head back. Frank used the opportunity to gain the upper hand.

It seemed to Cate, Travis might appreciate some backup. She stopped fishing for the gun and poked Frank with the stick a couple of times.

"Stop that!" cried Frank.

"I'll stop when you stop," said Travis. He wrapped his arms around his half-brother's arms again and locked his hands around the back of his neck.

"No, not you. That evil incarnate is poking me with a stick," snapped Frank.

Cate poked again. Frank grabbed the stick and pulled fast

and hard. Cate lost her balance and fell forward into the Jimsonweed and half across Frank. Travis had a hold of Frank's arms, so they were about as useful as wings on a frog. Cate scrambled to get out of harm's way. Frank kicked and thrashed to impede her progress. He managed a pincher hold on the hem on Cate's culottes.

"I've got you now," boasted Frank. Cate fought against the hold and scrambled for the gun. Failing that, she reached inside Frank's boot. No knife. She should have known. He would have used it if he had it.

Frank's strong fingers pulled on the hem. Cate thrashed her legs, one of which hit Travis. He let go of Frank with a yelp of pain, and Frank was on Cate in a flash.

She stretched her arm as far as it could go and grabbed the gun. Quick as a cricket, she pistol-whipped Frank. Frank let go of Cate and she scooted away from him. His stillness made her uneasy. She stood up and backed out of the Jimsonweed patch.

"Don't play possum with me," warned Travis, aware his half-brother had stopped struggling, but unaware as to why. "I'm wise to that trick."

Cate looked down at Frank's supine body in the Jimsonweed. "Is he dead?" she asked nervously. "I kind of need him to be alive."

"Why would he be dead?" asked Travis.

"No reason," lied Cate.

Travis felt around Frank's throat for a pulse. "He ain't dead," muttered Travis, letting go. "But he'll be wishing he was when he wakes up."

"Do you think you could roll him onto the trail so I could tie him up while I go get the sheriff?"

Travis snorted. "You want me to help you tie up my prisoner while you go get the sheriff?"

"Your prisoner?" asked Cate.

"That's right, my 'prisoner,'" Travis emphasized. "I'm a US Marshal come to transfer a prisoner to Fort Smith."

Cate contemplated the lie.

"Is that so?" she asked.

"It is," affirmed Travis. "You want that pardon for Mr. Gilbert, don't you?"

"You know about that?" asked Cate.

"O'course I do. Like I said, I'm a US Marshal," he insisted. "I got the papers here in my coat." Travis reached inside his coat, pulled out some papers and waved them around for her to see.

"You'll have to come out of that patch if you want me to read it," explained Cate.

Travis sighed. He was swollen from wasp stings, and he was sore from wrestling Frank. Nonetheless, he scrambled on his hands and knees in the direction of Cate's voice. When he could feel the beaten earth of the trail, he held the papers out again for her to take.

"Just put them down on the trail and back away," ordered Cate. "I'll come get them."

He put down the papers and edged back. She snatched them up quick, then stepped back. One was a writ to transport a prisoner, and the other was a pardon for Stumpy!

"They look official," she noted.

"O'course, they look official. They are official," he affirmed. He was one of the better forgers he knew. He took great pride in his "secretarial" skills, although he knew better than to boast of them. He continued his facade. "I'm a US Marshal. Now, just bring me back my horses and I'll take care of the rest."

Cate thought some. She pocketed the writ and the pardon, then she whistled loud and clear.

ʊ

Far up the hill Shadow's ears pricked. That was Cate's whistle. Shadow stopped. The Calvary horses stopped, too. Shadow looked down the trail. She looked up the trail towards the Lightning Tree. She looked down the trail towards town.

Shadow was Ann's horse. If Cate needed something, let Kiwi take care of it. Shadow was headed home and home was where she was headed. Shadow continued up the hill and the Calvary horses followed along.

ʊ

Over by the church, Lep pricked up his ears. Cate had tied him to the supply wagon and made him follow the whole way to church. She was "socializing" him. She was also humiliating him, putting him in last position like that. He considered Cate's whistle. Call me like I'm some sort of dog, will you, thought Lep. That uppity female needs to learn a lesson. He tugged on the slipknot that tethered him to the wagon, then with the leather in his mouth, led himself away.

ʊ

Kiwi and Stumpy had gone to Gup's Bend. Kiwi was grazing in the nearby meadow when she heard something. She pricked her ears. That was Cate's whistle. Kiwi sputtered and walked over and nudged Stumpy. Stumpy didn't want to get up. Kiwi bit into the back of Stumpy's new coat and lifted him up. Stumpy babbled and Kiwi snorted and pushed him along. Eventually, Stumpy decided to follow Kiwi and the two of them headed towards Cate.

ʊ

Back on the trail, Travis told Cate one white lie after

another. He was a smooth talker. Between all the telegrams Miss Darringer had sent, and all the things Opal Tamsen had told him, he figured he knew what to say to have her eating out the palm of his hands. Cate hung on every word. She was fascinated.

Travis's could see thin shafts of light through his swollen eyes. He could see the shapes of a horse coming towards him, and a man? Too tall to be the Sherriff.

Stumpy walked up to Cate. He was still a little hurt that she wouldn't sew on his button and now he didn't even know where it was. He had paid an acorn for it, too.

"Hey, Stumpy!" called Cate.

Stumpy forgot about being mad and he beamed at her.

"Do you think y'all could get Frank out of the Jimsonweed and onto a horse?" she asked Travis and Stumpy.

Jimsonweed? Travis's heart quickened. Wasps weren't enough? They needed to roll around in Jimsonweed?

Stumpy went through the sewing motions he had used earlier.

"Yes, Stumpy, I'll sew on your button, soon as we get these men on their way," smiled Cate.

Stumpy seemed immune to whatever nature sent his way, so he marched into the Jimsonweed bold as brass. Travis felt his way back to Frank and the two men half-carried, half-rolled Frank's unconscious form onto the trail. They had just hoisted Frank onto Kiwi when Lep showed up.

"Here comes your other horse," lied Cate.

She helped Travis get on Lep.

"You sure this is my horse?" asked Travis. The horse didn't seem to be the right height and feel.

"As sure as I am that frogs sing in the rain," answered Cate.

Lep waited patiently. Travis took the reins and clicked his tongue. Lep stood still. Travis clicked again. Lep stood still. Travis gave a little tug on the reins and Lep bucked into action. A near-blind man did not stand a chance.

It is a pity Opal Tamsen neglected to explain to Travis that Cate's mother, Ann, was a McGhee. The McGhee family hailed from the Show Me State of Missouri. Lying to a McGhee is just wasting your breath.

Lep snorted steam from his nostrils. He narrowed his eyes at Cate and sputtered, I showed you.

Cate smiled at Lep. Even an ornery horse can be relied upon if you know what behavior to look for.

Cate stood over Travis, who was now laying on the ground. "If you're done lying to me, I promise not to hurt you none while I take you both back to the jail."

Kiwi carried Frank, and Travis walked beside Lep and Cate while they made their way back to the jailhouse. Stumpy danced ahead.

Seeing the returning desperadoes, Howie and One-Eye counted their blessings that they had not been part of the botched escape.

The town only owned four sets of handcuffs. One of them had been bolt-cut. That left only three usable pairs, two of which were in use. With two men inside the jail and two men outside the jail, Cate ended up handcuffing one of Howie's hands inside the cell to one of Frank's hands outside it. She handcuffed Frank's other hand to one of One-Eye's hands inside the cell. Finally, she handcuffed the other of One-Eye's hands to Travis outside the cell. It was less than ideal, but it was the best she could think of under the circumstances.

"I don't like being chained to a cat killer," One-Eye protested.

"Who's a cat killer?" asked Cate.

"Frank," accused One-Eye.

"He's a cat killer?" asked Cate. "What kind of cat? Puma? Lion? Cheetah?"

"Alley cat," sniffed One-Eye.

"He killed an innocent little alley cat?" cried Cate.

"He did," affirmed One-Eye.

"On a Tuesday, too," Howie chimed in. "I reckon that's why his jailbreak failed."

Cate's boot must have slipped because suddenly the unconscious Frank let out a groan of discomfort.

With the men handcuffed, Cate kept her promise and sewed Stumpy's old elk button onto his new coat.

Cate rode Kiwi back to the church. Lep trailed behind. Stumpy disappeared along the way. Cate hoped her mother would return to the town with her to tend to the culprits. Even the guilty deserved care.

When Cate opened the reception hall door, her eyes popped. Her mother was dancing with the enemy! Cate had never seen her mother is such gay spirits before. Nor the judge.

The Judge considered Ann a most captivating woman. Spirited! Vivacious! A slender waist and nimble feet, too! In between songs he had been sipping a considerable amount of punch.

Cate showed the judge Stumpy's pardon. He did not remember signing any pardon, but there was his signature at the bottom. She had it in writing. He told Cate he would be delighted to pardon Stumpy, and the whole town heard him.

And to think, she did not even have to show him the button.

EPILOGUE

All things considered, the wedding and the reception that followed were successes. After all the hoopla died down, James, Ida Sue, Ralph and Nell made their final arrangements for Nigeria.

Cate made a few more attempts to talk her way into tagging along, but the attempts were increasingly half-hearted. Fretting over her mother when she was injured left an impression on Cate. She was beginning to understand how her mother must have felt when she had been in Peru.

It was a tearful goodbye when the explorers finally set off. James promised to write, which was greeted with a good deal of skepticism, seeing how he had managed to forget to write the note telling them all he was eloping with Ida Sue, a fact of which Cate was quick to remind him.

The driver had a schedule to keep, so that was that. The family watched them board the stagecoach. James hesitated a moment, then bent down and whispered in Cate's ears. She could hardly believe it! Juliette's dress had not gone up in flames! James had pulled it from the burn pile, washed it, ironed it and snuck it into her chifforobe when she was not looking!

Cate should have been thrilled, but instead it only reminded her of the kind of brother she was losing. She turned her face to hide her tears. James boarded the coach and in a moment the brave explorers were gone.

A few days later, Cate was sitting on the back porch swing, staring out across the yard. The past few weeks had been so busy, and now, nothing. Nothing but the doldrums of missing out.

The back door opened and her father came out to the porch. Cate looked over at him. She hoped someday to get a growth spurt and be near as tall as him, but so far, she seemed to be favoring her mother. She noticed he was carrying a small package.

"Cate," he nodded. "Mind if I join you on that swing?" he asked.

Cate scooted over to make room. "It's a free country," she shrugged.

Ian walked over and sat down.

"Cate," he uttered softly. She loved his voice. They had not spoken much of late and it was just nice to hear him talk. She could tell he was struggling to find words. She was fairly sure she knew what he wanted to say, and as much as she wanted him to say it, she was not going to say it for him. He would just have to man up and spit it out. She waited.

He grinned sheepishly. He was as headstrong as his young daughter, so eating crow did not come natural to him. "I, uh," he hesitated. He took hold of one of her hands. He studied it a minute. "Your fingernails look nice," he offered.

She pulled her hand away, crossed her arms and cut him a hard look. He would have to do better than that.

He looked away. He took a deep breath and sighed heavily. "I haven't had much time these past few days to tell you how sorry I am I testified against Stumpy."

"Don't matter, now," shrugged Cate. "He's a free man."

"Something he wouldn't be if not for you," noted Ian.

It was nice to hear him acknowledge her efforts, though she was still sore they were making her pay for a new door lock to the telegraph office. Seemed to her, they ought to thank her for showing them it was defective. She did not steal anything. She paid for the telegram. Not her fault she could not spell. If Miss Barris could not teach her any better than that, seemed to Cate, she's the one who should be paying for the new door lock. And Sheriff Dole would have sent the telegram if he had been there to send it. She hated making soap. Seriously, what was wrong with her parents that they could not come up with some other form of punishment? How could two seemingly intelligent people be so lacking in imagination?

Ian could see his daughter's mind was running like a locomotive with full steam. He fumbled with the small package in his hands, then handed it to her. "I made you something. I was going to save it for Christmas, but I think now is as good a time as any."

If you think you can buy my affections, you have another think coming, she thought. She eyed it for a moment, intent on refusing it, but her curiosity overpowered her. Cate uncrossed her arms and took the small package. She unwrapped it carefully in case it was something breakable. As she opened it, a smile flooded her face.

In the package was a puma claw necklace with beads, leather and even the curled feathers from a drake.

Cate hugged and kissed her father. Ian helped tie the necklace on. She closed her eyes and held the claws like they had magical powers and whispered a silent prayer.

Then, with a wild, loud "Whoop," she ran off the porch in search of adventure.

P.S. We nearly forgot to tell you:

To backup a spell, to the day the Stumpy Prison Break went haywire... Little Davy Burbank had been wandering up and down the storefronts of Okmulgee all morning. He had two dimes and a nickel that had been burning a hole in his pocket ever since the day before when he had earned them by nailing "Free Stumpy" posters all over town.

He had promised himself he would be good and save the money up for his education, but he got to fearing that he would never live that long, and that was a powerfully large sum of money to go to waste.

How to spend that windfall was a monumental decision. He had press his nose against every store window in town. Some windows he had visited more than once. He was crossing the alley to pay yet another visit to the general store when he looked down the way and thought he saw some kind of a furry lump. On closer investigation, he learned it was a dead cat.

Davy had a soft spot for cats, and this one was no exception. It was multiple shades of gray and black. It looked like it had had a hard life and had been in a scrap and lost.

Davy had always wanted a cat, but couldn't afford to keep one. He stroked its soft fur. The poor thing, dead in the alley like that. It did not seem right to him.

He reckoned he should do something quick before a musician walked by and decided his banjo needed new strings. Little Davy used the claw of his newly acquired hammer to dig a shallow grave next to where the poor cat was laying. He saw a smooth rock near by and reckoned it would serve as a small headstone.

Gingerly, he lifted the cat up and laid it to rest in the shallow grave. He bowed his head and closed his eyes and whispered a soft prayer. He took a handful of dirt and sprinkled it over the cat and the cat mewed!

Long short, we are glad to report that Little Davy Burbank took that little alley cat home and used his new found fortune to care for his new found friend, Lazarina.

About the Illustrator

LuAnn M. Conant was born in Portland, Oregon, then was whisked away by her parents to Lafayette, Indiana at the tender age of six months. Upon her return to Portland, in the third grade, she met Sally Stember. Sally immediately volunteered to share a desk with the new girl, with the confident announcement that they would be best friends. As always, Sally was right!

When not penning works of art, LuAnn assists her handsome, Viking husband, Lowell (the Red Neck with a Green Thumb and a Heart of Gold,) at Red Dog Farm in Goble, Oregon. She also has been a custom picture framer since 1986. Her framing business, Second Mouse Studio, is located at their farm.

LuAnn dreams of owning her own horse again someday, because being with a horse is like basking in warm sunshine, even on a cloudy day. In the past she has had an Appaloosa, a Morgan and a Kiger Mustang.

Have A "Cate" Day!

For
Sun Bear,
the hurricane beneath my wings,
the Dr. Who of my TARDIS.

Made in the USA
San Bernardino, CA
26 July 2017